SPECIAL MESSAGE TO

THE ULVERSCROFT FOUNDATION
(registered UK charity number 264873)

res   s.

The Green, Bradgate Road, Anstey
Leicester LE7 7FU, England
Tel: (0116) 236 4325

website: www.foundation.ulverscroft.com

After spending her early years in Lesotho, Beverley Eikli emigrated with her family to Adelaide, Australia, but was lured back to Africa after reading the diaries of her grandfather. There, she found work as a safari camp manager and met a bush pilot, whom she married after a whirlwind romance. Her husband's aviation career has taken them around the globe. Eikli now lives in Gisborne, a small town near Melbourne, with her husband and two daughters.

You can discover more about the author at www.beverleyeikli.com

LADY SARAH'S REDEMPTION

When Lady Sarah Miles becomes the sole survivor of a shipwreck, she assumes the identity of her ill-fated travelling companion to avoid an arranged marriage. Masquerading as governess to the daughter of dashing Roland Hawthorne, the mutual attraction between Sarah and her employer quickly turns to love. But Sarah's past returns to haunt her, revealing more secrets than just her false identity. Determined to redeem herself in Roland's eyes, she unwittingly plays into the hands of an unexpected adversary. With Sarah's honour at stake, can Roland's daring plan succeed? Or will the woman he loves be lost to him forever?

Books by Beverley Eikli
Published by The House of Ulverscroft:

LADY FARQUHAR'S BUTTERFLY

BEVERLEY EIKLI

LADY SARAH'S REDEMPTION

Complete and Unabridged

ULVERSCROFT
Leicester

First published in Great Britain

First Large Print Edition
published 2014

The moral right of the author has been asserted

A catalogue record for this book is available
from the British Library.

ISBN 978–1–4448–2038–6

Published by
F. A. Thorpe (Publishing)
Anstey, Leicestershire

Set by Words & Graphics Ltd.
Anstey, Leicestershire
Printed and bound in Great Britain by
T. J. International Ltd., Padstow, Cornwall

This book is printed on acid-free paper

For Sophie and Lillie

1

1819

'Do you suppose she's a dangerous siren come to bewitch us all, Cosmo?' Brushing aside a beech tree branch, Roland reined in his mount beside his nephew's. 'Or have I acted properly in taking her in?'

'I wasn't spying, sir!' Blushing, Cosmo turned in the saddle. 'When I saw the new governess had arrived, naturally I was curious — ' He broke off. 'If indeed it is the new governess.'

Roland followed Cosmo's gaze through the screen of trees, across the manicured lawns to the gravel drive where a carriage had just drawn up in front of the house. The slender young woman standing on the bottom step overseeing the removal of her trunk could have passed for any governess, anywhere in the country, she was so unremarkable.

Which was, of course, why Cosmo had sounded doubting and, understandably, disappointed. Miss Morecroft's appointment had been so vehemently opposed by Roland's sister-in-law, Cecily, that Cosmo had probably conjured up an image similar to the provocative siren suggested by his uncle.

Perversely, and despite his drollery, Roland was disappointed by this vision of ordinariness.

The young woman glanced briefly in their direction, before mounting the steps to the house. Her old-fashioned poke bonnet concealed her features at this distance but her outmoded, ill-fitting gown of faded puce lent her a homely air.

Cosmo stroked his chin, a new habit developed since he'd started shaving only recently, and asked, 'Will she be here long? Aunt Cecily says it's only until we find her another position. Caro says she's too old for a governess and Miss Morecroft won't last.' He shifted in the saddle then slid his eyes across to his uncle's face. 'You know what Caro's like, sir.'

Roland nodded absently, still trying to reconcile the image of the dowdy governess with his memories of the young woman's father. Any daughter of Godby's should be brimming with exuberance, flashing her ill-afforded finery with the same devil-may-care defiance as her ill-fated pater. Now Godby, his foster brother, was dead, snuffed out in a far distant land, forever denying Roland the catharsis of reconciliation.

'I know, Cosmo.' He sighed. He had as much desire to dwell on his obstinate daughter as he had on the new governess. 'I hope Caro and your Aunt Cecily will be kind to Miss Morecroft. First the death of the young woman's family, now this terrible accident — 'With a sigh he took up the reins. 'Go and pay your respects to your foster cousin, Cosmo. She is to be treated with respect and not judged on account of her father's actions.'

How, he wondered, as his mount picked its way over the stony ground to the rise at the far end of the western paddock, should he deal with Miss Morecroft? Any hint of kindness would be sure to invoke Cecily's wrath.

From the top of the hill he looked down upon Larchfield, the lovely home he'd never expected to inherit. Its honey-coloured stone glowed; mullioned windows twinkled in the sunlight. It looked like a fairytale castle. Once Roland had believed it was, until thieving passions had destroyed all that was good within its walls.

Until Godby, newly returned from war, had burst in upon their tranquillity. A boy no longer, he had changed the delicate balance, setting Roland against his brother, Hector. Three young men and only two women yet — despite her fortune — poor, ugly Cecily, Hector's wife, had still been discarded. Now she seemed to forget that Roland had lost a wife: his

3

exquisite Venetia. So beautiful. So beguiling.
So faithless.

Strange, reflected Roland as he turned his mount for home, how the pain still lingered, long after her image had blurred.

Now Godby's daughter was here and, in truth, Roland felt as much enthusiasm as his sister-in-law for having her at Larchfield.

The image of Miss Morecroft's quiet dowdiness was suddenly immensely reassuring. He felt confident Godby's daughter posed no threat to the peace at Larchfield, after all.

★　★　★

Cecily Hawthorne's critical gaze travelled from the top of Sarah's dowdy straw bonnet to the tips of her worn leather boots which peeked beneath her gown.

She sighed, tapping her fingers on the arm of the sofa. 'The truth is, Miss Morecroft, you're not what I expected and, to be blunt, nor am I convinced you will suit. Mr Hawthorne, however, was most insistent.'

'Then I am greatly obliged at being given an opportunity to prove myself.' Sarah had not considered a hostile reception when she'd embarked upon her rash charade. She'd thought it bad enough wearing the second-hand boots which pinched horribly and which the nuns had retrieved from the waterlogged trunk they'd believed was hers when she'd been saved from the wreck of the *Mary Jane*. She'd nearly wept with shame at having to appear in public wearing such an abominable gown. Now anxiety gripped her as she tried for a suitably grateful smile. She'd have to summon up all the humility she'd rarely had to use in her cosseted life to temper the threat to her plans that Mrs Hawthorne's hostility posed. Rarely, in her twenty-four years, had she felt at such a disadvantage.

The springs of the faux bamboo sofa creaked as Mrs Hawthorne shifted position, and the ormolu clock on the mantelpiece ticked loudly. They were the only sounds in this silent, oppressive house that was supposed to contain a brood of children.

Mrs Hawthorne sniffed. 'I'm told your French is flawless and you can play the pianoforte, but can you waltz? Have they even heard of the waltz in India?' Looking quite fierce, she added, 'A most inelegant dance, but Mr Hawthorne considers it an essential accomplishment. Caro is coming out next year.'

'I am an accomplished dancer, ma'am,' Sarah assented, trying to restrain her curiosity with regard to the novel hairpiece her employer had used to supplement her sparse ginger curls. She was sure the furry appendage peeping beneath the lappets of Mrs Hawthorne's white lace cap had once adorned a squirrel's behind.

'It's not a question of how accomplished you are, Miss Morecroft, but how accomplished you are at imparting these graces to Caro and the girls.' Mrs Hawthorne reached over the arm of the settee and tugged on the embroidered bell pull. 'No doubt you're anxious to meet your new charges.'

'Lovely.' Sarah smiled weakly, wondering how she'd survive the two or three weeks she needed to remain at Larchfield. She didn't like Mrs Hawthorne and, clearly, Mrs Hawthorne didn't like her.

'Girls, meet Miss Morecroft, your new governess.'

Sarah watched them weave their way amongst the clutter of occasional tables and spindly chairs to curtsy before her. The youngest gave her a shy, gap-toothed smile; the redheaded ten-year-old, a cheeky grin. In their wake came a tall, ungainly black-haired girl with hunched shoulders and dark eyes burnt into a sallow face.

'Caro!' Mrs Hawthorne squawked, and her hands flew to her cheeks.

'Sorry!' wailed the future debutante, struggling to right the brass Argand lamp in danger of toppling and singeing the fringed damask tablecloth.

The little girls sniggered and Sarah felt a rush of sympathy for the girl quailing beneath Mrs Hawthorne's withering scorn. Poor Caro was the most unprepossessing debutante Sarah had ever laid eyes upon.

'Never mind, Caro,' she said, 'it's in such an awkward position, I nearly did the same.'

This, of course, did nothing to endear her to Mrs Hawthorne. Nor did it appear to gain her any advantage, for Caro lanced her with a look of suspicion as she took her place beside the other girls.

Sarah had rarely encountered hostility in her life. It was an uncomfortable sensation. Swallowing, she managed to retain her smile. 'I'm sure we'll all deal together famously,' she said bracingly. For weren't little girls easy to win over? As for Caro, Sarah could well remember being a rebellious adolescent herself, to the despair of her beloved papa.

Her beloved papa.

She cut the thought off at the root. A little pain now while she saw through this vital element of her plan ensured she could soon resume her valuable role at his side.

All heads turned at the sound of footsteps in the passage before a tall youth with a mop of sandy curls above immensely high collar points put his head around the door.

'Aunt Cecily, forgive the intrusion,' said this eager young slave to fashion. 'I'd forgotten you were receiving the girls' new governess.'

His assessing eye as it roamed over Sarah gave the lie to his erring memory, though she would have expected more of an appreciative gleam. Smiling up at him, she consoled herself that one hardly looked one's best in someone else's cast-offs, and puce, which always reminded her of coagulating blood, was definitely not her colour.

'Master Cosmo is unaccustomed to the company of young ladies,' said Mrs Hawthorne after dismissing her nephew. 'He'll be returning home soon.' She rose. 'Let me show you your quarters.'

Sarah followed her new employer, listening to her strictures regarding the girls' education. ' — And you'll have to curb Caro's preoccupation with knowledge. The girl is likely to turn into a blue-stocking.' Halting at the end of a long passage, she threw open the door to a tiny chamber. 'You've just enough time to put away your things and change, Miss Morecroft. The girls have their supper at five.' Mrs Hawthorne turned on her heel. 'I shall see you in the nursery when you're ready.'

Sarah was too dispirited to take consolation

from the sight of the squirrel's tail now dangling at a rakish angle over her employer's left eye.

'Yes, ma'am,' she managed, disappointed nevertheless that the hairpiece retained its tenuous grip.

With dismay she took in her sparse surroundings. Apart from the bed, wash stand and chair, the garish rag rug provided the only splash of colour. On top of it rested her trunk — or rather, the other Sarah's trunk. After all the trauma she'd endured lately, she was visited by such a wave of loneliness and longing for home that she sank against the door frame and covered her face with her hands. Could she really endure a ticking mattress and coarse woollen blanket when duckdown and fine linen and all the other comforts she'd taken for granted were just a five-hour carriage ride away?

She'd have to, wouldn't she? she told herself as she sank to her knees and struggled with the corroded buckles. She might not have actively chosen this course, but she had endorsed it with her silence, thinking at the time it solved all her troubles. Just a couple of weeks was all she needed and then her darling papa would welcome her home like the prodigal daughter. Never again would he ride roughshod over her happiness.

Though her hands were still tender from their long immersion in icy sea water, making the chore more painful than difficult, she forced herself to count her blessings. Her maid was dead and poor Sarah Morecroft, the governess whose place she'd taken, was at the bottom of the North Sea.

The clattering of hooves on the cobble-stones outside was a welcome diversion. Throwing open the casement, Sarah looked down into the stable yard, wondering what other diversions Larchfield offered.

The horseman who'd just arrived raised his head at the sound and doffed his hat with a cursory glance at Sarah before dismounting.

Sarah retreated a little.

From this distance, he appeared to be in his late thirties. Mrs Hawthorne's husband? At a pinch their ages might make it possible, but surely not even a vast fortune could entice a man as elegant as this one to throw in his lot with Sarah's demanding employer.

His expression was serious, distracted, as he threw the reins to a stable boy and strode towards the kitchen steps.

Thick dark hair swept back from a high forehead and framed a pair of well-chiselled cheekbones. His manner was decisive. She noticed the way the servants bowed and scraped. The head groom tugged his forelock and the kitchen maid, scurrying across the cobbles with an apron overflowing with vegetables, curtsied and dimpled at his brief greeting.

Sarah strained forward to observe him better before he disappeared. This was no country bumpkin. Highly polished top boots reached the knees of a pair of buckskins that covered shapely, muscled legs. The immaculately cut coat of navy superfine that stretched across his broad shoulders was surely Savile Row.

Unlike Master Cosmo, there was nothing of the fop about him, although his attention to detail was apparent in his attire. A nonpareil, decided Sarah with satisfaction. And a particularly dashing one.

Dashing, just like James — Captain James Fleming.

She sighed. No point reflecting on the past. And she mustn't hold dear James entirely accountable for her predicament despite his *volte-face* regarding a marriage between them.

Sarah listened to the ring of his boots upon the stairs two floors below as she crossed to the tarnished looking-glass. A critical perusal of her reflection hardly bolstered her spirits. However, she reassured herself, with her chestnut tresses shining and her normally flawless complexion glowing, the lowly governess Sarah Morecroft would soon receive the same admiration to which she, the feted beauty, Lady Sarah Miles, was accustomed.

Feeling almost reconciled to her new life at the thought, she returned to her unpacking, only to gasp with horror as she pulled out the first garment that came to hand.

Dropping the drab, high-necked grey merino gown, she put her hands to her flaming cheeks. How could she possibly hold up her head in public wearing such a repulsive object? It would be more mortifying than anything she'd ever done in her entire life.

Swallowing convulsively, she reassured herself this must be the worst of the garments Miss Morecroft had packed. She'd probably tossed it into her trunk at the last minute.

But as Sarah began laying out the gowns, petticoats, chemises and other items in an orderly pile, her dismay grew. By the time she'd pulled loose a beige fustian gown adorned with two rows of badly sewn flounces that might just pass muster for eating nursery tea, she was close to tears. What was she to wear for family dinner in the formal dining room? Regardless of what Mrs Hawthorne said, there was no way Sarah was going to subsist on a diet of endless bread and butter, disgusting lumpy suet puddings and — she swallowed

— no Madeira for more than a week.

What, then, could she deck herself out in? She had no money. Her reticule had gone down with the boat. She fingered the gold cross at her throat. She'd have to pawn that, she supposed.

A cursory rap on the door heralded the entrance of a young personage who bustled into the centre of the room as if she owned it. Judging by her starched cap and apron, Sarah assumed she must be the nursery maid.

'Miss, you're not even dressed!' The stout, ruddy-faced creature, who looked as if she was in the habit of gobbling up all the nursery leftovers, scowled, hands on hips. 'And there's the little girls waiting for their tea!'

'They're hardly going to starve if I'm five minutes late.' Enraged at the maid's impertinence, Sarah pretended to examine the beige dress. Tossing it over the iron bedstead, she sank back onto the threadbare grey blanket and covered her face with her hands. 'I declare, the sea water's ruined my entire wardrobe. Isn't that a greater calamity than keeping a couple of children waiting for nursery tea?'

'Yes, miss.' Sarah's lofty tone appeared to have put the girl in her place. She shifted position, scuffing the oilskin floor covering with her toe as Sarah dragged herself into a sitting position. 'Right sorry we all were to hear of the accident, miss. First losing your family to fever in India and then nearly going yerself, afore yer time. Beg pardon, too, for me lack of manners, only the mistress gets on her high ropes when it comes to punctuality. I'm Ellen, by the way. And Mrs Hawthorne'll be bound to forgive you considerin' yer terrible ordeal, miss.'

'That's encouraging,' replied Sarah, getting wearily to her feet, her irony clearly lost on Ellen. 'I shall be down shortly.'

Struggling into the beige dress was an effort and the response she received from Mrs Hawthorne, who was waiting for her in the nursery, made no secret of the other's disparagement. But when Sarah cunningly and plaintively said, 'Oh, ma'am, two days floating in the ocean has done my wardrobe no favours,' a look of guilt immediately crossed her mistress's face.

'Of course not, my dear. I daresay there are a few of my things I no longer wear that can be altered. They may not be in the first stare, but that hardly signifies in your situation.'

No doubt they'd be simply hideous, thought Sarah, but at least they'd be of finer quality than Miss Morecroft's coarse cottons and serviceable woollens.

The nursery was as spartan as she had

feared, the expressions of her charges hardly compensation. Not one to be daunted by a trio of little girls, Sarah swept past them to the window.

'First lesson, girls! There's a difference between staring and paying attention,' she said, softening her stern tone with a smile as she turned. Despite the appalling deprivations she'd have to endure, there were compensations, she decided, her optimistic nature rising above the gloom. It could even be fun: the erudition of three sponge-like little girls. It gave her a sense of power she was unused to at home, despite her privileges.

'Yes, miss.' Their blank looks were replaced with curiosity. Even Caro did not look quite so hostile.

'And while we're waiting for the sumptuous fare about to be laid before us, you can tell me what you'd like me to teach you. I've no doubt I'll be the best governess you've ever had.' She warmed to her task. She loved to learn. Now she'd find out if she were as gifted in imparting her knowledge. 'I'm an authority on all the graces, with a special passion for the classics and, believe it or not, Caro, the sciences.'

Harriet looked down at her exercise book where she'd drawn a stern-faced insect wearing a monocle and lisped, 'I want to learn about worms, and Mama says Caro's going to need a lot of help if she's to catch a husband.'

'Worms? We'll make a worm farm, then.' Sarah spoke above Caro's protests. 'As for Caro — ' Her tone was thoughtful. Caro glowered and mumbled something incoherent as she stared down at her empty place setting.

'Enunciate, Caro.' Sarah spoke crisply. 'All I caught was the word 'ridiculous', and I do concur, it's a ridiculous notion you'll never catch a husband. Certainly you're no beauty, but that's sure to change. I was at my most unprepossessing at sixteen, and I remember girls far worse off who turned into veritable swans and waltzed off with nabobs and dukes.'

'You didn't hear, Miss Morecroft,' Harriet piped up as nursery tea — predictably, egg and toast — was served. 'Caro doesn't want a husband, but nobody ever listens.'

'Not want a husband?' Sarah frowned as she took her seat at the table.

'Finding a husband is not life's most noble pursuit,' mumbled Caro.

'Noble? There's nothing noble about securing a husband, but unless one intends to be a nun it's a young woman's most important enterprise. A girl must use all her wits and wiles to ensure she is as well-placed as possible.'

'Caro wants to be a blue-stocking,' said Augusta.

'Will you be of independent means some day?'

'What?' Caro was clearly affronted.

'Unless you are,' said Sarah patiently, 'an indulgent husband who will grant you the latitude to pursue your intellectual leanings is a far more desirable proposition than playing unpaid servant to those in the household who feel they have a legitimate claim upon your time.'

'You're not married,' Harriet pointed out, 'and you're much older than Caro.'

Caro sounded triumphant. 'So if there aren't enough of the good ones to go around — '

'There are,' Sarah interrupted. 'In fact, during my first season out I found the perfect husband after turning down half a dozen manageable suitors.'

'But you didn't marry him, did you?' Despite herself, Caro looked interested.

'He died on the peninsula two weeks before our wedding day.' Sarah toyed with her food. She was dismayed to have experienced only the slightest pang recounting this distant chapter in her life. Not so long ago she'd believed she'd never get over it. Could she really have lost her heart? Certainly, she'd lost it to Captain Danvers seven years ago. But was she now so old she was immune to the heady sensations that accompanied being in love?

When the girls pressed her she was tight-lipped. For one thing, she was not sure what the Hawthornes knew of Miss Morecroft's history. For another, she hadn't the heart to pursue the topic. Her first love had ended in tragedy, her second in disappointment. James, her distant cousin whom she loved like a brother, had betrayed her by supporting her father's cork-brained quest to marry the two of them off to each other, simply because James was next to inherit Lord Miles's title and estate.

'Not another word on the subject!' Sarah rapped upon the table for silence. 'Life contains many disappointments.'

'You must be very brave, Miss Morecroft.' Admiration shone from Augusta's serious dark eyes. 'You're not scared of spiders, are you? You wouldn't even be scared of Master.'

'Your dog?' asked Sarah, and Caro giggled.

'My father,' she said. 'Everyone's scared of him.'

'Goodness.' Sarah frowned. 'Nobody should be scared of their father. Why, mine's the world's most terrible ogre but I'm not scared of him. Or rather, I wasn't,' she amended hastily.

'You defied him?' whispered Caro, round-eyed as she fidgeted with her lilac sash, her food untouched before her.

Lilac! Sarah shuddered. Only the most unfeeling guardian would dress a girl of Caro's colouring in such a shade. Transferring her attention to the girl's intense expression, Sarah said, 'Not outright. That would have been to no purpose.'

'Then how did you manage such a thing?' Caro strained forward as if the question were of the greatest importance.

Sarah chose her words carefully. Caro might not be such a lost cause, after all. 'You have to work out how a person thinks.' She smiled. 'Learn cunning, while all the time appearing ever so meek and obedient. They think they're getting their way when, really, you're getting yours. Or, at least, you're not completely giving in to them. Take these eggs, for example,' she added, gaining inspiration from the soft-boiled eggs that were growing cold in front of them. 'Pass the charcoal, please, Harriet.'

Perplexed, the girls watched as Sarah drew a face on her egg. She pushed it towards Caro, together with the charcoal.

'Now draw the face of whoever frightens you most in the world.'

With great deliberation Caro pencilled in

sideburns and a head of wavy hair, adding a smart cravat before touching up Sarah's attempts at a face.

'You're quite an artist.' Sarah's tone was admiring. 'Obviously this is a man of consequence. Now, face him squarely and tell him what you feel. Then chop off his head!'

The girls looked at Sarah, horrified.

'I couldn't possibly,' gasped Caro.

'If you can't even tell it to an egg, small wonder the man himself reduces you to a quivering jelly. You're hardly going to get your own way if you lose your nerve every time he looks at you. So go on, face your egg sternly and tell it what you really think. Come now, Caro. Say: 'I despise the way you . . . '

Caro hesitated. Then taking a deep breath she hissed, 'I hate knowing you're ashamed of me; that you're so concerned at the impression I make upon people who in your opinion matter but who I don't ever want to see again. I hate the way you ignore me, think I'm ugly and stupid — '

'Right! Well, I'd be surprised if your egg hadn't got the message — ' Sarah cut in. Caro's voice had risen alarmingly. 'Perhaps now is a good time to cut off its head.'

'So I cut off your head! Like this! So I don't ever suffer the agonies of your ill opinion again!'

Seizing the bread knife, Caro sliced it through the air, wielding it with as much enthusiasm as any London executioner.

In shocked silence they all watched as the egg shot out of its cradle and hurtled through the air towards the door, levelling off at chest height . . . at the precise moment the door opened.

And as nursery dinner made contact with the immaculately clad torso of the handsome gentleman Sarah had made eyes at earlier that day, Caro cried out in anguish, 'Father!'

2

Silently, the object of Sarah's earlier admiration — no longer so immaculately attired — stared at the mess of yolk that now adorned his striped waistcoat.

'Such dreadful timing, sir!' muttered Sarah, seizing a napkin and dabbing at the sticky yellow patch. Conscious of the hard muscle beneath the two thin layers of clothing, and the fact that her enthusiasm in righting the damage was compounding the awkwardness, she stopped.

He removed the napkin from her grasp. 'Miss Morecroft, I presume?' Studying her through cool grey eyes, the gentleman tossed the linen upon the table.

Sarah was stunned into silence. No man had ever spoken to her like this. Like some erring minion. She could feel her cheeks burning. 'My apologies for the egg upon your waistcoat, sir, but it is decidedly me who has it upon her face, since I put Caro up to it.'

To her dismay the joke fell flat. Obviously the gentleman had no sense of humour. None of the sensual merriment she was accustomed to in her usual dealings with the opposite sex shone from his handsome, ascetic face. And indeed, it was a particularly fine face.

'Surely playing cricket with eggs falls within the domain of high-spirited young scamps, not gently nurtured young ladies?' He continued to frown at her, almost as if he couldn't make her out. 'I hope your curriculum, Miss Morecroft, takes account of the station in life to which these young ladies aspire.'

Sarah hung her head. 'Yes . . . Mr Hawthorne.'

'I came to welcome you into the household that was once your father's home.' Again, no smile to soften the effect of his earlier rebuke. 'I was sorry to hear of your misfortunes, Miss Morecroft.'

'Thank you.' She could not raise her voice above a whisper. Guilt stabbed at her once again. She was wicked. She would get her come-uppance, though at least she need not fear exposure from this quarter. The real Sarah Morecroft had been a child when her father had taken the family to India.

'And, while I appreciate your honesty in acknowledging your influence behind my daughter's uncharacteristically hoydenish behaviour, I suppose I should be glad your recent traumatic experiences have not sapped you of all spirit.'

Sarah's gratification at what she'd interpreted

as reluctant admiration was short-lived. There was not a jot of appreciation in his look as he scrutinized her. How dare he sweep his eyes over her with such scant regard, as if she were simply the — well, the mousy governess?

Glancing at a clearly mortified Caro, she felt a surge of anger replace her guilt. Yes, her own father might shout and try to cow her, but he peppered his fiery words with reluctant praise for her beauty, wit and intellect, damning her at the same time for not having been born a son.

Mr Hawthorne's tone still carried a warning as he put his hand on the doorknob to leave. 'Caro will have her come-out next year. Your father presented a very persuasive case for my employing you, Miss Morecroft. I trust you'll not disappoint his memory.'

'Sir — ' Desperate to detain him so as not to be abandoned to the girls in such a humiliating manner, Sarah strove for a disarming combination of entreaty and contrition. 'I realize what a great debt I owe you for the opportunity to prove myself as tutor to your children, especially Caro who I consider has great potential — '

' — For improvement, yes,' Mr Hawthorne cut in. 'Now, if you'll excuse me, my dinner guests are waiting. I merely put my head in to welcome you to Larchfield. I, too, have every

24

confidence Caro will make a shining debut in another six months — ' He levelled a meaningful look at Sarah ' — provided her new governess can impart the many accomplishments with which I was assured she was endowed.'

The door closed. Three seconds of shocked silence was broken by Caro's plaintive wail, 'He despises me!' as she plunged out of the room.

Harriet and Augusta exchanged looks, the latter remarking dryly, 'Uncle Roland wasn't very nice, was he?'

Nice? Sarah was furious. What callous brute would dismiss his daughter in such a manner? But diplomacy was her ally in desperate circumstances and she managed a dismissive, 'Your uncle is probably not feeling quite himself,' before she went in search of the distressed Caro.

Sarah's indignation had assumed monumental proportions by the time she finally retired to her poky little bedchamber, after trying to soothe Caro. She'd made some headway, but of course, what gains could she make when they'd barely met?

Mr Hawthorne was a monster. A cold, emotionless brute, completely derelict in the discharge of his paternal responsibilities. The way he'd treated the new governess was little better.

25

She tore out the pins securing her unflattering topknot with a serious of vicious tugs in line with her righteous anger, then shook out her hair. Mr Hawthorne would change his tune when she was done. In three weeks, as he acknowledged Caro and the miracles his new governess had wrought, he'd be begging her to stay.

Then her anger drained away. Covering her face with her hands, she slumped over the dressing table. It was a terrible thing to impersonate a young woman who'd died. And she was being justly punished.

The candle guttered, sending lonely shadows dancing upon the walls. Everything was hideous; alien. No elegant Argand lamp by which to read the classics or a thrilling romantic novel. No witty conversation, Madeira or tempting delicacy to round off the evening.

Yet this was the way governesses lived and it was her choice to have joined their ranks. Though, frowning, she thought that surely her own series of governesses had been pampered and spoiled. Then she recalled that they had had rooms just like this one and she'd not given a thought as to whether they might wish for surroundings less austere.

No point thinking about what could not be changed, she decided, as she returned to the trunk. There was no maid to tidy up after her and she needed to find a home for the last of the garments littering the floor. Perhaps that impertinent nursery maid had a brood of brothers and sisters and would be glad of them, she thought. She'd rather go naked in a blizzard than suffer the feel of such coarse, ugly material against her skin.

As Sarah pushed the threadbare garments to the bottom of the trunk her hand came into contact with a hard object. A book, by the feel of it. Intrigue quickly turned to scepticism. No point in pulling it out if Sarah Morecroft's taste in reading matter was as deplorable as her style.

But of course curiosity got the better of her and, taking a seat on the bed once more, she flipped to the flyleaf and studied the neat, heavily looped writing. Miss Morecroft's diary.

'So how do you find everything?' Once again, there was Ellen's inquisitive little nose poking around the door after the most cursory of knocks. Without waiting for a reply, she bustled across the room and settled herself upon the spindly chair beneath the window. Clearly she expected all sorts of confidences Sarah had no intention of sharing, though Sarah conceded in the next moment she might at least learn something of this strange household and her odd employers. Straightening up to sit on the bed and tucking the diary she now couldn't wait to read under her pillow, she asked, 'When I met Mrs Hawthorne I assumed she was married to the master.'

Ellen giggled. 'Lord, no! He thinks her the silliest thing under the sun, not but what he's always ever so civil.' She grinned, clearly delighted to find herself custodian of knowledge Sarah would want, and need, to know. Tucking a strand of lank brown hair back into her starched white cap, she went on, 'Mrs Hawthorne married Mr Hawthorne's older brother, Mr Hector, only he died seven years ago just afore Augusta was born.'

'What happened to Mr Hawthorne's wife?'

A cunning look crossed the nursery maid's face. 'Died in the same accident as Mr Hector. Mrs Hawthorne's kept house for the master ever since.'

Sarah, still discomforted by her meeting with her employer, was intrigued. 'So Caro is Mr Hawthorne's only daughter. He seems very hard on her.'

'That's because Caro's mother was a trollop!' Clearly, Ellen enjoyed a bit of gossip. 'She were running off with dashing Mr Hector when the carriage went off the bridge and they both was drowned. Not that it were the first gentleman she ran off with what wasn't her husband. Anyway, the poor master's terrified Caro might have inherited her mother's loose morals. She didn't inherit her beauty, that's for sure.'

Good Lord, poor Mr Hawthorne. Sarah frowned, calculating as she surmised, 'He must have married very young.'

'Just come into his majority.' Hugging herself, Ellen leaned forward. 'You ready to hear a tale of dastardly doings?'

Sarah decided not to dignify this with an answer, although she managed an expression that was mildly interested. Fortunately, it did not take much encouragement to set loose the nursery maid's tongue.

'When Caro's mother — Lady Venetia as she was called then — met Mr Hector he were affianced to Mrs Hawthorne. As you can imagine, the mistress were as much a beauty then as she is now.' She sniggered. 'But she came with a great fortune, whereas Lady Venetia was penniless. But so beautiful! You can see her portrait in the gallery.'

She sighed, then added matter-of-factly, 'Only good thing to say about 'er, really. Anyway, she begged Mr Hector to choose her, instead. Oh, he was tempted, but the money talked louder and he and Mrs Hawthorne were married.' Ellen made a moue, parodying the late Lady Venetia's apparent disappointment before continuing, 'So poor, spurned Lady Venetia turned her attentions to Mr.

Hawthorne, the master, as is, now.' Her eyes darted to the door and she lowered her voice. 'Word was that Lady Venetia's reputation was ruined with all her carryings-on. And that young Mr Hawthorne's honour — which was a great deal stronger than his brother's — was prevailed upon. Anyway, the poor man was smitten so it didn't matter what she'd done, and besides, he had money enough. A rich inheritance from a doting aunt. So he married her . . . to his eternal regret, for there never was a less loving or grateful wife.'

Sarah hoped she did not appear as intrigued as she was. What a delicious scandal. It was hard to imagine the austere man who'd presented himself just now in the nursery smouldering with passion for a heartless beauty.

'What was she like?'

'She were the vainest creature what ever lived. She ate men for breakfast — leastaways, she did until she met 'er match in the villainous Sir Richard Byrd, only that's another whole story.' She sighed, as if hankering after this bygone era. 'I could tell you a thing or two about Lady Venetia and this household that would make yer hair stand on end. It were a lot livelier then!'

The magnificent oil painting of the late Lady Venetia, commissioned by Mr Hawthorne as a wedding present, hung near the mullioned windows at the end of the parquet-floored gallery.

Poor Caro, thought Sarah, as she stared up at the proud, fiery eyes that gazed out beneath disdainfully arched brows. Although her eldest charge possessed her mother's fine dark eyes and coal-black hair, all similarities ended there. The slight upturn of the late mistress's full and sensuous mouth hinted at some private satisfaction while her sumptuous gown and rich jewels indicated a love of finery.

She wondered if Caro's refusal to make any attempt at improving her appearance was simply rebelliousness. Well, she'd soon set the girl straight.

She also wondered if the swell of Lady Venetia's creamy white breasts above her daringly cut evening gown still had the power to move the master when he stopped to admire the likeness of his late wife.

Sarah glanced down at her own awful gown. Last night she had borrowed needle and thread in order to launch a serious attack upon her wardrobe. Instead of dropping hemlines she'd worked hard to increase the deleterious effects of shrinkage and staining. Surely Mrs Hawthorne would remember her offer of cast-off clothes.

'My mother was the most beautiful woman

in Dorset,' came a cool voice beside her, and Sarah turned to see Caro at her left shoulder staring dispassionately at the portrait. 'Hard to believe when you look at me.'

Sarah hesitated, sensitive to her adolescent charge's vulnerability. Though she'd always been confident of her own beauty, she still remembered the uncertainties of her adolescent friends and cousins. 'There's little resemblance, but your eyes are finer.'

Caro arched her brows. 'False flattery, Miss Morecroft.'

'What would you say if I told you I was considered a great beauty where I come from?' countered Sarah. Laughing, she added, 'Your silence wounds me. But what if I told you that clothes, the artful application of my favourite Liquid Bloom of Roses and my hair styled *à la Greque*, instead of this unflattering topknot, would make me the toast of the town?'

At Caro's sceptical look Sarah's amusement grew. 'Just wait, Miss Hawthorne. When I'm done you'll see that you can be both a beauty and a blue-stocking.'

Sure enough, Sarah's ploy with a needle and thread worked upon Mrs Hawthorne's conscience, for several days later Sarah returned to her room to find three day dresses and an evening gown upon her bed.

Their flounces and furbelows screamed their decrepitude (three seasons ago!) but Sarah was as gifted with a needle in creating wonders as she was in wreaking havoc.

She was gratified by the admiration in young master Cosmo's eyes as he greeted her on the stair the following day.

'Oh, miss, you look lovely,' breathed Harriet when Sarah entered the schoolroom; and although Caro said nothing, Sarah, who was watching her closely, registered the surprised widening of her eyes.

'All it needs is the right bonnet,' Sarah announced, stooping for the copy of *The Iliad* which lay upon the table. 'I thought you girls might like to go into town and help me choose one.'

Harriet and Augusta regarded her as if she were mad, while Caro actually choked.

'Did your previous governess never take you on shopping expeditions?' Sarah looked up from her task of selecting a passage from the text. She had surprised herself at her desire to devise a curriculum for the girls that was both instructive and entertaining.

'Oh miss, do we have to read that?' groaned Harriet.

Sarah snapped the book shut. 'If society decrees that your social success depends upon your being a beauty, my job is to ensure you are at least a well-read one.'

'Governesses have not the means to go shopping,' Caro pointed out virtuously, raising her head from *The Revd Huckerby's Treatise Against Sin*, ignoring Sarah's last remark. 'And Papa would never countenance such frivolity.'

'But he *has* countenanced a visit to the circulating library. The carriage is being brought round as we speak. Naturally we'll need refreshment, also. And it would be foolish to walk right by a milliner's if one happened to get in our way — don't you think?'

The younger girls were vociferous in their agreement. And although Caro said nothing, at least she didn't object when Sarah ushered her out of the schoolroom and down the stairs.

★ ★ ★

For the first time since she'd survived the shipwreck, Sarah was enjoying herself. The fresh spring air and the warmth of the sun on her face as they sauntered through the prosperous little town were balm to her soul. The visit to the circulating library, however, was cursory as she chivvied Caro to make her selection so they'd have time to do the important chores — such as visit the milliner's, where Sarah had noticed a very pretty chip bonnet in the window.

'You can't possibly mean to buy that?' Caro gasped when she saw the price.

'Indeed I do,' Sarah assured her. 'Only I have one more errand. Caro, here's money for currant buns your aunt was generous enough to donate to the occasion. Now I want you to look after your cousins and I'll meet you here in ten minutes. No, you can't come with me.'

Shameless she might be, but little girls had a habit of innocently revealing all, and Sarah's visit to the pawnbroker's was not something she wanted Augusta happily divulging to her mother or uncle.

With no regret, she handed over her necklace in return for a sum that would keep herself in the luxuries necessary to make the following couple of weeks tolerable.

The next visit was to the apothecary's. Caro might disapprove of her purchases: Royal Tincture of Peach Kernels, Olympian Dew and, of course, the essential Liquid Bloom of Roses. Mr and Mrs Hawthorne *certainly* would.

With these items carefully concealed in brown paper, Sarah gave a sigh of satisfaction and stepped out onto the pavement.

Right into the path of Mr Hawthorne.

'Good morning, sir,' she said, endeavouring

to maintain her composure and wishing heartily the three girls were in tow.

She was upon the point of calling them, pretending they'd disappeared round a corner, and then excusing herself and supposedly dashing after them, when he remarked dryly, 'While I am glad you had delicacy enough to shield your charges from a pawnbroker's, might I ask what supervision they currently enjoy?'

'Caro is buying the girls currant buns — ' Sarah tried to sound as nonchalant as she could. 'I considered ten minutes' absence in the care of their cousin who, after all, might be married within the twelvemonth, safe enough. And of course, as you yourself remarked, I couldn't take them to a pawnbroker's.'

'Not a pawnbroker's . . . no.' He waited expectantly, the sun at his back throwing his lean, athletic body into relief.

Sarah sighed. 'Sir, my clothes have been ruined by salt water. As I had a necklace I was able to pawn, I did so in order to make those additions to my wardrobe necessary to do honour to the family which employs me.'

Mr Hawthorne looked unimpressed. 'Mrs Hawthorne, I believe, generously donated four fine gowns and shawls of her own.'

'From three seasons ago,' objected Sarah before she could stop herself.

His disapproval was palpable.

36

Quickly, Sarah continued, 'Of course, she *was* very generous but — ' She put out her hands, as if exhorting him to concur. ' — there were the other necessary additions . . . like a new bonnet, and slippers. And of course, gloves.'

Her defence was not having the desired effect. Mr Hawthorne was positively glowering.

'Miss Morecroft, such frivolity is not countenanced in my household. Your father assured me of your sober temperament. I paid your passage and offered you a home upon the death of your late mother — '

'Oh, sir!' Sarah caught her breath in what she considered a heart-rending manner. Running the back of her hand across her eyes, she darted a surreptitious look from between her fingers. Yes, this was proving a most effective way of quelling his diatribe. She could see his immediate self-recrimination was genuine. 'You have been kindness itself!' She hiccupped, unable to continue, for her tears were suddenly no longer feigned. She thought of her darling papa, who must be mad with grief. Guilt bubbled up inside her. Nor had she any right to deceive the decent, if somewhat grim, gentleman before her.

But how to extricate herself?

Mr Hawthorne's frown was now one of deep concern. Taking her by the elbow, he led her into a narrow alley, away from the curious looks of passers-by.

Sarah stared at her feet, encased in their ugly, serviceable second-hand boots, bit her lip and gave another hiccupping sob.

'Miss Morecroft, I apologize.'

Raising her head, she was struck anew by his fine grey eyes regarding her with . . . compassion? She was even more surprised when he put his hand on her shoulder and said with genuine feeling, 'My behaviour was unsympathetic and ungentlemanly.'

Her heart gave an unexpected lurch. To cover her awkwardness she managed a brave smile as she said briskly, 'You had every right. Please, sir, if I promise never to set foot in another pawnbroker's, may I be forgiven and fetch the girls? I must get them ready for nursery tea.'

His normally severe expression softened. The extraordinary transformation only increased Sarah's loss of composure.

'I hope you did not pawn something that was precious to you, Miss Morecroft. I will gladly redeem it. That is, if you do in fact promise to approach me before you consider setting foot in such a place again.'

'It was nothing precious, sir.' Though her heart was beating quickly, Sarah ventured a wicked grin. 'Merely a trinket I happened upon during my brief visit to the ocean floor.'

'The girl is quite unlike Godby's description of her.' Roland scowled at Mrs Hawthorne, who was stitching an elaborate pastoral scene that consumed most of her daily hours.

With speed and deftness she worked the needle and coloured threads. Roland often wondered how she could spend so many hours by the fire — in all weathers — when the garden beckoned, beyond.

She picked up a skein of gold and glanced at him. 'I believe excessive sea water in the system can unhinge the mind. Her manners are lax. I did warn you, Roland, but hopefully time will reveal a more sober nature.'

Roland raked his fingers through his hair as he kicked a burning log further into the fire. 'I'm not about to turn her out.' He sighed. 'I owe her father too much. But when all's said and done I must act in Caro's best interests. I cannot risk her being corrupted by a frivolous and hoydenish young woman.'

His scowl deepened as he reflected on their encounter the previous afternoon. Yes, the girl was quite unlike Godby's description of her, and Roland was dangerously discomposed. Both by Miss Morecroft, and his response to her.

Mrs Hawthorne clicked her tongue before

adding, 'Indeed, Caro is in the greatest moral danger . . . through no fault of her own.' She bent once more over her work and shook her head to emphasize her point.

Not for the first time, Roland looked dispassionately at the bobbing ginger corkscrew curls which his brother had so cruelly derided before he'd married Cecily for her money, and wished his sister-in-law could bring herself to feel a little more kindness for his daughter.

'Caro is old enough to eat with us at table,' he said abruptly, ignoring Cecily's dire prediction. He didn't want to risk her dredging up the past, yet again. 'With her governess. That way we might better observe Miss Morecroft's manners.' Picking up a small plaster bust of a cupid wearing a seraphic smile, his frown became even more pained. 'If she proves unsuitable we will have to find her another post.'

★   ★   ★

'Sit at table with my aunt and father!' With a shriek, Caro leapt up from the nursery table and threw herself against the window sill, her hands to her face. 'Oh, that's worse than anything!'

Sarah's smile faded. 'But you'll do them

40

such credit.' She stepped forward and put a reassuring hand on the girl's unresponsive shoulder. 'I'll teach you how to deport yourself with confidence. We'll turn you into the toast of the town.'

'I don't want to be the toast of the town!' Caro sobbed. 'I want to be left alone to read my books.'

It took two days before Sarah finally persuaded Caro to submit to her cache of beauty aids. Afterwards she cajoled Ellen into helping them both with their hair using tongs, a jug of water laid before the fire, and sugar to set the curls.

Sarah had again been busy with her needle and thread. The little girls had been her willing assistants, happily parroting French conjugations as they handed her the various coloured threads and other tools she needed.

Now it was the day of reckoning and she was ready. As the dinner gong reverberated through the house, Sarah allowed herself a moment of self-congratulation. Then she hastened Caro to her own room to look in the tarnished mirror which rested on the chest of drawers.

'A credit to your father, don't you think?' Her eyes raked her young protégé with pride.

Caro's dull cheeks had been enlivened with a discreet touch of Liquid Bloom of Roses. Her best dress, once a utilitarian and modest gown of Pomona green velvet, had been remodelled to resemble something in the first stare.

Sarah's heart leapt with anticipation. She could not wait to present her handiwork and earn her employers' admiration.

'Are you ready, Caro?' she asked, and was gratified by the spark of wonder in the young girl's eyes as she continued to stare at her reflection.

'I don't look anything like myself,' she whispered, her tone indicating this was a good thing.

'You look beautiful,' Sarah said, and meant it. 'Just don't spoil it with poor posture. You need to make your entrance with pride and dignity.' She gave the girl's arm a quick squeeze. 'Just you wait. Your father will be overcome!'

As Sarah had anticipated, amazed silence greeted their entrance. She smiled demurely at her employers as she sank into her seat. Lowering her eyes to her plate, she waited for the praise.

Silence.

Clearly, they were lost for words. She had obviously excelled at her self-appointed task of transforming Caro into a vision of loveliness.

Only as the silence lengthened did she feel the first stirrings of doubt. She raised her head to glance first to her left, where Caro was cringing with unconcealed embarrassment, not daring to look at anyone; then to the head of the table where Mr Hawthorne sat.

Her heart missed a beat, then uncertainty turned to anger. What father would look at his daughter with such undisguised recrimination? As if it were a crime for a woman to try and improve herself.

But it was Mrs Hawthorne, clutching her scrawny throat, who shrieked, 'Have you been using complexion enhancers, Caro?'

The direct accusation stirred Caro to retaliation. Her cheeks took on a feverish hue. 'Do you mean like Mother?' she ground out. 'Yes, I found them once in her dressing table drawer and decided to use them tonight.' She took an unsteady breath. 'I did not realize Mother was considered *such* a harlot!'

Shocked silence greeted her outburst.

Caro gave a choking sob as she added, 'Forgive me, Father, for *daring* to remind you of her.'

Sarah bit her lip, watching Caro confront her aunt and father. Both looked increasingly concerned as Caro, now in full swing, went on, 'Poor Mother — it's a good thing she's not alive to see what a hideous creature she brought into the world. But then, how much easier it will be to eschew the vices and wickedness which brought her down. I recall you saying something along these lines once, Aunt Cecily.'

Mrs Hawthorne turned puce. 'Really, Caro,

I don't recall ever — '

But it was Sarah who finally took charge, saying brightly — despite having to quell her own trembling — 'I read in the news sheet that the prince regent's banquet for more than a hundred guests at Carlton House is the talk of the town.'

Hopefully that would deflect attention from Caro, who appeared on the verge of a breakdown. Caro's fears and insecurities must have been feeding on gossip for years. Sympathy washed over Sarah. Outrage, too.

She took a spoonful of lobster soup. 'Delicious,' she pronounced.

When there was no response she glanced up again. Why was everyone staring at her as if she had somehow scandalized them as much as Caro had? Caro was glancing at her nervously. Mrs Hawthorne, even more puce now, was looking as if she'd like to turn Sarah into a lobster and then into soup. And Mr Hawthorne was regarding her as if she had already turned into, if not a lobster, then certainly something very much resembling a spiky, hideous crustacean. At least Cosmo was gazing at her with undisguised admiration. That was some solace.

Sarah raised her chin. 'Sir, do you not believe Caro's appearance tonight vastly improved? It will increase her confidence and,

44

in turn, her chances.'

A succession of emotions seemed to flit across her employer's face. His slate-grey eyes, seemingly darker, settled disapprovingly on her bare arms before he fixed her with a cold, level stare. 'Clearly, Miss Morecroft, you had eyes only for the description of the Gothic chapel in which the royal entourage dined; of the fifty-six haunches of venison, ninety-three brace of pheasant and two dozen turtles that were devoured. You were unmoved, it would appear, by the news sheet's report on what I suspect you'd consider a fairly minor occurrence at St Peter's Fields in Manchester.'

Sarah stared at him.

'An orderly meeting of fifty thousand people wished for an audience to hear their grievances. Like the high cost of bread. The average labourer breaks his back so his landlord can dine on *le jambon à la broche* and truffles, yet his wage cannot support his family.' His expression became thunderous. 'Then the cavalry moved in. Eleven people were killed, and more than four hundred injured. Should we countenance such things in civilized society? Are you teaching my daughter respect for worthy values, or filling her head with frivolous nonsense?'

Sarah was lost for words. She had heard her father rant and rave on such topics. Only,

45

he came from the opposing side.

Carefully, Mr Hawthorne pushed together his knife and fork. 'Miss Morecroft — ' His glittering eyes lanced her with scorn. ' — I would like to see you in my study after dinner.'

★　★　★

Sarah's prepared speech, she believed, incorporated a fine balance of contrition with just a dusting of flirtation. Yes, she took her role as governess seriously, but while she sympathized with the families of the dead there was a place for frivolity. She was quite happy to agree that if she knew what the cost of bread was, it was undoubtedly too high.

By the time she had finished Mr Hawthorne would be begging her pardon for having maligned and misjudged her.

But reflecting on the scorn and anger in his turbulent grey eyes unsettled her in a way that was entirely alien.

3

What was he to do about the girl? Roland paced before the fire which warmed his study. His sanctuary. The only room in the house where he was safe from Cecily and the silly, chattering acquaintances she liked to entertain.

Yet he did not feel at peace.

He drew back the curtains and stared out into the starlit night. As cold and black as his soul.

The girl was not at all what he had been led to believe.

But what was worse than her apparent preoccupation with life's worldly pleasures was her resemblance to her father. To his old schoolboy companion and foster brother, Godby Morecroft. Oh, not in features, but certainly in character.

The way her eyes glittered with challenge in that beautiful face of hers when she was gainsaid. The mutinous set of her rosebud mouth when she was waiting to put across her opposing point of view. Why, it was Godby all over again.

He did not turn immediately as he heard

her enter. He knew only too well the look she would level at him. He could almost hear Godby's voice: smooth, cajoling, with a hint of humour intended to ameliorate his anger.

He would not allow her the chance to speak first in order to defend herself. Somehow Godby had always managed to make him feel a killjoy Puritan when he had as much desire to enjoy life as anyone. Just not as thoughtlessly as Godby.

'My daughter is not to have her head turned by foolish fancies.' He came directly to the point, waving Miss Morecroft to a chair while he returned to stand in front of the fire.

If she would just bow her head and show a little contrition it would be a good start, Roland thought. *Don't be like Godby, who could never admit he was wrong.*

'Foolish fancies?' Her smile was guileless. She was confident, no doubt, that she was incapable of doing wrong. Just like her father.

His heart hardened.

How different from when she had landed on his doorstep, penniless and orphaned. Nearly a victim of the high seas. At the time it had seemed she'd not even good looks to recommend her.

But then some extraordinary metamorphosis had occurred. Within the space of a few days Miss Morecroft had been transformed;

like a water rat she had emerged, sleek and jaunty and ripe for anything.

'Sir, your daughter is in little danger of having her head turned. All she thinks about is improving her mind.'

Her gaze was steady, her bearing composed — very different from the way he felt. He tried to retain his dignity as she stared at him from the depths of her leather armchair.

'Caro,' he managed to say evenly, 'is not a beauty, and you will only make her look a fool by trying to turn her into one.'

'With respect, sir, the sad truth is that a woman's face is, more often than not, her fortune.'

Until now — well, recently — Roland had not appreciated what a fine face Miss Morecroft possessed. Her eyes were amazing, glowing bright with life and humour; her cheek bones were well defined, her chin slightly pointed so that her face appeared heart-shaped when combined with the effect of her coiffure: a fashionable 'V' parting with cascades of shining ringlets tumbling from the band which secured them at the top of her head. And her dress. He frowned. Cecily's gown — he remembered it, now. A drab, russet confection once adorned with too many frills and furbelows. What a transformation. This girl had obviously worked wonders with

49

her needle and thread. She would have got on famously with Venetia.

Venetia . . . and Godby.

His heart turned to stone. However persuasive Miss Morecroft's argument, his armour was back in place.

Oh dear, thought Sarah, this man really was a Puritan. The moment she even mentioned 'worldly pleasures' he seemed to tense. And the way he spoke of his daughter made her blood boil! But she went on blithely, 'I have always believed confidence and wit among one's greatest assets. If Caro is to be presented next year she'll be competing with a great many beautiful and accomplished young ladies.'

Now why was he looking at her like that? Sarah wondered indignantly. Had she dropped sauce upon her dress?

Instantly she saw him colour and his eyes return to her face, where they were now fixed grimly. She stifled the impulse to smile. Oh ho, so the master did appreciate a pretty face and figure. Only right now he was doing his best to fight it.

The observation gave her confidence.

Yes, Sarah had learned a thing or two about men since storming her way out of the schoolroom as a precocious fifteen-year-old to play hostess at her father's parliamentary dinners after her mother had died.

Mr Hawthorne, however, was unlike any of the men her father entertained. Dangerous radicals like Roland Hawthorne did not receive invitations from Lord Miles.

Yet he hardly looked the threat to law and order, as her father would have maintained. Larchfield, with its exquisite grounds and works of art, was a testament to refinement.

Mr Hawthorne himself was a fine specimen of civilized manhood, far more to her taste than the pleasure-seeking rakes and popinjays her father entertained and who regularly made up to her. Well, as much as she would allow them. She quickly tired of their vanity and pomposity, although she'd pretended to encourage it. It was, after all, what was expected.

She flashed him another smile and was surprised and gratified by his brief awkwardness.

Clearly, there was more to her employer than met the eye. How intriguing. If this was a man who could smoulder with passion for a heartless beauty seven years ago, thought Sarah, she would be more than interested to find out what excited his passions now that he had apparently adopted a more sober outlook on life.

She bowed her head. 'I accept your

censure, sir. I will not turn Caro's head with foolish nonsense. And I shall read the news sheets, for I must admit, I had in fact been reading some gossip column whose talk of the Carlton House Set I had thought might divert the girls — ' She stopped, adding ingeniously as she interpreted his glowering look, ' — with examples of deplorable behaviour to be condemned.'

Mr Hawthorne seemed to struggle for words.

'Miss Morecroft,' he said finally, 'you are here to instruct the girls in simple arithmetic, spelling, French and drawing. Not to provide moral guidance. That,' he added crisply, 'is something you can leave to me.'

He nodded in dismissal.

Sarah hesitated, about to cast one of those seductive lures which came naturally and which had successfully hooked many an admirer in the past.

No. Coquetry was not going to win over Mr. Hawthorne, despite experience showing her men liked their women beautiful and vacuous. She paused, turning, her hand on the doorknob. He nodded stiffly, his eyes nevertheless lingering upon her.

Her heart gave an unexpected little skip. She couldn't remember when she had last felt such anticipation.

4

'She's a mean old cat and I'm not going down.'

'Yes you are.' Sarah bared her teeth in what she'd intended to be a saccharine smile. 'Now, shoulders back and get rid of that scowl.' She took Caro's arm and propelled her to the nursery door. 'Whoever conjugates the 'to be' verb first can have my portion of suet pudding,' Sarah said to the younger girls. 'Just think, Caro,' she added, as they descended the stairs in answer to Lady Charlotte's summons, 'in six months you'll be dining on caviar and champagne instead of suet and roly poly pudding.'

The notion failed to rally Caro. Glumly, she said, 'It's Papa's idea I be presented.'

'Surely you want to reflect well upon him?' With a sigh that wasn't devoid of affection, Sarah tucked an errant curl behind Caro's ear as they reached the drawing room door.

Lady Charlotte was a fascinating creature whose like Sarah had not met. With an acerbic wit and political leanings in sympathy with Mr Hawthorne's, her view of the world was a revelation. No sooner had Sarah and

Caro seated themselves than they were regaled with a scathing oratory on the heavy-handed tactics used to quell the Peterloo Massacre, as Lady Charlotte referred to it. Sarah suspected her father would have advocated that the cavalry move in to break up the 'rabble-rousing crowd', muskets blazing.

Now well into middle age, Lady Charlotte had the bone structure and a porcelain complexion that would see her a beauty at eighty. Once she had finished her diatribe she relaxed into her blue chintz seat and, with a sharp look at Sarah, observed, 'You favour your father, Miss Morecroft. Do you not think so, Cecily?'

'In manner, there is a strong resemblance,' replied Mrs Hawthorne with a disapproving twist to her thin mouth.

'Then we must hope you don't follow the same dangerous path.' Lady Charlotte looked grim as she added, 'And that you appreciate gratitude better than your father.' She sighed. 'How thoughtless of Godby to foist a brood of brats upon your poor mother on nothing more than soldier's pay. Still, he had no one else to blame for losing out on the fine inheritance he'd been expecting.' She shook her head at Sarah. 'I daresay your father could do no wrong in your eyes.'

So that was the story, thought Sarah. Or, at

least, part of it. 'He was my inspiration,' she murmured, determined not to be cowed by Lady Charlotte's bully tactics. Not a page of the first half of Sarah Morecroft's diary was without some glowing reference to the apparently incomparable Godby Morecroft. The diary also did not seem to contain much else of interest, which was why Sarah had left most of it unread.

'Not, I trust, the kind of inspiration that leads to similar disgrace and penury.' Mrs Hawthorne's tone was sharp.

Sarah realised her error. Clearly, she needed to learn more about the relationship between the late Godby Morecroft and her employer if she were not to land herself in worse trouble.

When Mrs Hawthorne excused herself to attend to some domestic matter Sarah tried a more subservient approach. She glanced at Caro. The girl seemed immersed in her own thoughts. 'Pray, Lady Charlotte, my mother made it clear what a great debt we owe Mr. Hawthorne and yet — ' She bit her lip. 'How am I to avoid my father's mistakes if I don't know precisely what they are?'

'Good Lord! Your father said *nothing* of his disgrace?'

Sarah shook her head.

Lady Charlotte adjusted her lorgnette. She

looked undecided. After a quick glance at Caro, still daydreaming, she said, 'You know that your father's advancement was on account of the especial fondness old Mr Hawthorne — Roland's father — had for him. Of course you do. Well, better get it over with before Cecily gets back. If there are two things that require us all dashing for the burnt feathers it's mention of — ' She lowered her voice. ' — Caro's mother.'

Resuming a more normal tone, she went on, 'Your father was the son of old Mr Hawthorne's estate manager and even from the age of eight, which was when old Mr Hawthorne first took an interest in him, he was a charmer. He and Mr Hector were the same age and great friends. Cut from the same cloth, too,' she added, disapprovingly, 'unlike the present Mr Hawthorne, who was born three years later. Your father's destiny was the local dame school and perhaps an apprenticeship, had not old Mr Hawthorne decided such a gifted lad ought to be tutored with his own sons and then bought a commission in the 10th Hussars. If you don't know what a pretty price a pair of colours that would have set him back it's not my place to tell you! It was commanded by the prince himself, for nothing but the best would do for your father, but it was his eye for the ladies that was his undoing.'

Sarah was fascinated. What a marvellous story. What could the rakish Godby Morecroft have done to have landed up in apparent ignominy, in India?

'Your mother was a comely lass of seventeen, and your father barely a year older when she . . . er . . . caught his fancy. A publican's daughter! Of course, he could have done a great deal better for himself but honour prevailed, or rather, old Mr Hawthorne's honour did, and your parents were married . . . in fairly timely fashion, for shortly afterwards you were born.'

Sarah blushed. 'So that's why my father was disgraced.'

'Indeed not!' exclaimed Lady Charlotte. 'I can't image to what purpose you've been shielded from all these . . . tawdry details, though I suppose Godby left it too late to tell you, as usual,' she added, with what Sarah considered great lack of feeling. 'Well, old Mr Hawthorne was far more generous to the newlyweds than your father deserved — Ah, Roland.' Lady Charlotte's cornflower-blue eyes widened almost coquettishly.

Not so long ago just such a smile would have come naturally to Sarah, but now she was tongue-tied, and her heart was skipping a little too fast for her liking.

'Ladies.' Mr Hawthorne acknowledged them with a small incline of his head, standing aside as Cecily re-entered the room.

'Sit down, Roland,' commanded Lady Charlotte, 'and tell me what else you know about these barbarians. I'm all for one knowing one's place but I do believe in an honest wage for honest toil.'

A shadow crossed Mr Hawthorne's face. Glancing at Sarah he hesitated, almost as if he was of a mind to plead his excuses and retire. When he took the only vacant seat just a foot from her, she was conscious of his nearness in a way she hadn't been since as a debutante she'd fallen in love with Captain Danvers at first sight.

Unaccountably awkward, Sarah glanced away as Lady Charlotte launched into an animated monologue on the likely outcome facing the ringleaders of the uprising. She hoped her high colour, if noticed, would be attributed to the heat of the fire.

Mr Hawthorne, dark and brooding, was the antithesis of her lost love whose Roman nose and blond curling hair had fired her adolescent senses.

Within weeks of gushing to James all those years ago that Captain Danvers was the only man she'd consider marrying, she was mourning his death and declaring her intention never to wed. She recalled, with painful affection, James's endless patience during her grief. Poor James. He'd be beside himself, thinking her dead right now. What was worse, he'd be so terribly wounded if the truth came out that she'd actually pretended to have drowned to avoid marrying him. Her plan was simply to turn up on her father's doorstep in a couple of weeks claiming to have been washed up on a beach and cared for by local villagers. Her grief-stricken father would grant her anything, then.

'Isn't that so, Miss Morecroft?'

She jerked her head round at the sound of Mr Hawthorne's mellifluous tones and stammered her apologies.

He regarded her a moment, smiled, then repeated, 'I was telling Lady Charlotte of your admirable approach to teaching Caro values and restraint.'

Lady Charlotte, looking dubious, responded, 'I'm not sure the gossip sheets are something Caro should even know about, but if you condone it, Roland, I daresay there are moral lessons to be learnt if approached in the right manner.' The way she was looking at Sarah suggested a healthy scepticism about Godby's daughter having any handle on morality.

Sarah looked past her and caught the glint of amusement in Mr Hawthorne's eye. Her heart did a little somersault. She smiled back.

The air felt suddenly charged between them, despite Lady Charlotte's and Mrs Hawthorne's presence. The darkening of Mr Hawthorne's pupils revealed he felt the same. Sarah had not spent the last six years encouraging or warding off the approaches of potential suitors without learning to recognize the signs of a male's interest.

Then it struck her anew that it was just as likely that, even if Mr Hawthorne was flirting, he believed he was doing so with a mere governess; that likely he was simply making atonement for his harsh words of earlier. It was a dampening thought. Squaring her shoulders, Sarah rose to the challenge. When the time was right she'd face Mr Hawthorne on equal ground.

'So there you have it, Caro,' she said, as they passed through the nursery on their way to Caro's bedchamber. Ellen was putting the younger girls to bed. 'I am the product of vice and sin, the granddaughter of a lowly publican. No wonder I was only reluctantly elevated to the dining room.'

'Don't say such things,' Caro muttered. 'My father believes people are distinguished by their actions, not by their rank. Lady Charlotte should never have said such things!'

'Your father faces a tough battle if he thinks

the baker's apprentice and the fishmonger worthy of a seat in the House of Commons.' She lit the candle on the bedside table. A very different code of morality existed in the circles in which she had grown up. Rank was everything. As for morality, Sarah knew many of the aristocratic matrons who visited her home at Thistlewaite were guiltlessly indulging in extramarital affairs, having dutifully produced the required male heir.

'My father is not a radical,' Caro said angrily, pulling on her night rail. 'Nor does he believe in turning rank on its head. He is a good, honourable man who hates the inequities of society. At least he has the courage of his convictions. He fought a duel for them once.'

Sarah raised her eyebrows. 'Over your mother?' she ventured ingenuously, helping Caro into bed. She'd like to hear more about the fascinating Venetia.

'My father would *never* fight a duel over a woman.' Caro's voice was full of scorn. 'He is far too principled to commit murder over something so . . . . unimportant.'

'Yet not too principled to fight a duel over something else.' This time it was Sarah's turn to sound scornful.

'Obviously you care nothing for the people to whom Papa has devoted his parliamentary career championing,' said Caro through gritted teeth as she reached for her book. 'You're lucky you're not a man, Miss Morecroft. It was an argument just like this that Papa had once in the House of Commons. Lord Miles challenged Papa to the duel right there and then.'

One minute Sarah was directing an indulgent, slightly mocking smile at Caro, the next she was wincing at the sudden roar in her ears. For a moment she truly thought she was going to faint. She sat heavily upon the bed.

Caro didn't notice. She was too busy thumbing the pages of her book with unusual energy, a snarl upon her face. 'Narrow-minded bigot! That's what Papa called him, and said it demeaned him to have to answer his challenge.'

Blinking rapidly to clear her head, Sarah murmured, 'I never heard about it.' She gazed at the brushes and combs lined up on the dressing table.

Her own father, fighting a duel with Mr Hawthorne! She tried to imagine it: Her red-faced, apoplectic father, trembling with the passion of his convictions, seeing nothing but a dangerous radical as he stared down his opponent.

No doubt Mr Hawthorne coolly stood his

ground. Compared with her father he was a very controlled man.

'It was lucky they both didn't have to resign from Parliament,' said Caro, 'because of course he thought it was ridiculous that honour decreed he must fight.'

'What happened?'

'Papa shot wide and Lord Miles missed. Well, he grazed Papa's shoulder but it was only a flesh wound.' Caro shuddered. 'Why drive a man to murder for pride?' She hugged her book to her chest, rolled over and presented Sarah with her back.

Sarah did not leave, as Caro had clearly indicated was her desire. Instead, she rose and went to the window.

'It's called passion,' she murmured, drawing aside the curtain to look into the darkness. 'Sixteen-year-old girls are not supposed to know about such dangerous emotions.'

Her voice trailed away as she contemplated if she had ever felt passion.

'I'll never fall victim to my passions,' mumbled Caro.

Sarah quirked an eyebrow at the huddled bedclothes, then returned her gaze to the darkness beyond the gardens. Not even a sliver of moon touched the landscape with light. 'Really?' Her tone was droll. She sighed. Such talk made her restless. She wanted to feel desire but it was as if in this household love, desire, passion . . . had destroyed the trust of a generation. Passion at Larchfield was the handmaiden of sin and vice. If Caro were lucky enough to experience the same spark of feeling which Sarah found so necessary to sustain her enthusiasm for life, she'd be forced to extinguish it long before it took root and blossomed.

'Do you not wish to fall in love, Caro?' she asked. 'Is it not the desire of your aunt and father that you marry a good man? That you marry for love?'

Caro said nothing.

Sarah sighed again, the girl's pubescent virtue suddenly irritating her. Caro would be dried up by nineteen.

She turned back to the window. 'Do you not long for the embrace of the man whom you admire beyond all others? The caress of his hand upon your cheek . . . ?' Her voice dropped to a whisper as she added, 'The sweet, gentle touch of his lips upon yours?'

Turning at the loud thud of the book thrown forcefully upon the floor, Sarah realised she'd gone too far.

It was time to apologise and take herself off to bed before she reversed all the gains she'd made with her difficult, but increasingly endearing, charge.

5

As Roland turned into the gallery, he was arrested by the odd sight of his sister-in-law on her toes upon the window seat, peering through the mullioned windows.

She swung round, red-faced — with anger not embarrassment — at the sound of his footstep. 'If Harriet's new dress is ruined I want Miss Morecroft dismissed upon the spot.'

Roland put out his hand to help Cecily to the ground. 'I wonder if their expedition will be as successful as last time?' His tone was mild. 'Harriet and Augusta tell me they captured a dozen inmates for their new worm farm.'

Cecily glared at him. 'I do not share your amusement, Roland. Miss Morecroft is impulsive and wayward and as such, highly unsatisfactory.'

Unsatisfactory? With an effort Roland kept his expression neutral as an image of Miss Morecroft's lovely face, eyes dancing with merriment, mouth trembling with barely suppressed laughter, appeared before him.

Steeling himself against the extraordinary

and dangerous yearning to possess that which he knew could only bring heartache, he asked through gritted teeth, 'How could I refuse Godby's wife?'

Cecily stamped her foot. 'What Godby did to you, not to mention to his men in battle, can never be forgiven. His daughter is cut from the same cloth, Roland. Do you see the way she courts attention? It's a good thing Cosmo's returning to his own home — '

'Miss Morecroft may not be as docile as her mother led us to believe, but she is capable and the girls are fond of her.'

Cecily glanced over Roland's shoulder at Venetia's portrait and her eyes narrowed. 'Surely you are not suggesting Caro model herself on Venetia!'

Roland turned away from the venom in her eyes, even though he acknowledged the many good reasons Cecily had to despise his late wife. 'I am suggesting nothing of the sort.' Though his response was mild, he could feel the blood pumping through his veins under great pressure. Normally he avoided Venetia's name, but now he felt it was pertinent.

Striving to keep his growing anger in check, he went on, 'However, Venetia was her mother. I believe Caro tries too hard to be everything Venetia was not.'

'Of course Caro must endeavour to be

everything Venetia was not!' Cecily flared. 'And if you think I am responsible for the whispers, you are wrong.'

Roland looked at her steadily. Her face was red, knots of anger protruding from her scrawny neck. Anger had been his first impulse, too. Now he merely felt sorry for Cecily. How cruel of his brother to have made no secret of his enduring love for Venetia, while happy to take Cecily's money. Hector and Venetia should have married. They'd have made each other miserable very quickly instead of drawing the rest of them into it . . . the survivors who had to keep living with the memories.

'I have always admired your discretion, Cecily. It is the servants who are not so reliable.' He seated himself on the window seat and beckoned to his ugly, red-faced, trembling sister-in-law who was not a bad woman by nature, but who had never got over being so ill-used. He sympathised. It was hard to live with the betrayal of the only person one has ever loved. How much worse, though, to be a woman and seeing oneself age with little, if any, prospect of love on the horizon to ameliorate the damage of the past.

She sat, and he took Cecily's clasped hands between his. 'I have long suspected that Caro has been aware of the whispers.'

Cecily jerked her head up. 'You must refute them. Deny everything!'

With a sigh, Roland dropped her hands and rose. Changing the subject, he said, 'You will, of course, launch Caro next season. I trust it's not an imposition, for I realize I am sometimes guilty of taking your good offices for granted. Perhaps you might enjoy a little enforced gaiety.' He managed a smile.

Cecily was in no mood to respond with similar good humour. 'I consider it a duty I am happy to discharge, Roland,' she said through pursed lips. 'Hardly a pleasure! Ugly old women like me are fools if they deck themselves out in frills and furbelows to seek out pleasure.'

'Good,' said Roland, ignoring her last remark. 'In the meantime I thought a little practice in advance of Caro's come-out would be in order. I plan to hold a small ball at Larchfield for Caro's seventeenth birthday next month. Just twenty or so people from the neighbourhood. Caro will, of course, hate the idea but I think Miss Morecroft might be just the person to bring her round.'

Seeing her stiffen, he tried a final approach. 'Come now, Cecily,' he cajoled. 'With your deft touches and skill at organization the evening is sure to be a success.'

'It'll be a disaster!' wailed Caro, twisting her handkerchief around her fingers and looking at Sarah as if for corroboration.

Unmoved, Sarah bent over Harriet's shoulder to correct her French translation. Caro, opposite her, gripped the back of Augusta's chair as she fixed Sarah with a tragic look.

'The evening will be a disaster, or you will be?' Sarah enquired gently, not looking up.

With a huff Caro began pacing around the table. 'Both,' she said finally. 'I will be a disaster and so bring great shame and embarrassment to Papa.'

'Oh, so you do recognize the correlation,' said Sarah, as if discussing a lesson in logic. 'I'm glad, Caro. It's time you learned that how you deport yourself reflects upon those who reared you. If you behave charmingly your father's guests will go home saying, 'How fortunate Mr Hawthorne is to have a daughter with such pleasing manners. What a credit she is to him'.'

Caro was not such a fool she could not recognize the sarcasm in her governess's tone. But when Sarah looked up she was taken aback by the anger in the young girl's eyes.

'You understand nothing!' Caro hissed. She

thrust herself across the table to glare at her governess. Harriet and Augusta looked up in alarm. 'No, nothing!'

Sarah eyed her with concern. 'Calm yourself, Caro,' she soothed. She did not fancy another hysterical outburst with consequences worse than last time.

'Do you think I'm insensible to every nuance of my voice?' demanded Caro. 'Or that I am not afraid every time I smile that I might be creating the wrong impression? If I smile 'charmingly' as you put it, how is that different to the enticing way my mother smiled? She used her 'pretty manners' and enhanced her beauty to enslave men. Do you think I wish to be called a harlot, too?'

Sarah did not interrupt. Her heart went out to the girl.

'This birthday ball of mine — ' Caro put a hand to her temple and closed her eyes briefly. 'I shall feel like an — an animal in the zoo. Everyone will be watching me, studying me, making comparisons. They won't come with the object of helping Mr Hawthorne celebrate his daughter's birthday. They'll be there to see if his daughter is as beautiful as her mother, as flirtatious as her mother, as gay and lively and . . . and likely to be as immoral as her mother.'

She sank down upon the paint-chipped

70

nursery chair and covered her face with her hands. Sarah stifled the urge to go to her. A brisker approach, she decided, was safer.

'You've made some interesting observations, Caro, and with your permission I should like to conduct an experiment.' She smiled from across the table, her tone matter-of-fact. 'I have an aptitude for charades and amateur theatricals, I am told, which will enable me to show you how to create any impression you want.'

Caro looked at Sarah as if she were speaking nonsense.

'But the experiment is to be conducted in the evening, when your aunt and father are out visiting. I believe they are to play cards with Colonel Doncaster and his wife tomorrow night?'

'What do you want me to do?' Caro sounded suspicious.

'Oh, *you* don't have to do anything, except observe and — ' Sarah crinkled her brow. ' — supply me with one of your mother's old dresses.' She gave a satisfied smile at Caro's look of horror. 'One of her most alluring.'

★ ★ ★

Despite Caro's apparent reluctance, the girl's curiosity clearly overrode her aversion to

71

looking through the scandalous, diaphanous wisps of fabric that had once clothed her mother. A sense of devilry obviously made her select the most scandalous, diaphanous of them all.

Sarah was still wearing her own evening gown when Caro came to her tiny bedchamber while Ellen put the girls to bed. The garment had been bequeathed to her by Mrs Hawthorne but Sarah had transformed it into an eye-catching sheath of peony-red *gros de Naples* with three rows of gold trimming around the hem. She'd noticed Mrs Hawthorne's gimlet eye stray towards the creation throughout the evening. Mr Hawthorne's ill-concealed admiration had, however, been more gratifying, even though he'd addressed her with the same studied coolness.

'Wait for me in the drawing room,' instructed Sarah, relieving Caro of her mother's evening gown.

'Why can't we go down together?'

'Because I am the one issuing instructions and it's my desire that you take a seat by the fire and pretend you are simply a guest. I shall come down in one guise, take my seat at the piano, and pretend to entertain my audience. Remember, you are merely to observe. I shall then leave, and return, as another person — '

'You mean my mother.'

'It doesn't matter. Perhaps I will pretend I am Lady Venetia, or perhaps I will pretend I am Caro who is pretending to be her mother. You will know, believe me. Just do as I say, Caro.'

She leapt into action the moment Caro had closed the door. Out of her trunk she pulled the real Sarah Morecroft's most hideous garment and, with satisfaction, struggled into the drab grey merino gown with its ill-made trimmings. She then rearranged her hair to fall in two unflattering loops over the sides of her face and topped it with a poorly sewn toque adorned with a sadly drooping feather.

Regarding herself with satisfaction, she proceeded down the stairs. At the door to the drawing room she turned her attention to her posture. With shoulders slumped, neck thrust out, and eyes darting suspiciously from side to side, she made her way to the piano.

Executing a clumsy, self-conscious curtsy as if she were about to perform before a small audience, Sarah's voice was a flat monotone as she muttered in Caro's general direction, 'I shall play 'Hey, Betty Martin'.' Placing the music onto the stand, she dropped ungracefully onto the piano seat and began to play haltingly. The music's lack of feeling was matched by Sarah's unemotional rendering of the words.

Once Caro's dutiful clapping at the end of

the piece had died away, Sarah rose. Staring over Caro's shoulder into the middle distance, she collected the music sheets, shuffled them nervously, then muttered an incoherent thank-you before exiting the room.

She took the stairs two at a time. A few minutes would be needed to transform herself, though she did not want to take too long about it.

'Ellen,' she called in a loud whisper as she passed the nursery, and was glad the girls had obviously gone to sleep so that Ellen was free to assist her.

The nursery maid's face was a picture of horror as she stared at the barely decent dress Sarah held out to her.

'Quickly, help me put it on,' Sarah ordered, as she pulled off the grey merino and stood in only her chemise and short stays.

'Lordy, what are you doing?' Ellen squeaked. 'You'll lose yer job! That dress don't belong to you!'

'The master's out. This is for Caro's benefit,' Sarah explained. 'I'm showing her the difference confidence and poise can make. And don't look at me like that. I charged Caro with the task of finding me something suitable of her mother's, and this is what she selected. Now quickly!'

The dress fitted like a glove, once Sarah

had removed her chemise in order for it to hang properly. Then, on an impulse of pure wickedness, she dashed water from her pewter jug onto the garment and began to smooth it through the folds. Admiring herself in the full-length cheval mirror she had purloined from Caro, she was gratified by the seductive effect created as the diaphanous garment clung to her limbs.

'Dear Lord,' whispered Ellen, stepping back after she had hastily worked Sarah's hair into an attractive topknot of tumbling curls, 'I'm right glad the master's out. He'd drop dead at the sight of you. Reckon it's the dress m'lady wore the night everything blew up with Sir Richard.'

'Who is Sir Richard?' Sarah had heard his name before.

'Another of m'lady's lovers, only he were the worst.' Ellen looked more scared than eager to impart gossip. 'She met her match, all right. He were a true villain. Gave her a pearl necklace wot cost more 'n diamonds so's she'd run off with him, only she soon came back, she were that scared.'

'Good Heavens. How many lovers did Caro's mother have?' Sarah adjusted a curl.

'Well, there were Mr Hector and of course — ' Ellen shot Sarah a quick look, hesitated, then added, 'and . . . Sir Richard. So I s'pose that ain't too bad.' She bit her lip. 'Just don't let the master see you, for it *were* the dress m'lady wore when she came back a week later and Mr Hawthorne had to fight Sir Richard.'

'Mr Hawthorne seems to be in the habit of duelling,' Sarah remarked, her tone dry though her heart beat loudly.

'Reckon this was the only one. Only lover, I mean. He's a good shot, the master.'

'What happened?'

'He winged Sir Richard. After that, the fellow was exiled for debts.'

Sarah hurried down the stairs to the large, lovely drawing room where Caro waited patiently. The longer she spent at Larchfield, the more intrigued she became. Poor Caro. Even running a comb through her hair must fill the girl with doubt as to whether she was doing it to court admiration, or simply to get the knots out.

Well, this was a great lesson in demonstrating the vast middle ground between being a self-conscious dormouse and a raging coquette — and it was fun!

Confidently she threw open the door, boldly meeting Caro's eyes above her ivory fan. Oh, she knew how to use her eyes to great effect, and she did so now, playing to her young charge as if Caro were the most handsome, gallant gentleman in a room crowded with them.

'Since you have asked me so charmingly to play for you, sir, how can I refuse?' she asked, inclining her head coquettishly and sweeping Caro a smouldering look from beneath downcast lashes. '*Any* requests from such a handsome gentleman, will be happily acceded to.'

Caro's eyes widened at the double entendre though she stammered, obligingly, 'Perhaps, miss, you would regale the company with 'Over Yonder Mountain'?'

Sarah affected a show of false modesty. 'Oh, but you will think my singing very poor after what you have already heard this evening.' With a dazzling smile, she took a deep breath so that the swell of her breasts could not fail to be admired above the line of her low-cut evening dress. 'However, if you insist.' Sarah sank gracefully onto the piano stool and began to sing in tune to the emotional music.

Everything this evening had been play acting. But this, her singing, was real, and her voice was exquisite. She knew men found her attractive, but the many sincere compliments she'd received on her voice were even more gratifying. She adored music. Until now, she hadn't realised how much she'd missed it in this sad, songless house.

Soon Caro, who Sarah knew worked hard

to maintain a cynical exterior, was dashing tears away.

The strains of the last chord drifted into nothing but Caro did not applaud; she just stared at her governess with wonder while Sarah was filled with a sudden sadness for the home she had left behind, and the lovable, tyrannical father who would probably be out of his mind with grief.

Footsteps sounded from beyond the open French doors that led onto the terrace behind her. Alarmed, Sarah half turned, then rose and stepped out from behind the piano stool.

The footsteps stopped. There was silence. Mr Hawthorne stood on the threshold to the garden, his face blanched by moonlight. He looked as if he'd seen a ghost.

Sarah's hand went to her breast, as if to still her thundering heart. Her mouth went dry.

Passionless? Had she once thought this man passionless?

The seconds became an agony of eternity as she waited for him to come to her. She watched the play of emotions roil in the tortured depths of his dark grey eyes. She thought he looked like a man who'd found Nirvana and would risk his life to cross the crocodile-infested raging torrent to lay claim to it.

In three strides he'd closed the distance between them. Then she was in his embrace. Thrown backwards over his arm, helpless and not wanting to be anything else, his mouth came down, swiftly and all-consumingly, upon hers.

She did not struggle. Objection was the last thing on her mind.

Breathing in his familiar smell of sandalwood and leather, she twined her hands behind his neck. She could feel the pounding of his heart beneath his waistcoat of watered silk, his hard chest pressed against her breasts.

It was not a gentle kiss; rather the kiss of a man who fears his chance may not come again and wants to plunder what he can before all is taken away.

Sarah did not need gentleness. With her mind in thrall to her body she surrendered herself wholeheartedly. The redoubling of his passion signalled he'd registered her enthusiasm.

Clearly, he hadn't registered her true identity.

Sarah wilted with want, bent to his will, consumed by a primal determination to take everything this fascinating man could give her before he realized his mistake.

She'd had many admirers but as a young,

unmarried woman she'd been kissed by only one man: her fiancé. This was infinitely more exciting.

She arched her back to achieve a more snug fit, and he responded, skimming his hand the length of her body from cheek to thigh while his other arm bore the full weight of her.

Waves of desire hit her with increasing force, coursed hotly through her veins, and pooled in her lower belly.

She gasped with disappointment when his mouth left hers. Compensation was swift as he thrilled her body with a feathered line of kisses down her throat. He trailed them over her collar bones, tracing the contours of her cleavage before returning once more to plunder her mouth.

She never wanted him to stop. Arching deeper against him, she raked her hands through his hair.

Then Caro screamed.

6

Sarah stumbled as she was released abruptly. Dear Lord, how could they have forgotten the girl? Endeavouring to master her breathing, she stared across the chasm that separated her from Mr Hawthorne. His expression was inscrutable. He ignored his daughter who whimpered from the settee, and Sarah wilted inside as she saw the passion drain from his face.

At Caro's second scream, shock reflected like a flame, quickly extinguished, in his dark eyes. Instead of going to her, he turned on his heel, the doors clicking shut behind him as he disappeared into the moonlit darkness.

'What has Father done?' cried Caro, throwing herself at Sarah.

Sarah stumbled backwards and sank upon the piano stool while Caro slid from her shoulder to weep at her feet.

'So wicked! Terrible! Mother's spirit must've been in that dress and bewitched him. Poor Miss Morecroft!' Her muffled voice came in choking gasps.

Still dazed, Sarah realised the need to make Roland appear blameless in his daughter's eyes.

'Perfectly understandable,' she said with a briskness she was far from feeling. 'I had no right to deceive him like that.'

She patted Caro's head, then, seeing the concern still in the girl's raised eyes, reassured her, 'Have no fears on my account. I didn't find it horrible.'

'Roland!' Cecily's voice drifted, disembodied, from the depths of the house.

* * *

Roland gripped the door handle of the library to steady himself, closed his eyes to ward off the memory of what had just happened, and waited for Cecily.

'Roland, there you are. Have you seen Caro? Ellen says she's not in bed yet. I was just about to retire when I thought I heard her scream!'

Cecily stood at the top of the stairs. The pins and hair pads had been removed and her hair hung lankly and unflatteringly down the sides of her anxious, drawn face.

'I saw her just now.'

Turning his back on her, Roland slipped into the library and closed the door firmly behind him. His first priority was to pour himself a fortifying brandy. It was easier said than done. He was shaking so badly he had to steady himself against the mantelpiece as he removed the glass stopper.

Closing his eyes, he took a long swallow of the amber liquid, hoping to burn away all traces of Miss Morecroft's kisses. Kisses, which lingered like rose petals upon his lips.

★ ★ ★

Sarah was still trembling as she sat on the edge of her bed and peeled off her stockings. Ellen had unbuttoned the tiny row of pearl buttons at the back of her dress, but now she was alone — haunted by the look in her employer's eye as he'd stood in a shaft of moonlight and gazed at her, believing her to be his dead wife come to life.

She touched her lips. They still burned. The hunger in his eyes was branded on her mind. No one had ever looked at her with such longing and ardour.

She didn't know what to make of him. Nor did she know what to make of her own tumultuous heart. Would she feel the same if just anyone kissed her?

She feared not.

Drawing in a ragged breath, she contemplated the difficulties. Mr Hawthorne had kissed her while conjuring up his dead wife. A great deal of delicacy would be required on her part to counter his mortification upon seeing her again.

And if that that was how Venetia had been revered by her husband, Sarah had her work cut out to compete. For compete she must. The feelings he'd whipped up could not be discarded lightly.

She blew out her candle and climbed into bed.

It would be a long night.

★　★　★

'Dancing!' Caro blanched. 'I already know how to dance.'

Sarah cocked her eyebrow. 'But not to waltz. I don't believe I've ever heard of a debutante who doesn't waltz in this day and age. Excuses like that are the preserve of dried-out spinsters, like me.' Sarah held out her hand to Caro. 'Come, Lady Charlotte has brought her three nieces to visit. They're in the drawing room and anxious to meet you.'

Reluctantly, Caro followed Sarah downstairs.

Sarah entered the room with a smile. 'Lady Charlotte, this is just what Caro needs: company, and a spur to learning her dance steps. We are short of gentlemen, however my mama used to employ a broomstick on occasion when teaching us, and I'm sure there is very little difference.'

Lady Charlotte waved an imperious hand from her seat by the fire. 'This is young Georgiana and her older sister Philly who will be coming out with Caro next year. I have the dubious pleasure of playing duenna to the young ladies while their mother is indisposed. It hasn't taken me long to discover that young ladies need a great deal of amusement.' She looked as if she were already fatigued by her duties.

'My, and don't I know it,' exclaimed Cecily, catching her last words as she entered the room. 'Certainly, useful recreation is to be recommended, and dancing, while some might reckon it distinctly un-useful, is an indispensible accomplishment.' She directed a pointed look at Caro as she seated herself upon the piano stool. 'I shall accompany but first we must find Cosmo. Yes! And Mr Hawthorne too, for it is intolerable to have no gentlemen with whom to practice when there are two perfectly able-bodied ones in this very house. Mabel,' she said to the parlour maid who had just answered her summons, 'fetch Master Cosmo and Mr Hawthorne. Tell them to present themselves in the drawing room at their earliest convenience. Also, find Dorrington to arrange for their dancing shoes to be brought down.'

Mention of Mr Hawthorne made Sarah's heartbeat do a little dance while heat rose in her cheeks. She pushed Caro into the centre of the room.

'What a treat to have an impromptu dancing lesson, Miss Hawthorne,' said Philly, dimpling as she smoothed her sprigged muslin skirts over her ample hips. Her round, ruddy face was flushed with pleasure. 'Aunt Charlotte is sponsoring me for the season, you know. She says you're not fond of dancing, but surely it is an accomplishment a girl cannot do without.'

'That and never revealing when she feels at a disadvantage,' came Lady Charlotte's stentorian tones.

Well, no one was going to know the extent to which the governess felt at a disadvantage, thought Sarah, as the door opened and Mr Hawthorne strode into the room.

It was immediately clear that Mabel had not elaborated on the nature of the summons, for it was Mr Hawthorne who looked at a complete disadvantage, greeted as he was by a room full of expectant ladies and his sister-in-law jumping up from the piano stool saying, 'How very good of you to come so quickly, Mr Hawthorne. The young ladies are eager to be put through their paces. We are having a dancing lesson, don't you know.'

Sarah felt a wave of sympathy as his dancing shoes were thrust in front of him.

'I fear, Cecily,' he said, looking pained and studiously ignoring Sarah, 'that I am not going to satisfy your demands for excellence. Surely the young ladies have been doing country dances since they could walk?'

'Oh, not country dances, Roland. No, we mean to perfect the waltz.'

His eyes widened, but Sarah was able to say soothingly, 'Here comes Cosmo. Perhaps he would prefer to take a turn with one of the young ladies.'

'A waltz.' Cosmo beamed at the unexpected but obviously welcome sight of such a large female contingent. 'Why, I should love to render my assistance. Who shall go first? I should hate to set the cat amongst the pigeons by favouring one pretty girl above the other.'

Clearly gratified by their blushes and giggles, Cosmo glanced up as he changed his shoes. 'Miss Morecroft, I daresay waltzing does not fall within the curriculum of most governesses, but since you are a breed apart, is it too much to wonder if you felt up to partnering me?'

'With pleasure.' Sarah felt no embarrassment as she stepped forward and placed one hand upon his shoulder while he clasped the other and rested his hand upon the small of her back.

'Ready?' asked Mrs Hawthorne, and she began to play.

However, Cosmo proved no very great proponent of the dance and was soon relegated to the sidelines by his critical aunt.

'You're all over the place, Cosmo, and half the time upon poor Miss Morecroft's foot. Roland, you're an excellent dancer. Step up and take his place.'

Sarah turned, smiling slightly, in time to see Mr Hawthorne's dismay, quickly masked by a look of cool indifference.

But while her own heart was being exercised somewhat more than usual, and not just by the energy required in twirling around a room, she managed, to her surprise, a smile that was not at all tremulous.

'Shall we show the young ladies how it's done, sir?' she said clearly and for the benefit of all, smiling over her shoulder at Caro, for she wanted to reassure the girl she did not consider herself in the evil clutches of some shameless villain.

He could not look at her. 'Yes, of course.' Fortunately, his dancing was not as stilted as his manner. Roland was, as Mrs Hawthorne claimed, an excellent dancer. Sarah felt herself perfectly matched, light on her feet and expertly led as they twirled around the room.

She adored dancing, and it had been a long time. Trapped in his arms, feeling the heat of his body and moving in time to the music was joy to her senses but after a few moments, she acknowledged Mr Hawthorne's grim expression. Clearly, he had not lost himself in the dance as she had. Her pleasure drained away. Pique turned to indignation. She pushed it back down, murmuring, when they were in the farthest corner of the drawing room, 'I fear you are angry with me, sir.'

He jerked his head up to look her in the eye for the first time. 'Angry with *you*? Obviously Caro put you up to it. The charade, I mean. Giving you Venetia's dress to wear. No, my behaviour last night was reprehensible.'

'I'm afraid it was entirely my idea. But if you're not angry with me, perhaps you could look a little less like you are — ?' Sarah paused as he raised her a little off the ground to compensate for dancing her too close to a potted palm. He was not just adept on his feet. It was a relief to surrender herself to his skill on the dance floor knowing she could say anything, it appeared, without risk of being tripped up over the rug. His scowl was unsettling, but it was his nature, and Sarah was determined to reduce the frequency of such signs of unhappiness. When the time was right. For now, his obvious discomfiture gave her the advantage. 'At least for the benefit of the others. And for my reputation,' she suggested mildly.

'Forgive me. My manners have deserted me. I'd also understand completely, Miss Morecroft, if you wished to give notice and leave Larchfield directly.'

'My notice?' Sarah gasped. Such a thought could not have been further from her thoughts.

His eyes narrowed as if he suspected the turmoil in her heart. 'It would be entirely appropriate for you to wish to hand in your notice,' he said carefully, as he set their course for their audience. 'As your employer I have behaved unacceptably.'

Without giving her a chance to reply, he deposited her amidst the others. 'And that, Caro, is how your mother and I used to dance when the waltz was still considered quite daring.' He smiled at her. 'I am sadly rusty, but Miss Morecroft has shown how it can be performed with skill and elegance. Come Caro,' he invited. 'It would be kinder to all if you tread first upon your father's feet before you are let loose to injure other inno-cent parties.'

Sarah's thoughts were in such disorder it was a relief to have half an hour to herself before putting the children to bed. Snatching her shawl from the hook on her bedroom door, she made for the ornamental lake.

Would Mr Hawthorne really let her go so easily when she knew he reciprocated her feelings? Dismay replaced her confidence as she wondered if he considered *she* were the one to have exhibited a certain laxness by not pulling out of his embrace earlier. Surely not? He'd made it clear he regarded himself as entirely at fault. He'd also made it clear, whether he later chose to refute it or not, that he found her entirely irresistible.

Yet he'd offered to let her go, as if he did not care either way.

She would not go. She'd been at Larchfield nearly three weeks but her task was not finished. Caro's birthday was coming up and Sarah needed to see her through it. After that it would be time to leave. But she'd return . . .

And she'd return as Lady Sarah Miles, Mr Hawthorne's equal, with a thoroughly convincing reason for having done what she'd done.

'Miss Morecroft.'

She turned, her heart lurching at the familiar voice.

Burnished by the setting sun, Mr Hawthorne looked like a mythical creature emerged from the waters of the lake. But though Sarah managed a smile of polite enquiry, he exhibited no answering pleasure.

'My apologies for my behaviour in the drawing room this morning,' he began. He ran one finger inside his cravat, as if it were tied too tightly. 'It was unpardonable that the apology should have been prompted by you when I had every intention of offering my sincerest regrets, in person.'

'I had no right to wear your wife's dress,' said Sarah lightly, trying to make it easier for him.

'You must not think that I — '

'Oh, it has occasioned no alarm or dread on my part, sir.' Sarah wished his brooding look really did inspire the pique she now strove for, rather than making her want to kiss and stroke the lines of strain away from his face. She went on in the same unconcerned tone, 'For I cannot for one moment think that it was desire for a mere governess which prompted your uncharacteristic behaviour.'

Frowning, he advanced a few feet. 'The 'mere governess', as you term yourself, should feel properly protected. Do not imagine I am in the habit of preying on the vulnerable members of my household.'

Her heart thundered but her voice was soft. 'Let us walk,' she suggested, stepping onto the worn path that led towards the wood. He hesitated, then fell into step beside her.

'You are very like your father, Miss Morecroft,' he observed. 'You have his fearless spirit.'

'Tell me about him.'

'Our golden youth?' His tone was ironic. 'I'll happily recount those halcyon days if you promise not to press me further, Miss Morecroft. Godby was closer to me than my own brother. But boys become young men, and life becomes complicated.'

They halted in a copse shaded by leafy elms. The air was damp and in front of them was a grotto, overhung with ferns. Dominating the small cleared space was a memorial stone dedicated to Venetia and Hector Hawthorne.

'Venetia died seven years ago, yesterday,' he said, clearly glad to change the subject as her gaze went to the posy of flowers at its base. 'I gather Caro didn't mention it?'

Sarah evaded his look. 'She mentioned it.'

'Since Caro turned twelve she's refused to accompany me here. She says she hates her mother. Can I ask you what she said to you?'

Weighing up whether to spare him the truth, Sarah stared at the limp dewdrops upon the woodleaf floor. Everyone at Larchfield had remarked upon the anniversary yesterday. Seven years after her death Lady Venetia and her powerful influence over her husband — amongst other men — continued to provide the servants with a rich source of gossip.

When it was clear he intended waiting for her answer, she said hesitantly, 'Caro asked why her father would erect a memorial to a harlot.'

To her surprise he looked amused. 'Caro has spirit. It's not customary to cultivate the society of our adolescent daughters. They can seem like strangers on occasion.'

Sarah thought of her own father. He had not been customary in his approach to her upbringing, throwing at her books she must read, quizzing her, arguing with her. He even took her shooting when only close friends were visiting.

She felt a pang, but as ever her resolve hardened when she thought of his parting words: 'Marry James, or my doors are closed to a crotchety spinster who insists on spurning life's bounties.'

Well, she'd be going home soon, if only to prepare herself for her return to Mr Hawthorne.

'Yes, she has spirit. Like her mother.'

Boldly, Sarah moved closer, putting her hand on the mossy surface of the rock face for balance. He did not step back but the gaze he levelled at her was harsh.

'Venetia was a poppy eater. Did the servants tell you that?'

Shocked, she shook her head. It explained so much.

'Her addiction made her moods volatile and unpredictable.' His eyes left hers and he gazed over her shoulder. His reflective smile suggested happier memories. 'When Venetia needed me she was everything I could have wished for — ' He gave a short, wry laugh, adding, almost imperceptibly, 'Well, almost.' Sarah saw his pain as their gazes locked. 'It's one thing to be needed, Miss Morecroft.' His voice was now so low she strained to hear him as he finished, 'Quite another to be loved.'

She was not prepared for such a revealing confidence. Nor what he required of her. Sympathy? Understanding? But it was her heart, not her head that dictated her next impulsive move. As if it were the most natural thing in the world, Sarah raised herself upon her toes and put her hands on his shoulders. She closed her eyes. An instant later she felt the answering touch of his lips upon hers. His hands cupped her face, and her senses were assailed by sandalwood and leather, yearning and desire as his strong, hard body pressed her back against the stone.

She might have been a seasoned flirt, but Sarah had little experience of physical desire. Tingles of sensation rippled through her as she twined her hands in the short hair at the nape of his neck and felt the roughness of his skin against her cheek, the sweet gentleness as his tongue skimmed her upper lip before he deepened the kiss. Her bones became jelly as he rained kisses upon her lips, her eyes, her neck. He kissed her like a drowning man replenishing himself, and Sarah responded like a flower soaking up the sun.

He released her suddenly. Breathless, she steadied herself against the rock behind. The turbulence in his eyes revealed mixed emotions. She could see he wanted her still. Against his will.

The rapid rise and fall of his chest mirrored the turbulence of her own reaction, but she was aware of the need for restraint.

'A gentleman would apologize to you, Miss Morecroft.' His voice was strained as he stepped back. 'Yet I'm not sure I'm entirely to blame.'

She felt stripped bare, from the inside out. Unable to respond, she touched her lips.

'It shan't happen again.' He turned, but she could not let him go.

'If I am to blame, then forgive me,' she ground out. If he didn't blame her, he was blaming himself, and hating her for it. She couldn't bear it.

'Pretend it never happened.' She lurched towards him, stopping herself before she stayed him with a hand upon his sleeve. 'Don't let it spoil what was between us.'

He turned, his eyes drinking her in. There was more than just regret in his expression, as he responded, 'There was, and is, nothing between us, Miss Morecroft.' At the devastation in her look his tone gentled. 'Nor ever will be.' He sighed. 'I'm sorry.'

He was wrong, but now was not the time to persuade him. Smoothing her skirts as she stepped away from the memorial stone, Sarah managed at last to control her trembling mouth and in a voice that was light and careless, said, 'It's getting late. We should return to the house or Caro will wonder what's become of us.' With an inviting smile she indicated the path and was relieved when he began to walk with her. 'Which brings me to the matter of Caro's birthday ball.' Her chatter was deliberately inconsequential. 'I was hoping you'd do me — and Caro — the great honour of allowing me to be final arbiter of the choice of Caro's gown. Mrs Hawthorne, you see, has her heart set on

primrose. Caro exhibits great fashion understanding when she declares that in primrose
she'll rather resemble Banquo's ghost dressed
for a wedding.'

7

Georgiana and Philly were constant visitors to Larchfield in the lead-up to Caro's ball. The daily curriculum of dance practice, deportment lessons, drills in how to use a fan to convey a hundred moods and meanings, and how to execute the perfect curtsy had been gruelling. Despite that, the girls' enthusiasm seemed to have rubbed off on Caro.

In another couple of weeks her work here would be done, thought Sarah with a pang. Caro, her 'special mission', had proved far more amenable than expected, which was not surprising. Caro was like any normal young girl. A boost to her self confidence, and a few friends, had made an enormous difference.

Mrs Hawthorne, inferring at the outset that a lowly-born piece of goods like Sarah would know nothing about such matters, had soon entirely discharged to her all duties related to Caro's initiation into the adult world.

Mrs Hawthorne's ill opinion amused Sarah. Mr Hawthorne's feelings were another matter. He ignored her. No amount of persuasion from the young ladies would induce him to partner them in their dance lessons. Sarah knew she was the reason.

She felt hurt. He had confided in her. The connection had not only been physical. Clearly, he feared his attraction for Sarah, the lowly governess.

If it were to be a battle of the wills, she thought, fluttering her fan as she dropped a curtsy in mock deference to Caro at the conclusion of a minuet, practiced in the drawing room with the chairs and tables pushed against the walls, hers would prevail.

But for once, she was not entirely convinced that her powers of persuasion matched her powers of attraction.

★   ★   ★

Roland watched the spray of droplets catch the light as two birds bathed with rapturous abandon in the birdbath a few yards from his study windows. It seemed a lifetime ago that he and Godby had bathed in the river that ran through Larchfield, splashing water at each other with similar abandon. Venetia had eaten his heart for breakfast the day he'd met her, and made short work of the rest of him. He had nothing left of himself to offer anyone. When Miss Morecroft had made it clear she thought otherwise, he'd responded with a resurgence of symptoms indicating his dangerous susceptibility to her overtures. How nearly he'd become a fool in love yet again.

He groaned inwardly, trying again to turn his mind to the accounts with which his bailiff had presented him. The man was breathing over his shoulder, waiting for him to endorse his monthly summary so Roland could send him on his way.

Roland turned the inked paper over in a useless gesture, while he re-lived his encounter with Miss Morecroft at the grotto. Godby's daughter, charming and as apparently careless and forthcoming with her affections as her father, was never far from his thoughts.

Through the open window his eye caught a flash of white-sprigged muslin. So much more interesting than the paper in his hand. His gaze followed Miss Morecroft's graceful figure down the path across the sloping lawn towards the woods. Flanked by the two little girls, the three appeared to be chatting easily. He smiled as he imagined Harriet insisting on another worm expedition.

As if she knew she was being observed, Miss Morecroft turned to look over her shoulder. She smiled in his direction, then returned her attention to Augusta, who was pulling her arm and pointing.

With a final, lingering look at the disappearing figures, he picked up his pen and dipped it in the inkpot. In a moment Cecily would knock on the door to show him the guest list for Caro's ball. Launching Caro in the hopes she'd find a suitably connected and indulgent husband was Roland's immediate priority. He hoped Caro would never suffer the disappointment that had blighted her mother's happiness. But Caro, less beautiful, more practical, had become increasingly grounded in reality since Miss Morecroft had entered her orbit.

★   ★   ★

Caro entered the nursery, tying the ribbons of her bonnet beneath her chin. 'I'm ready, Miss Morecroft.' There was excitement in her voice.

Sarah gazed at her with approval. The girl's simple white muslin gown with its blue sash flattered Caro's slender figure and set off her striking combination of dark hair and pale skin. The ensemble had been selected by Sarah after a battle of wills with her employer. Mrs Hawthorne was reluctant to countenance any expenditure upon her niece, even though Mr Hawthorne paid the bills.

'I'm afraid you younger ones must stay here,' Sarah told them from the doorway. 'This is Caro's special treat.'

'How can you bear them clinging to your

skirts, Miss Morecroft?' grumbled Caro as they descended the stairs. 'I daresay you're used to it, with so many brothers and sisters.' Clapping her hand to her mouth as she remembered her error, she turned on her heel. 'I'm so sorry, miss. They're all gone now. You're alone in the world.'

Sarah could not feel personal sorrow for the death of all those Morecroft children she had never known, but she felt a pang at the fact she had no siblings. She enjoyed Augusta and Harriet's happy chatter *and* the way they clung to her skirts. 'I don't dwell on what can't be changed,' she said briskly. 'Now what do we need? Ribbons for you and — '

Caro skipped across the black and white flagged entrance hall. Turning at the sweep of the stone stairs, she said with an impish grin, 'And something for a fine gown for *you* to wear for my birthday ball.'

Sarah laughed. 'How do you suppose I might pay for that out of my wages, Miss Hawthorne? No, I shall refurbish your aunt's cerulean blue velvet. You won't recognize it.'

Caro slanted her a secretive look as they made for the bridle path that led over the hill to the village beyond. 'Perhaps you'd relish an even greater challenge. Like constructing a garment entirely from new.' Her eyes shone as she looked at Sarah. 'Of *any* material you

103

choose. I asked Father yesterday and he has given his consent.'

Before Sarah could respond, Caro rushed on, 'I said I couldn't possibly enjoy my birthday ball unless Miss Morecroft, who loves fine clothes far more than I do, had the prettiest gown of her imagination. We're going to the village today to choose a bolt of fabric, and all the trimmings, for you!'

Caro laughed at Sarah's silence and the expression of shock on her face. 'You'll enjoy sewing it yourself, won't you? There's plenty of time.'

Sarah beamed. 'I couldn't think of a nicer surprise,' she said, clapping her hands together. 'What a capital girl you are, Caro.'

In the village shop Caro deliberated over a bolt of Egyptian brown sarsanet and a silver-grey lutestring called Esterhazy.

Sarah felt moved beyond words. There had been more than a few occasions when she'd wondered if her young charge positively *dis*liked her. How curious, she reflected, that this home-sewn gown, conceived by Caro and sanctioned by Mr Hawthorne, filled her with more honest excitement than any extravagant creation she had devised with her seamstress.

'Hardly an appropriate colour for one's foray into the world, Caro.'

They turned to see Lady Charlotte, flanked

by her nieces, regarding their choices with disapproval.

Sarah sent a swift look at Caro to indicate she would deal with this, but with a petulant tilt to her chin Caro announced, 'I intend wearing scarlet to honour my mother, Lady Charlotte. This is in fact for Miss Morecroft.'

Sarah's heart sank. 'Caro should not have spoken like that,' she apologised, but Lady Charlotte ignored her.

'Mr Hawthorne must pay you handsome wages to teach his daughter decorum and respect if you can afford such finery, Miss Morecroft. Georgiana, Philly.' She put a hand on each girl's shoulder to shepherd them out of the shop. 'Your visit to Larchfield this afternoon is cancelled due to Caro's gross incivility.'

Caro looked abashed but her eyes flashed defiance when she turned at Sarah's gentle rebuke. 'That woman has never said a kind word about either you, or mother,' she began. However as Mrs Willow, the shop proprietor, returned to show them a selection of ribbons that would complement each fabric, Sarah decided not to pursue the matter.

Caro had regained her former ebullience by the time they'd left the shop, and when she saw Philly and Georgiana running towards her across the village green, she beamed.

'We're so sorry Aunt Charlotte was such a gorgon.'

'How did she agree to you coming out again?' Caro asked.

Georgiana giggled. 'We had a harpsichord session, and Philly did lots of very loud singing, until Aunt Charlotte positively begged us to leave her in peace. Oh Caro — ' She took her friend's arm and fell into step. 'Isn't it exciting to have so many men in red at the ball? What a boon that Hetty Siskin's brother is so well connected. Your father has agreed, hasn't he?'

Caro nodded.

'And is he inviting Mr Hollingsworth?' Philly's tone was urgent. 'Please say you've asked him?'

'Who is Mr Hollingsworth?' Sarah's tone was sharp.

The three girls gasped. 'Talk of the devil,' said Philly. 'He's over there. Do you think he could have seen us and come out specially?'

Before anyone could respond, a tall, smiling gentleman strolled up to them.

'Ladies.' He removed his low crowned beaver with a bow. 'You all look especially lovely this morning.'

When the introductions had been performed, Sarah silently observed the newcomer's disquieting effect upon the three girls.

He was, she judged, several years older than herself, with the kind of handsome looks, detail to fashion and personable manner calculated to win him female admirers. Caro, Georgiana and Philly crowded round him, chattering as if they'd known him forever.

'And where do you hail from, if I may be so bold as to cut in?' Sarah asked eventually. Not only was it growing cold on the damp grass, but there were some who'd consider it unseemly for all the world to witness the young ladies feting an unfamiliar gentleman.

His smile was as warm for the governess as it was for the young ladies. A shrewd touch. Sarah wondered for whom he might have a possible interest.

'I've leased Hawthornedene for the season.'

Caro took Sarah's arm. Sarah had rarely seen her so animated. 'Uncle Hector's house. Well, he owned it though he didn't live there, of course. It's beautiful, Miss Morecroft.'

'You must be my guests some time,' the young man said. 'I shall organise a picnic by the lake.'

This was greeted by squeals of enthusiasm. Sarah realised it was hardly fair to criticize him for looking so self-satisfied, but when she'd dragged Caro away from the group she demanded, 'Since when has Mr Hollingsworth become your latest bosom-bow?'

'I did not think it a crime to speak to a young man.' Caro's tone was defensive. 'Or that you'd think ill of me, Miss Morecroft. He's a friend of Hetty Siskin's brother. I've met him several times on walks and once when we were at Hetty's house.' Caro wrapped her cashmere shawl more closely around her and stuck her nose in the air as they walked across the common.

Wrapping her own, more serviceable woollen shawl around her shoulders, Sarah followed. 'Don't be cross with me, Caro. I must be accountable to your father and aunt.' She put her hand on Caro's shoulder and was relieved that her conciliatory gesture wasn't rebuffed.

'It seems I'm to be criticised whatever I do,' Caro grumbled. 'Aunt Cecily harps on at me to be more sociable, but she's such a high stickler that only means being nice to Lady Charlotte and mean old cats like her.'

'That would have been a good start.' Sarah's tone was dry. 'But now we are nearly home, so let's say no more about it. I was not criticising you for talking to Mr Hollingsworth, but merely executing my duty as your governess by ensuring he's a nice, suitable young man worthy of your addresses.'

Caro halted and fixed her with an intense look. 'Oh, he is, Miss Morecroft,' she breathed.

8

'There are not nine pence in a shilling, Augusta,' Sarah snapped, tossing the gown she was sewing onto the nursery table.

Remorse was swift as she saw Augusta's trembling lip. She sighed as she acknowledged she was taking her frustration out on the girls as she drilled them, in between sewing straight seams and fine pin tucks. 'I'm sorry I was sharp,' she said more kindly. 'Tell me the cost of a loaf of bread, and there'll be no more sums for today.'

But they could not, and Sarah did not know the answer herself. She tried to bolster her spirits but it was no use. What was the point of the lovely creation taking shape? Mr Hawthorne would pay her no attention. He'd gone to pains to keep his distance since their encounter at the grotto. He'd hardly seek her out at Caro's birthday ball.

'I have a secret,' announced Augusta from her cushion at Sarah's feet, recovering her spirits.

'If it's about Caro, then I already know it,' said Harriet, who was sitting beside her. 'It's not nice to gossip about people behind their backs.'

'I'm only telling Miss Morecroft.' Augusta stuck her tongue out at her sister. 'She'd not get Caro into trouble.'

'And what is this secret?' asked Sarah mildly, hiding her disquiet.

'I saw her with Mr Hollingsworth in the churchyard . . . alone,' said Augusta in weighty tones.

'The churchyard in the middle of the village?' Augusta's tone was scornful. 'Where everyone in the village pays their respects to the dead?'

'Well, I nearly didn't see them,' said Harriet. 'I was with Ellen and she was hurrying me along. But it *was* Caro *and* she was in the shadow of the yew trees where I'd seen them talking the day before, too.'

'I hope you don't mean to gossip like this to your mother,' reproved Sarah, biting off a thread.

The girls looked indignant. 'We never tell Mama anything! Not even when we hear the servants gossip about *her*.'

'That is most wise,' remarked Sarah with irony. 'Not that your mother is the kind of woman to excite a great deal of gossip, I would imagine.'

With her heart — not to mention her dignity — bruised and battered by Mr Hawthorne's rejection, it was difficult to concern herself with much else. She held up a seam for inspection, her eyes blurring as they ran across the stitches while she remembered the finality of his let-down.

Why? When she *knew* he was not insensible to her?

'Mama never does anything scandalous,' sighed Augusta, as if this were her greatest failing.

'And never did,' said Harriet. 'She was never a beauty, like Aunt Venetia. Do you think I will grow up stout and turkey-necked like Mama, Miss Morecroft?'

'And that Caro will stop looking like a long-necked goose?' asked Augusta.

'Girls, girls! Where do you hear such things?' asked Sarah, sounding more shocked than she felt.

'The servants, of course,' Harriet replied, as if she were stupid. 'They talk about such interesting things.'

'Only they think we don't understand because we're children,' said Augusta. 'You didn't know that Aunt Venetia ran off with my father and it was their sin which killed them, did you?'

Sarah was about to open her mouth and say that indeed she did, thereby upping her status in the girls' eyes, when Harriet said with a sly roll of her eyes, 'But Father wasn't her true love.'

111

'Harriet!' her sister hissed, with a meaningful look at Sarah.

Sarah knew she should nip such gossip in the bud, but she wanted to know how Harriet's version differed from any other. She pretended unconcern as she worked the cloth in her hands, hoping they didn't notice how her fingers trembled. 'You're obviously dying to tell us this latest piece of unreliable servants' gossip, unless you're just making it all up.'

'I'm not making anything up. Ellen and the other servants say her true love was Uncle Godby,' said Harriet.

'It was not!' cried Augusta with another meaningful look at Sarah.

Harriet looked suddenly guilty. Pretending concentration as she stuck pins into her cream sash, she mumbled, 'Sorry, Miss Morecroft. I keep forgetting you're Uncle Godby's daughter.'

'So do I.' Sarah's voice was distant. She hoped her creased brow would be attributed to shock at this bombshell regarding her supposed father. They wouldn't know she was mentally digesting the implications of this altered history.

Hope surged through her. Had she just stumbled upon the real reason for Mr Hawthorne's rejection of her?

'Why are you smiling, Miss Morecroft?' Harriet asked.

'I have an eyelash in my eye.' She covered her face with her hands to hide her joy. There was hope, after all.

* * *

In the small, gloomy antechamber which accommodated Venetia's enormous wealth of sumptuary display, cobwebs hung thickly.

Roland had had to use his pocket handkerchief to wipe the dust from a window pane to let in enough light to see the location of Venetia's fashionable, elegant furniture, much less what was contained in the drawers.

He was so absorbed in his examination he did not hear the soft-slippered approach of his sister-in-law. But he nearly dropped the rope of pearls that he held, suspended between two hands, at her screech.

'You're not giving Caro *that*?'

'It would appear you're not in the habit of visiting Venetia's old apartments.' Roland wiped a finger through the dust on the windowsill as he raised a disapproving eyebrow.

'I swore I'd never enter these rooms again.' Cecily shuddered. 'I told the housemaids to stay away, too, but when I saw the door open . . . ' Her voice trailed away. 'Even after all these years these rooms *still* smell of her.' Her lower lip trembled as she looked at Roland.

When he offered no sympathetic rejoinder she begged him, 'Give them away, throw them away. They're bad luck.'

'I note the absence of one or two of Venetia's favourite pieces. No, I don't blame you, Cecily,' he added quickly, at her look of outrage. 'Hector used your dowry with little regard for you. I'd be the first to sanction your behaviour. But these — ' He swung the strand of gleaming pearls closer to her face. 'Do you know how much these are worth? A perfect pearl . . . rare and priceless. And dozens of them on this one strand. All because Venetia demanded — '

He stopped abruptly as Cecily shrank back, her mouth bared in a rictus of a snarl as she hissed, 'They're worth more than a king's ransom, which is all the more reason not to give them to Caro.' Her bulbous eyes flashed anger. 'You surely weren't thinking of it, Roland?' she demanded again. 'They're tainted. *You* didn't buy them. They cost you nothing.'

'They cost me my wife.'

Cecily stamped her foot. 'If Sir Richard was prepared to spend that sum on his mistress and bankrupt himself in the process then he was a fool!' She spat out the words with no regard to his feelings. 'Though much good it did him. Venetia soon moved on to greener pastures, didn't she?'

'She came back to *me*,' Roland observed dryly.

Cecily put her hand to her stringy neck and her lip curled. Had her look not been so venomous, Roland might have smiled at the sight of a dusty spider's web adorning the finely pleated rows of lace on her fashionable high-crowned cap.

'You should have closed your doors to her forever, Roland.'

'When Caro was crying for her mother, every night?' Roland put his hand on Cecily's shoulder. 'Why can't you put the past behind you? You'd be so much happier.'

'Like you, Roland?' Cecily's tone dripped scorn. 'You still live in the past, so don't preach to me.' She turned on her heel. 'You've not forgotten your interview with Miss Morecroft? Don't be soft with her. I fear she's insinuated her way into your affections just as her father did. It was a mistake to take her in.'

'We made the decision jointly.'

'In a moment of weakness when her poor mother all but swore she'd cut her own throat if we didn't. Now, I'm going to see cook.'

She was gone before he could reply.

Venetia. On a whim he withdrew her likeness from his desk drawer, once he had returned to his study.

Proud and confident of her beauty, she stared back at him. Dispassionately, he studied her features: the lustrous dark hair, curled at the front and cascading in ringlets from a high crown; the rosebud mouth, so divinely kissable when that was what she had desired.

Oh, she had taught him how to please her. It was just that he, alone, was not enough for one of her . . . vanity? He preferred to think that was the reason she'd strayed rather than that the fault lay with him, alone.

Replacing the miniature with the usual disquiet he felt every time he thought of her, he moved to the window. A team of gardeners was clipping the topiary-adorned hedge beyond the rose arbour. He watched them as he prepared himself. It was not Miss Morecroft's position that was at risk in this upcoming interview; it was Roland's heart and integrity.

At the gentle tap on the door Roland turned, unprepared for the sudden drumming of blood in his ears, although his voice was steady and cool as he said, 'Please sit down, Miss Morecroft.'

So that she was under no illusions as to the

nature of his request for her company, he said without preamble, 'I hope I've not interrupted any plans you may otherwise have had for the engagement of the girls. However, I have promised Mrs Hawthorne to investigate a matter which is of concern to her.'

The young woman looked at him enquiringly while she settled herself in one of his large armchairs with that peculiar grace of hers.

Roland tried not to be distracted by the tendrils of chestnut hair which brushed the high planes of her cheeks in such an artless fashion. He cleared his voice and frowned but this did not have the desired effect, for she merely deepened her smile as she waited for him to elaborate. The smile insinuated its way like warm honey through the cracks of his heart, thawing the ice which sheathed it. He fought to remain impervious.

'Yesterday,' he went on, feeling at a distinct disadvantage, 'Mrs Hawthorne brought to my attention a matter which she considered betokened negligence on your part. Apparently Lady Charlotte observed my daughter conversing with an unknown gentleman in the street in front of the haberdasher's.' He paused, waiting for her to colour at the recollection. When she did not — in fact her smile broadened — he continued in more sonorous tones, 'Caro was alone and unchaperoned.'

'Scurrilous gossipmongers!' Miss Morecroft shook her head. 'To report such tales reflects badly on *all* parties and is deeply insulting to Caro. It so happens that as we stepped into the haberdasherer's yesterday afternoon to purchase some last-minute trimming for Caro's gown, Caro was greeted by Mr Hollingsworth who, I'm pleased, you saw fit to invite to her birthday. Not wishing to interfere directly, I remained just within the building and listened to Caro and Mr Hollingsworth discuss the weather and his pleasure at having been included on the guest list for Friday's entertainment. Shortly afterwards the young gentleman bade her good day and moved on again. I would say the exchange lasted about one and a half minutes.'

Despite her smile her fine hazel eyes were alight with challenge. 'If you wish to verify my story, Mrs Willow, who works in the shop, will corroborate everything.'

'That will not be necessary,' Roland said hastily. 'It was merely incumbent upon me to investigate the matter at Mrs Hawthorne's request. Please be assured that I, personally, have no concerns regarding your care of my daughter.'

He should have left it there. Should have

nodded politely, risen, and shown her the door. But he couldn't help adding, 'Caro's confidence has increased under your tutelage. I would not want to disappoint her.'

The last was a thinly veiled warning. He did not need to elaborate. Miss Morecroft must be fully aware of her danger in making an enemy of the mistress of the house.

Expecting her to thank him and take her leave, Roland nodded in dismissal.

She rose.

'So I am in danger, then, of losing my position, Mr Hawthorne?' she asked bluntly. 'Once people like Mrs Hawthorne decide menials such as myself no longer give satisfaction it is usually not long before we are given our marching orders.'

He regarded her with a level look. 'I have said I will protect you, Miss Morecroft.' He nodded in the direction of the door. She had to go, now. He wasn't sure how much longer he could trust himself to refrain from reassuring her, in the most unseemly fashion, of her security. The knowledge made his expression sterner, his stance more rigid.

She took a step towards him. 'You are to leave for London this afternoon for several days.'

He registered the rise and fall of her chest, the concern in her eyes. 'That's all the opportunity Mrs Hawthorne needs. After all, I am in charge of her girls, as well as Caro. What then, sir? Remember, I have nowhere else to go.'

Retreating, he turned to stare out of the window. 'I am not one to tolerate injustice, Miss Morecroft.' He could feel his breath quickening and the blood surging to his extremities. This was madness. She had to go. Now!

'Yes, you are a fair man,' she said, angling herself so that she was within his vision.

He ignored the rustle of her gown but the scent of orange flower water made him turn his head.

'And that,' she said, the shadow of a smile upon her beautiful face, 'is why I want to stay. That, and my sincere affection for the girls. Your warning suggests it would be wise to explore alternative avenues of employment.' Her eyes were dark with entreaty. 'I do not know whether the fault is mine alone, or whether my father's wrongs have sealed my fate, but I do know that I love it here, Mr Hawthorne — working for you — and that I don't want to leave.'

'Yes, yes,' he said, suddenly finding himself in possession of her hand. He had no idea whether he'd taken it in response to her distress, or whether she might have offered it to him. 'You have, I assure you, given every satisfaction.' He stopped, colouring at his choice of words, and did not like the fact that she smiled back, rather like a cat, her face tilted to one side, her eyes bright with mischief beneath demurely lowered lashes.

What might have happened next, had footsteps not sounded in the passageway, he did not care to dwell upon, for his actions were not about to be dictated by his head — he was uncomfortably aware of that. But the sound of Cecily's voice was like cold water upon him and the next thing he could remember, he was leading Miss Morecroft to the door and bowing to her in polite dismissal.

The turmoil in his breast did not abate at her departure.

He stared at the papers on his desk and knew he'd be unable to concentrate. Then he headed for the door. Perhaps a bracing ride would help cast out the madness that was beginning to consume him.

9

'Papa, you should see the ballroom.' Caro was barely able to contain her excitement. Sarah knew she could claim some of the credit for the girl's recent transformation, but not all. Love was in the air.

Caro's eyes shone. 'Bows and flowers everywhere. People will talk about my birthday for months to come.'

She smiled at her father in happy expectation. The house had been a hive of activity and the air was thick with the anticipation of tomorrow night's ball.

Sarah watched Mr Hawthorne finish the carp on his plate. If this couldn't wipe the scowl from her employer's face, she thought, nothing could. He'd not addressed a single word to his daughter or sister-in-law the entire meal. That he'd said nothing to Sarah hardly signified. Two afternoons ago, though, before he'd rushed off to London . . . She tried not to think about it. If Mrs Hawthorne hadn't trumpeted her orders to the house-maid right outside the study door, who knew what might have happened.

With careful precision, Mr Hawthorne put

together his knife and fork and directed a reproving look at his daughter. 'Just remember you are of the privileged minority, Caro. Few people in this country, much less the world, are as fortunate.' His voice was chilly.

Indignation on Caro's behalf replaced Sarah's romantic ruminations on what might have been. She bit her tongue to prevent herself from voicing a tart reminder that Caro was the last young lady who put her own pleasure above the needs and suffering of others.

Only the click of the ormolu clock on the mantelpiece broke the tense silence.

'Tonight we dine in luxury while a large majority of Englishmen and their families will barely fill their stomachs. Tonight a dozen wives are weeping for husbands condemned to death for challenging a society which denies them a fair wage for an honest day's work.' Mr Hawthorne glared at Caro, impervious to her quivering lip.

Sarah couldn't help herself. 'I do not think Caro's enthusiasm is a reflection of her indifference towards those less fortunate than herself.'

Mrs Hawthorne snapped her head around and looked at Sarah as if she had suggested they open their doors to the starving masses and serve them personally. 'I do not believe,

Miss Morecroft,' she said in clipped tones, 'that your opinion was solicited.'

This had the opposite effect of dampening Sarah's defence. 'I deplore injustice as strongly as you,' she bit back. 'Caro said nothing to warrant her father's criticism. It was unjust to accuse her of selfishness when she is naturally excited about her ball tomorrow night.'

'Injustice!' Mrs. Hawthorne cried. 'You accuse my brother-in-law of injustice when I can think of no other man who has expended more time and energy fighting for the rights of the working man.' With an agitated hand she repositioned her vermilion toque, which was favouring one ear, and nearly dislodged the squirrel's tail hair piece. For once, Sarah was in no danger of succumbing to unwise giggles. Caro had started to cry. Though no tears came Sarah could see the trembling of her thin, white muslin-clad shoulders. She turned to Mr Hawthorne. Surely he knew he was in the wrong?

He was staring at the silver epergne centre-piece, clearly resolved to have no part of the argument. Anger seared through her.

'How dare you answer back to your betters!' cried Mrs Hawthorne. 'Leave the table at once, Miss Morecroft.'

With a cold, hard stare at her employers,

Sarah rose. 'I am sorry if the truth offends you,' she said with quiet dignity. Passing close to the back of Mr Hawthorne's chair as she made her regal exit, she hoped he could feel her anger.

He had been vastly unjust. Surely he must realize it.

Then she heard his voice — music to her ears, despite its arctic tone. 'Wait for me in my study, Miss Morecroft. I will see you there when I've finished my dinner.'

*   *   *

Five minutes waiting for him had fanned the flames of Sarah's fury to a blaze. Swinging round from the fireplace, she seized the initiative.

'I've not had time to pack my bags, sir. No doubt Mrs Hawthorne has instructed I be dismissed on the spot.'

Wearily he waved her to a chair. 'Be seated, Miss Morecroft.' He took her place in front of the fireplace. Standing a little to one side so he didn't block the heat, he removed a gold enamelled snuff box from his coat pocket and toyed with the lid. Finally his eyes travelled from the apparently fascinating object to meet hers.

The hunted look in their intense depths

125

shocked her. He ran a distracted hand through his dark hair and said, 'Contrary to what happened at dinner, Mrs Hawthorne does not override my authority. The irony is that my reaction to the terrible injustice meted out to the men charged in relation to the Peterloo uprising blinded me to the injustices perpetrated at my own dinner table. I apologise.'

She was caught off-guard by the plea for forgiveness in his smile. Then she realised his apology was meant as a dismissal.

She would not be that easy to be rid of. She smiled back. 'You fight your battle on many fronts, Mr Hawthorne.' They were not the words of a governess, but then, theirs was not a conventional relationship. She eased herself from the depths of the armchair and moved towards him.

He stood his ground. The wary look in his eyes amused and angered her. He had every right not to trust her.

She stopped inches from him, forcing him to lower his head to look at her. 'I admire a man who holds to principle with such passion.' Her voice was low. 'My father was more interested in passion than principle, it would seem. I've heard whispers that connect him with your late wife and I can only say how sorry I am for the damage caused.'

She had to stop herself from reaching up to caress the vein that throbbed at his temple. Anticipation crackled between them but he made no move to touch her.

Unsteadily, she went on, 'I apologise if my frankness offends, but as my days are numbered I want the satisfaction of giving voice to my feelings.'

He said tightly, 'I have already assured you, Miss Morecroft, your position is safe.' He deposited the snuff box on the mantelpiece and clasped his hands behind him. 'At Larchfield the principles of fairness I hold dear are enshrined. Last night, Lord Miles's calls for bloodletting drowned out my entreaties for reason but at least I am master of my own home. I repeat, your position is safe.'

He would have gone on. Perhaps he did. Sarah had no recollection of what happened next. She could only register deep, stultifying shock.

'Miles? Lord Miles?' The words forced their way through her constricted throat. She covered her face with her hands.

Lord Miles, her own father. She couldn't bear it. Blinking, she dropped her hands to stare at her employer. Then, unable to bear her agitation, she took a few steps towards the window, gripping the heavy gold curtain as she turned. Anguish for her darling father swamped her, replaced by the realisation her position was hopeless. Her feelings for Mr Hawthorne had just been consigned to a dusty grave. She really was the daughter of his nemesis, only this time it was no lie.

'Yes, Lord Miles,' Mr Hawthorne ground out, staring into the flames. 'Crusader for the status quo. God knows how he can harden his heart to such suffering.' He became silent, his frown deepening. 'But grief changes a man.' He turned slightly, but did not meet her eye. There was hesitancy in his voice as he went on, 'It can open his heart to compassion, or harden his heart through fear.'

Helplessly, Sarah watched him. She was losing him. With every word, their distance increased.

'The fear of being hurt twice, Miss Morecroft, will drain the courage of most men. Slice away at our legs and our arms, but don't tamper with our susceptible hearts.'

She searched vainly for an appropriate response. But what could she say? 'I am not the daughter of the foster brother who betrayed you — I'm the daughter of your sworn political enemy'? The silence lengthened and she lost her opportunity. He turned and when he addressed her directly the passionate undertone had left his voice.

'Lord Miles, pity the man, is deranged with grief at the loss of his daughter, but he hardens his heart when it comes to the loss of others.'

Sarah closed her eyes as she continued to grip the curtain with both hands. She was in orbit. Her world was spinning. Mr Hawthorne's words taunted her. Shame, remorse and fear at her deception swamped her. The curtain, worn with age, tore and she stumbled forwards. Unable to focus through her tears, she started blindly towards a chair. Had he realized? Was disgust about to replace his earlier grudging admiration?

'Miss Morecroft!'

Before the ground met her, strong arms swept her into the air and against his chest. She squeezed shut her eyes, drinking in the heat from his strong, hard body, breathing in his comforting, familiar smell. Exhaling on a sigh of disappointment as he lay her on the leather sofa, her senses snapped back to life as he knelt, his face inches from hers.

'You are ill. Shall I send for a doctor?'

She reached for his hand, unable to open her eyes. Or unwilling? His anxiety would only be further reproach.

With a small shake of her head she whispered, 'It's nothing. I shall be myself in a moment.'

Unconvinced, he raised her head with

gentle hands to push a cushion beneath.

'So weak and foolish of me.' She turned away and covered her face with her hands. Tears threatened and her voice wavered. 'I've never succumbed to the vapours, yet your talk of injustice fuelled my fears for my precarious situation.'

It was true enough. No artifice required here. Without a shadow of a doubt she'd be punished for a situation entirely of her making. She had no one to blame but herself. Once the truth were known, her father would hate her . . . and Mr Hawthorne would hate her even more. It was enough to reduce the strongest of women to heart-wrenching sobs.

Sarah could not hold them at bay. Here was Mr Hawthorne at her side, on his knees in fact, yet her life lay in tatters. Her selfishness had resulted in this terrible situation of her own making. He'd never forgive her.

'Please, don't cry.'

The depth of feeling in his whispered entreaty sounded a breath of hope. This was her moment. She must tell him now. But as his arms encircled her and she was pulled against his chest and set across his lap, and she knew he was about to kiss her, her resolve melted. This was the clearest and most passionate declaration she'd had yet of his feelings. She had not the courage to test them to such an extent.

'Forgive me,' he murmured. He cupped her cheek and with his thumb, gently traced her lower lip. 'I've unfairly attributed to you Godby's disregard for the feelings for others.'

Sarah closed her eyes against the heart-breaking concern in his eyes. In a moment the tables would be turned. She'd be the one uttering the apology and she felt sick with apprehension. She chose her moment before he could kiss her again, knowing she'd never have the strength to utter her confession afterwards. 'I'm not Godby's daughter.'

She took a quavering breath, tensing for his response, but he misunderstood. Brushing an escaped tendril of hair from her brow, he said hoarsely, 'No, Godby has no part in all this. You are a woman, whom I must judge in your own right.'

His breath tickled her ear and sent shivers down her spine. She cried even louder, and fearing he was holding her for the last time, sobbed into his neck, 'I don't ever want to leave you.' He'd certainly send her away after that admission.

He did not. In the heartbeat and a half it took him to digest the enormity of her confession, she felt him stiffen. She opened her eyes and stared into the depths of his tortured soul before their hearts collided. With one hand supporting her head, the other cupping her cheek, his mouth claimed hers.

It was a kiss that demanded surrender.

And she surrendered everything, except the truth, for she knew now that would be the death knell of all the hopes and dreams that were at last being satisfied here, on the Chesterfield in his library.

She met him at every level. The initial urgency of his hunger became the rapture of discovery as he trailed kisses along her jawline, her throat, her collar bone and she responded, leaving him in no doubt as to the intensity of her feelings.

'Father!'

They heard Caro's cry in the passage before she threw open the door and burst into the room, leaving them just enough time to rise to their feet.

'Father, you can't let Miss Morecroft go!' Breathless, Caro gripped his coat sleeve. 'Aunt Cecily says she won't tolerate any more impertinence, but Miss Morecroft was only defending me. She is the most wonderful governess I've ever had — and I love her!'

Mr Hawthorne cleared his throat. Above his daughter's dark head he gazed into Sarah's face, as if he were seeing it for the first time. She saw the softening in the depths of his intense dark grey eyes.

With a rare, sweet smile, he said, 'Miss Morecroft is going nowhere. She will be very busy making sure tomorrow is everything you could have wished for. After that — ' The look he sent Sarah made her tremble. ' — I think it's time to review the current arrangements.'

* * *

Caro and Sarah stood in the centre of the ballroom Venetia had had built and gazed with satisfaction at the huge vases of flowers placed on plinths in each corner. Swathes of pink muslin tied in bows — Sarah's idea — adorned the gilt chairs arranged around the walls.

'I hope I don't spend my evening occupying one of those,' sighed Caro.

'You'll be so sought after you'll want nothing more than to rest your tired feet sitting in one of those,' Sarah prophesised. 'I'll wager there are more than a couple of eligible gentlemen, as we speak, who'd like to engage you for every waltz.' She squeezed Caro's shoulder as they turned their attention to the refreshments table, before adding slyly, 'Perhaps that nice Mr Hollingsworth is one of them.'

Caro blushed. 'Philly is much prettier than I am,' she mumbled, pretending concentration on a silver urn filled with Lilies of the Valley.

'Only if one prefers plump, giggling girls.' When she saw Caro was staring at her, eyes wide with expectation, she added, 'In my opinion Mr Hollingsworth appears far more interested in tall, dark, serious young ladies.'

Caro put down the urn with a clatter and clasped her hands together in a semblance of entreaty. 'I don't suppose I could borrow a touch of your Olympian Dew?' she asked.

'I thought blue-stockings didn't approve of such artifice.' Sarah pretended to sound prim as she took Caro's hand and led her to the stairs. 'Only three hours until the guests arrive. We might as well start preparing ourselves now.'

When they reached her tiny room, Caro sat on her lumpy bed while Sarah rummaged in her drawers for the pot of magic ointment.

'Didn't you say it was possible to be both a blue-stocking and a beauty?' Caro asked.

'I did.' Sarah unscrewed the lid and dipped in her finger. 'Aren't I just such a manifestation? Now you shall have just the merest suggestion of a blush of roses upon your cheeks, if you will allow me to do it. Exercising restraint is the secret. With your lustrous dark curls to set off your perfect pale skin, a tinge of colour will instantly transform you.'

Caro returned to her own room to finish dressing with the help of Aunt Cecily's maid, Betty, but was soon back so that Sarah could complete her toilette. Betty could not be trusted with tales of Caro's use of complexion enhancers.

'What a couple of beauties,' declared Sarah as they stood side by side in front of the small tarnished mirror which balanced on her chest of drawers. 'Your father will be so proud of you tonight.'

'And of you,' replied Caro. But when Sarah glanced suspiciously at her she was met by Caro's ingenuous smile. She swallowed down her nervousness as she recalled Mr Hawthorne's expression when he'd vowed she'd remain. Dear Lord, dare she hope it would all end well?

'Let me help you into your dress, Miss Morecroft. I haven't seen it yet in all its glory.'

'Only because I sewed the last stitch at four o' clock this afternoon.' Sarah was pleased with the finished work. The Esterhazy lutestring, the colour of rain-darkened sky, was cut low and fell in shimmering folds from just beneath the bust. A sense of devilry had inspired her to use the silver-grey netting from one of Mrs Hawthorne's cast-off gowns for the puffed sleeves and a decoration of leaves around the hem which ended at Sarah's ankles. She still had the unusual silver and green dancing slippers beneath her bed which Caro had given her the night she'd supplied her with Venetia's clothing for her demonstration.

Caro gasped. 'I cannot believe that with just a simple bolt of silver fabric you have made . . . this! You should be a modiste.'

Sarah preened at the compliment. 'Your aunt helped,' she said, smiling at Caro's open-mouthed amazement. 'You remember her grey round dress from last season which she gave me? The one with the ugly, bulky rouleau just above the hem? I unpicked the rouleau, smoothed it out and cut from it the sleeves and leaf decoration.'

Caro giggled. 'I can't wait to draw her attention to it. She'll look like a boiled chicken.'

'Now, now, Caro,' Sarah admonished mildly. 'Life has dealt your aunt a poor hand, whereas you can look forward to a glittering future. As to becoming a modiste, it is a hard way to make a living but more than that, I'd miss you too much.'

Caro stared at her for a long moment. 'You

won't ever leave Larchfield, will you?'

Studying the silver-backed brush in her hand, Sarah weighed up her response. The lie she was living had turned into a nightmare. She longed to unburden herself, but how could she under present circumstances?

'Not willingly,' she said, unable to predict Mr Hawthorne's response to her deception. So much depended on how she conveyed to him the truth.

She gave Caro a quick hug and pushed her towards the door. 'Your aunt and father will be looking for you. It's nearly time to start receiving guests downstairs.'

Apparently satisfied, Caro turned the door-knob then hesitated, her thoughts now focussed on herself. She looked suddenly stricken. 'What if I'm not good enough?'

'Good enough?' Marching over to her, Sarah grasped her shoulders and looked into her face. 'You, my dear,' she said severely, 'will be the toast of the town.'

Caro's frown vanished. Smiling, she stepped across the threshold. 'My mother would have been proud of me, I think.'

Sarah watched her disappear down the stairs, her fondness for the girl suddenly replaced with terror at her own imminent entrance. It was ridiculous. She'd been to dozens, if not hundreds of balls, all far grander than this small, country birthday celebration for Caro.

But Mr Hawthorne would be there, and that changed everything. She swallowed nervously as she smoothed her hair, which she had dressed with ribbons to match her dress.

When it was time, she took the stairs from her bedchamber to the ground level. Servants scurried about, making last minute preparations, replacing the occasional wax candle that would not sit straight, glancing anxiously out of the window as the crunch of gravel heralded the first arrivals.

From halfway down the stairs, Sarah watched Mr Hawthorne greet his daughter as she was about to progress into the ballroom.

'I have never seen you in greater beauty, Caro,' he declared, as she curtsied.

His gaze moved on to Sarah. She saw admiration flare into astonishment and her heart pulsed into renewed life. In a state of self-conscious turmoil, she took the last few steps to the bottom.

'Miss Morecroft,' he murmured, the touch of his lips sending shivers of excitement fizzing through her veins as he bowed over her hand, 'you are without equal.'

'Roland, there you are — ' Mrs Hawthorne stopped abruptly as she rounded the corner. She frowned at the trio, her eyes drawn to Sarah's dress. 'I had no idea you possessed such a fine gown, Miss Morecroft.' She slanted a suspicious look at her brother-in-law.

'Miss Morecroft has done a magnificent job making up the fabric we gave her, hasn't she, Papa?' Caro burst out. 'It's a pity you didn't ask her to make your gown, Aunt Cecily.'

Bridling as she glanced at her own gown of ruby velvet, adorned with every embellishment, Mrs Hawthorne presented Sarah with her back as she took Caro's arm. 'Lavery is admitting the first arrivals. It's time you and your father did your duty.'

Mr Hawthorne ignored the departing pair. His gaze locked with Sarah's. Laughter pealed in the hallway. Sarah recognised it as Philly's. She heard the click of the front door closing, the approach of voices, the rustle of silk. The lengthening silence was heavy with a thousand unsaid words, but Mr Hawthorne's eyes reflected everything she longed to hear. With a final lingering look at Sarah, he stepped back, ready to do his duty by his daughter but not before he'd asked in a voice hoarse with longing, 'Promise the first waltz to me?'

Unable to speak, she nodded, admiring the way his evening clothes hung on his strong, athletic body and the confident way he carried himself as he strode into the saloon after Caro. Like a schoolroom miss, she shrank against the wall and covered her eyes with her hands, shivering with excitement.

He loved her! She'd known it from the start. And Caro endorsed their union. Arriving at the entrance to the ballroom she was still shaking, though now fear outweighed her excitement. She was going to have to exercise every piece of cunning and understanding of Mr Hawthorne's character if her heart's desire were to be realised.

Chattering and giggling, Philly and Georgiana entered the ballroom by the door opposite, accompanied by their dignified aunt. Sarah watched as the girls crowded around Caro, marvelling at her fine dress and improved looks. Some time later, their entrance was followed by a group of officers, dashing in scarlet, who stood rather awkwardly in the centre of the room, casting surreptitious glances at the young ladies.

Sarah's mouth curved into a smile which took on the added joy of being collaborative as Mr Hawthorne joined her, observing, 'The boys admire the girls when they think they're not looking, and the girls pretend ignorance, ogling the boys the moment their backs are turned.' Leading her towards a corner, he plucked a glass of orgeat from the tray of a passing footman.

She accepted it with a grimace. 'I trust

you'll serve something a little more fortifying later this evening.'

'You perplex me, Miss Morecroft.' He looked puzzled. Unconsciously, it seemed, he'd led her into semi-seclusion behind the luxuriant fronds of a lush indoor fern. 'When has champagne been the diet of a poor governess?' His hand moved to a small, faded scar above her wrist. Tracing it with the forefinger of his gloved hand, he smiled up at her as she trembled. 'There is so much more I want to know about you.'

Not yet! a voice screamed inside her head. *When the time is right* . . . She swallowed and put her hand to her bosom to control her erratic breathing. Light strains of music drifted from the annexe where the orchestra was tuning up. The room filled with guests, but here they were alone. In a cocoon of intimacy.

'How can you possibly have escaped marriage — ' His smile faded and his gaze grew more intense. ' — when you are so very lovely?'

Still she could not reply. He went on. 'Or did you always wish to be a governess?'

Sarah tore her eyes away. Carefully, she said, 'I became a governess because my father wished me to marry someone I could not care for. Not as a husband, anyway.'

141

Clearly, her response astonished him. 'Godby — ?'

She cut him off quickly. 'My father wanted me to marry my cousin. We were more like brother and sister. My cousin didn't want to marry me, either, but when a parent believes he knows best — ' She shrugged. ' — drastic action is sometimes called for.'

'I would not have thought it of your father,' he murmured.

'I nearly married — ' She nearly said in her first season but stopped herself. She was treading a tenuous line between giving the truth and a reason for her actions. She could not risk being caught out, yet.

'Was it a match of your choosing?'

'We were mad for each other.' Over Mr Hawthorne's shoulder, Sarah regarded the group of young men in the centre of the room chatting amongst themselves. What callow youths they appeared compared with Mr Hawthorne. She slanted a glance at him. He regarded her soberly, the flirtation gone from his manner. He understood she wanted to give an account of her past as straightfor-wardly as she could before she was ready to embrace the next phase.

If her courage didn't fail her. 'Two weeks before our wedding his regiment was called to fight. He did not return.'

'I'm sorry.'

'Yes, but that is nearly six years ago now.' She met and held his eye. 'Nearly as long ago as your wife died. At the time I believed I'd never get over it, but one can't forever mourn for what one cannot have.'

'One can mourn for what might have been.'

'Only hopeless dreamers do that. And not forever.'

Mr Hawthorne's smile held admiration. 'Your presence at Larchfield has been good for us all,' he said. 'The change in Caro has been remarkable. See, a young gentleman has just engaged her in conversation and she doesn't look as if she's about to sink through the floor.'

'That's Mr Hollingsworth, whose innocent addresses to Caro nearly cost me my job.' She gave him a wry look. 'He's renting Hawthorne-dene until the end of the hunting season and appears a personable fellow. Certainly, he's charmed Lady Charlotte, who seems to want to push Philly his way.'

A group of young ladies brushed past Mr Hawthorne. When he stumbled against Sarah he did not move away. Sensation charged through her. She could tell he felt it, too. His breath stirred the tendrils that curled about her ears. 'I need you about the place, Miss Morecroft — ' His smile was self-deprecating.

' — to keep me from descending into a crotchety dotage.'

She could have adopted the light, bantering tone he'd employed, perhaps to put her at ease. Could have said such a thing was a long way off.

'I am not the governess you think me,' she blurted. There! She'd exposed herself, at last. The truth had to be in the open before they could proceed. She tensed for his horror, his outrage.

Instead, he transferred her glass from her trembling fingers to the depths of the urn so he could grip both her hands.

'No, for I misjudged you. You are *so* much more, yet I've been blind to the truth, and for that I offer my humblest apologies.' He lowered his head to gaze into her eyes.

'What?' Confusion swamped her.

'I believed any daughter of Godby's must share his disregard for the feelings of others. You have proved a true and loyal friend to my daughter. You have the courage of your convictions. You have earned my esteem and admiration — '

Oh, dear Lord, I must *tell him the truth.* She stepped backwards, drawing her hands from his grasp. Sick with fear, she struggled for the right approach. How could she not be tarnished, however artfully she offered her

144

excuses? She had embarked upon her charade as a spoilt and thoughtless young woman. *But I am no longer that young woman*, she screamed inside. *I was once as careless as you believed, but you have shown me how to view the world with a new understanding.* She lay the palm of her hand upon his heart and fixed him with an intensity she had never felt before now. 'Whatever happens, I hope I will always be worthy of your regard — '

'Father, Miss Morecroft, allow me to introduce to you Mr Hollingsworth.'

Dropping her hand, Sarah turned, forcing herself to smile. Clever green eyes set into a handsome, chiselled face smiled back. He had the kind of looks that would make the heart of many a young girl beat more quickly, thought Sarah, forcing her mind into the present. Dark brown curls swept back from a high forehead and pronounced sideburns followed high cheekbones above a strong chin and stylishly high pointed collar. In the final decider, his cravat could not have been more dextrously tied.

A quick glance at Caro confirmed that she was far from immune to his charm. Mr Hollingsworth, though of similar age to many of the young men here tonight, had an air of assurance which set him apart.

After he'd brushed his lips across the back

of Sarah's hand and complimented her, Sarah excused herself. This was Caro's moment. She needed to win her father's approval of her new beau. And, Sarah needed time to rally her defences and embark upon a fresh approach before she was completely undone.

En route to the supper table she was waylaid by Mrs Hawthorne and Lady Charlotte. The latter peered at her through her lorgnette. 'The silver lutestring I had thought so unsuitable for Caro makes splendid finery for yourself, Miss Morecroft.' Her tone was cool. With a start she added, 'Is that not the grey net from your old dress, Cecily? Why, Miss Morecroft, if you should unexpectedly find yourself without employment here, perhaps I shall take you on as my dressmaker.'

Sarah inclined her head while anger bubbled up inside. 'Mr Hawthorne reassures me that he and Caro have become far too attached to me to let me go.' She forced a thin smile. 'And nor shall I be tempted to leave, no matter how great the inducement.' With a haughty nod, she left them.

The refreshments table was not far from the dancing but was afforded some privacy by its separation through open double doors. Sarah began making her selection as she watched Mr Hollingsworth lead Caro onto the dance floor to join a set for a country dance.

'It was not an auspicious moment to be interrupted, but nor was it the ideal place for such a conversation, Miss Morecroft.'

Sarah started. She'd been unaware of Mr Hawthorne's approach.

His smile was artless and her heart somersaulted as he said, 'We shall enjoy more privacy on the dance floor.'

Retrieving the slice of ham Sarah had dropped upon the tablecloth with a fork and placing it on to her plate, he added, 'Although I think perhaps one dance may not be enough to say all that needs to be said.'

She hesitated. 'I think it might be unseemly to engage the governess in even one dance.' She'd been weightless with joy earlier, but the truth of her situation could not be ignored. She was in an impossible situation and had not the least idea how to extricate herself.

He laughed and Sarah was struck by the transformation. The warmth of his expression erased the deep lines etched from nose to mouth, and his eyes glowed with humour and affection.

'I am master of Larchfield and tonight's host. You would do me a great honour if you reserved for me each of the three waltzes on tonight's programme, Miss Morecroft. I think it would send rather an unequivocal message to the rest of the company as to how matters stand between us, don't you?' he murmured.

Sarah swayed towards him.

'May I take it you'll grant my request?'

What could she say? Her whole being screamed to be enfolded in his arms, the truth no longer a barrier as he rained kisses upon her face and lips. Well, perhaps he'd reserve that for once they'd left the dance floor.

Her longing must have been plain for briefly he cupped her cheek, his expression tender. 'I hope I'm not being too presumptuous in taking that for a yes,' he murmured before he left her.

The Sir Richard de Coverley was in progress. A dozen couples participated, performing their steps with endless repetition.

In the meantime there were more arrivals: a group of noisy young men in regimentals, causing the half-dozen wall flowers to raise hopeful heads in their direction.

Sarah stood near a group of neighbourhood matrons, pointedly ignored by Mrs Hawthorne. She tried to calm the turbulence of her emotions, tried to whip up the sense of delicious empowerment she'd have felt not so long ago at the prospect of Mrs Hawthorne's reaction when Mr Hawthorne led Sarah off the dance floor at the conclusion of the third waltz. But she knew she'd not be released from the grip of her overpowering dread and apprehension until her conscience was clear.

She returned Mr Hollingsworth's smile as he passed by with Caro on his arm. There was no point making some trite enquiry as to whether Caro were enjoying herself. Sarah had never seen her look so happy, nor so poised and beautiful.

Had Caro just discovered the antidote that would banish her demons forever? Sarah had no doubt that Mr Hawthorne had invested in herself the care of his damaged, passionate heart. It was a weighty responsibility. She prayed she would not fail him.

She shivered at the chill gusting in with the arrival of some latecomers: more young men, self-consciously adjusting their high pointed collars after they'd been relieved of their outerwear by Lavery. She smiled at the stir of feminine interest.

A smile soon replaced by dismay as the assembled group broke up, revealing a young man whose sheer height and breadth and thick red hair set him apart. Only that was not what drew Sarah's attention, and soon all those nearby.

Run! screamed the voice of salvation in her

head. *It's all over for you. You've lost your chance and you can never be redeemed.* But horror curdled into sick inaction, rooting her to the spot.

The ringleader, a blond tousle-headed young captain, rose from his bow with an engaging smile, and glanced about the room. 'Mrs Hawthorne, ladies. Forgive us for being so late. Is Aunt Charlotte here? I daresay I deserve the earful she'll no doubt dish out, but we are here at last and — Sarah!'

She hadn't realised how tensely she'd waited for it.

'Sarah?' the red-haired man asked again, his voice now low, questioning. He advanced a few steps. Sarah retreated in the face of his stricken look. Pale-complexioned with a dusting of freckles across his nose, and hugely broad shoulders, his presence filled her with as much affection as alarm. She hadn't realised she'd missed James so much. Her heart pounded. She wanted to throw herself into his arms then drag him from the room and tell him everything, but she could not with so many eyes upon her. Her future happiness hinged on how she dealt with the next few moments.

She was aware of Lady Charlotte's gimlet eye trained upon her. She forced herself to give a little laugh as James approached. *Be calm*, she exhorted herself. *If you lose your composure now, it could be all over for you.*

'Hello, James.' She grasped his wrist. How she kept her voice steady, she did not know. Smiling, keenly aware of the interest still trained upon her, she pulled him a few feet away. She realised she could not bask in admiration all evening without exciting the glare of publicity at such an interesting change of tone. 'Goodness, you look as if you've seen a ghost. Had you not heard I'd taken a position as governess for Mr and Mrs Hawthorne? No?' *Please*, she prayed. *Not here. Don't let him unmask me in front of everyone.* Taking advantage of James's confusion, she went on quickly, 'It's a long story and I can't wait to catch up with all you've been doing. Only you'll have to excuse me as I've promised the next dance.' In a low hiss she added, 'Meet me at the supper table in two minutes.'

Shaking, she made her escape. She soon gave up trying to load up her supper plate, instead watching beadily as Mrs Hawthorne quizzed the red-headed newcomer across the room.

A few minutes later James was by her side. Gripping her arm he exhorted her, 'Dear God, Sarah, you know we all thought you were dead? How could you — ?'

151

'Please, James!' she entreated under her breath, for another couple was now helping themselves to food nearby. 'There's a terrace just outside. I'll be there as soon as I can get away. I promise I'll explain everything! Just don't tell anyone who I am.'

She pulled away, leaving her plate upon the sideboard. Her breath came in short, sharp bursts as she hurried towards the double doors. Caro smiled at her over her shoulder as she waited in line to perform her dance steps. Lady Charlotte cast her a narrow-eyed look as she slipped from the room.

Sarah steeled herself as she stepped from the passage out onto the terrace, heedless of the chill upon her bare shoulders.

In just a moment she'd be calling on all her reserves of remorse and tact to soothe the feelings of a kind and honourable man who had every reason to feel hurt and betrayed.

Poor James, she thought as she prepared to sink her pride. Her spirits sank even lower as she reflected that her ordeal with James was just the prelude to her mortification.

10

Trembling, Sarah paced the gravel terrace just around the corner from where the doors opened wide upon the garden outside.

The final chords of the Sir Richard de Coverley were followed by a smatter of clapping. Sarah chewed her knuckles. After a short interval the orchestra would break into the exciting, romantic strains of the waltz. She stifled a sob of disappointment. If she could tell James the truth quickly, she might be back in time. The fear of James revealing her true identity battled with her fear that Mr Hawthorne would come looking for her.

She continued to pace, her mind in a panic, oblivious to the soft tread upon the gravel until she virtually collided with him.

'James!'

'Sarah!'

Seizing his arm, she pulled him into the seclusion of the shrubbery.

'Do you realize your father is half mad with grief?' he demanded angrily. 'Not to mention the agonies *I've* suffered on your account. I can't believe you've done this!'

His words were like barbs in her already

battle-scarred conscience. She couldn't bear to see the pain and anger that roiled in his hurt, angry green eyes.

'You don't understand, James. I had to leave.'

His chest heaved but he said nothing, though he quirked an eyebrow in invitation to go on.

'It was because of you — '

'*Me?*'

She reached up to put her hands on his shoulders. 'Papa was pressuring me to accept your offer. I knew you didn't really want to marry me — '

'That's not true!' he interjected, but his voice lacked conviction.

'Oh James,' Sarah sighed, hooking her hands behind his neck and wilting against him. She wanted him to forgive her but she didn't want to be forced into revealing the full truth. Not now.

'It *is* true. And as I wanted to marry you as much as you wished to marry me — ' She shrugged, nestling her cheek against his chest. ' — I thought that disappearing would be the best way of winning Papa round.'

James grunted as he stroked her hair, the sounds of the next waltz drifting through the open windows. 'Lord Miles would hardly have forced you to the altar against your wishes. Sarah, come back!' He made a lunge for her as she disengaged herself and ran towards the house.

'I'm promised for this dance.' Frantic, she skirted the bushes which separated the terrace from the French doors leading into the house. 'Say nothing. *Please*,' she begged over her shoulder. 'My entire life's happiness depends on this waltz.'

She was reassured more by his expression of dawning understanding than his attitude of resignation. But she'd known James her whole life. He'd often looked at her like this. And he'd never yet let her down.

* * *

Smiling, Roland watched Miss Morecroft weave her way over to the supper table. For such a slender young woman she had a hearty appetite. It was the second time this evening she had piled her plate so high. A frisson of excitement ran through him as he anticipated their forthcoming encounter on the dance floor.

'Know you'd have me whipped for the sentiment if you could, Hawthorne, but I wasn't sorry to see those trouble-makers swing.'

Roland turned with a resigned smile. He'd

known it wouldn't be long before Colonel Doncaster espoused such sentiments. Wrinkling his claret nose, his oldest friend and neighbour went on, 'They'd turn England on her head if they could.'

Now was not the time to enter into a spirited debate on politics, justice and the social system, though Roland knew this was what the colonel was angling for.

'Colonel, we are celebrating my daughter's come-out.' He smiled a warning before greeting Mrs Doncaster with genuine pleasure. A sensible, good looking strawberry blonde in her early forties, she knew how to keep her husband in check.

'You've picked up a pistol for less, Roland,' the colonel reminded him.

It struck a nerve. 'I was a callow youth.'

Mrs Doncaster put a gentle hand on her red-faced husband's sleeve. 'Roland has more sense now. It's time you married again, Roland,' she told him. 'The days of Venetia and duelling and risking your life for your beliefs are over.' There was a glint in her eye. 'I know several young ladies who would suit you very well if you'd let me introduce them.'

'Frances prides herself on being the canny one in matters of the heart,' her husband said, putting an arm about her waist, 'but I'd wager something's already in the wind if

Roland won't talk politics with me.'

Roland gave a good-natured laugh. He'd lost sight of Sarah though he'd scanned the room several times for her. The Sir Richard de Coverley was winding down and he was aching for the promised waltz.

Unconsciously he shifted position to ease his growing anticipation, and was whisked into the present by Frances remarking slyly, 'I believe you're right, Seb! Tell us, Roland, is Cecily's position as mistress of Larchfield about to be usurped?'

Roland blinked. Was he that transparent?

Laughing, she observed, 'You always were one to wear your heart on your sleeve, which is why I know there's been no one since Venetia.'

'Frances, you're embarrassing the poor man.' The colonel's tone was full of disgust. 'Men of sound mind do not wear their hearts on their sleeves like namby-pamby boys or swooning maidens.'

'But my dear, I well remember Roland doing just that when you brought me here as a new bride,' she objected, undaunted. 'He was captivated by Venetia, just as you were captivated by *your* new bride.' She patted the colonel's arm as his complexion took on the deep ruby hue of her gown.

'Excuse me.' Roland left them with a bow

and a smile. 'I am under an obligation to claim the next dance.' Full of expectation, he left their good-natured circle in search of Miss Morecroft.

'Caro, you haven't seen Miss Morecroft?' he asked his daughter, who was being escorted onto the dance floor yet again by Mr Hollingsworth.

'No, Papa. Aunt Cecily, have you seen Miss Morecroft?'

'Miss Morecroft?' Her aunt sniffed while Lady Charlotte indicated the doorway. 'Left a couple of minutes ago. Seemed quite discomposed by some fellow who'd just arrived.'

With a final, worried glance around the room, Roland turned into the passage as the orchestra tuned their instruments. Waltzing with Godby's daughter would cause far more of a stir than dancing with a mere governess. Had Miss Morecroft taken it upon herself to *spare* him?

Impatiently, he waited outside the mending room set up for minor repairs to the ladies' gowns. He could think of nowhere else she'd be. She wasn't downstairs, Augusta and Harriet were in Ellen's care, and Miss Morecroft would hardly be out in the chill night air.

He willed her to issue through the doorway; to look him up and down in that assessing way of hers which always reassured him she didn't find him wanting.

Pacing impatiently, he pictured her in his mind's eye. Like Venetia, she was beautiful and proud. But Venetia had been venal and calculating. Venetia had taught him how to reap the rewards of desire: how to pleasure a woman and what unexpected pleasures a man might likewise enjoy at the hands of a woman. He'd been a willing pupil, hurling himself headlong into a surfeit of lust. And when he had totally surrendered to her all he had to give — his heart, his body, his every waking thought, almost his own sense of self — he had realized her pleasure had been largely in his surrender, in her ability to conquer.

Then she had moved on, like a predatory shark, to fish other waters.

But Miss Morecroft was not like that. Miss Morecroft had kindness and sincerity to compensate for the traits she shared with Venetia.

'Mary, have you seen Miss Morecroft?' he asked the maid who opened the door of the mending room. Hearing the urgency in his voice, he added, 'Caro is looking for her.'

Instantly he was ashamed of himself. Was it necessary to conceal from one of his employees that it was he, himself, who wished to find the governess?

No, he didn't care what Mary, or Cecily, or anyone thought. Miss Morecroft was the most divine, spirited, engaging woman he'd ever met. He'd thought keeping her at Larchfield as the girls' governess would be enough. Now he knew he had to marry her.

Instead of being dismayed, he exulted. For the first time in his life he was about to yield to his desires with supreme confidence in the outcome. They would make each other happy. He was certain of it.

His frustration increased as the orchestra launched into the waltz he had looked forward to with such anticipation.

'I saw her running outside just a few minutes ago, sir.' The maid looked disapproving as she rose from her curtsy. 'Not even a cloak or shawl to keep her poor bare shoulders warm this freezing night.'

Thanking Mary, he stepped through the French doors. He was worried now. The sharp air stung his face and he stamped his feet and rubbed his hands together to warm them. Why on earth would Miss Morecroft rush outside into the freezing night when she was supposed to be enjoying the warmth of his embrace? He thought of a dozen reasons to reassure himself as he crunched his way along the terrace. Perhaps she'd fallen ill, or felt faint, then re-entered the house by another door.

He scanned the immediate area as far as the light from the windows penetrated, then continued along the side of the house to where the terrace disappeared around the corner, half shrouded by shrubbery.

Hearing voices, he moved closer.

'Oh, James . . . ' There was anguish in the young lady's voice. He could not see her, obscured as she was by the shrubbery, but it was clear by the sigh and tone of her voice as she continued, that she was in company with someone familiar to her.

Caught between making his presence known, and the natural impulse to eavesdrop, Roland was on the point of retracing his footsteps to the house when the urgency in what only now he realised was Miss Morecroft's voice arrested him.

'I wanted to marry you as much as you wished to marry me.'

Disgust infected Roland's veins with cold, sluggish blood as he heard her next words. 'I thought that disappearing would be the best way of winning Papa round.'

Then the young man answered. 'Lord Miles would hardly have forced you to the altar against your wishes. Sarah, come back!'

Roland stepped back against the bushes as

she ran past him. He heard the doors slam shut behind her. The low groan of the now deserted young man was followed by the sound of his footsteps disappearing in the opposite direction.

Roland's breath rasped on the icy air as he stumbled towards the house.

Sarah scanned the room from her secluded corner vantage point while she regulated her uneven breathing. There he was, talking to Colonel Doncaster on the far side of the room.

Surely, she thought, Mr Hawthorne could not be thinking her a flirt or a jilt for missing their appointed waltz? A sudden call upon her time by one of the girls, a torn skirt, or twisted ankle was far more likely.

He appeared not to be aware of her as she brushed past him and the colonel. Glancing over her shoulder, she tried to catch his eye as she wove her way through the crowd. Her ploy was not successful.

For a few moments she stood alone by the double doors which separated the card room from the dance floor. Her glass replenished, but not her spirits, she frowned at him as he disengaged himself from the colonel. If she didn't know better she'd think he was ignoring her.

Out of pique?

She felt sick. Mr Hawthorne couldn't imagine she was playing games with him — could he?

James had engaged Caro for the next set. Caro smiled, acknowledging her governess with a wave as they passed nearby. To Sarah's relief, James pretended ignorance of who she was.

Growing fear twisted her gut. Miserably, she watched as Mr Hawthorne stood, grim and woodenly, conversing with Lords Digby and Denning, ancient acquaintances of her father. It felt as if the evening were closing in on her.

Sarah positioned herself a little away from Philly and Georgiana so as not to bring attention to her solitary state while she waited for an opportunity to waylay him. He must know she was here. All evening she'd been thrillingly aware of his eyes following her around the room.

Watching him discuss a matter that was apparently of weighty concern, she was gripped with longing as he raked his hand through his hair in that familiar gesture of his.

Was he talking of universal access to education and male suffrage? Such notions would send her father into paroxysms. He'd certainly have paroxysms if she informed him she intended marrying Roland Hawthorne.

With a determined tilt to her chin, she

pushed her shoulders back. Marrying Mr Hawthorne was exactly what she intended doing.

Lord Denning shook his head with sudden vehemence and Lord Digby scowled. She wondered what Mr Hawthorne could have said. Both men were her father's age, with a propensity towards apoplexy — on little provocation. Just like her father. She felt a pang, then rallied. Soon, this whole charade would be at an end.

As he extricated himself from the group Sarah seized her moment and glided into his path.

'Forgive me, Mr Hawthorne, for missing the waltz I promised you. I was called away suddenly.' When her apology was not greeted with the immediate pardon she'd expected, she stammered, 'Calls on my time come from all quarters and the little girls required me for a moment. I am merely the governess, after all.'

He frowned down at her. 'Ah, yes, merely the governess.'

Discomposed, she suggested, 'Perhaps the next waltz?'

'There will be no more waltzes for me tonight,' he said. 'Forgive me.' He bowed and was about to pass on but she stopped him, alarmed.

'Mr Hawthorne, Have I angered you? Surely you understand — '

'Indeed I do, Miss Morecroft. If you will excuse me, there has been distressing news this evening. I am poor company in my current mood.'

With another cursory bow, he was gone.

Sarah stared after him, fear and disappointment wrestling one another.

Think! It was perfectly reasonable, she told herself, that a man with such a powerful social conscience would need to mull over events in private. She'd do herself no favours badgering him for the cause of his distress.

Ignoring Mrs Hawthorne's beady-eyed stare, she rested against the large urn where he'd caressed her arm. Longing tore through her. And uncertainty. Perhaps he'd call her into the library to apologise later.

'I've been trying to put my finger on it all evening, Miss Morecroft, and at last it's come to me.'

Sarah met Mrs Hawthorne's gloating smile across the top of the plinth. She didn't intend straightening out of deference.

'Those dancing slippers belonged to Lady Venetia. I recognise them.'

'You don't think I — '

'I'm not accusing you of theft, Miss Morecroft. Merely recalling the last time they graced her ladyship's dainty feet.'

Sarah said nothing. Mrs Hawthorne clearly would enjoy telling her.

'When the men brought her into the house from the river I asked my brother-in-law if he should like her buried in them.' Mrs Hawthorne touched her necklace with bony fingers, feigned wistfulness twisting her features as she gazed at the couples on the dance floor. 'Poor Venetia looked so lovely in death, her white gown clinging to her, her dark hair loose around her face.' She fixed Sarah with a hard look. 'In that moment I felt closer to her than I ever had.' With a nod at the offending dancing slippers, she added, 'I even felt sorry for her when Roland said he hoped they'd carry their deceiving baggage to hell.'

11

'Master wishes to see you, Miss Morecroft.'
Ellen put her head around the bedroom door
and eyed Sarah speculatively.

'When? Now?'

'At your convenience, miss.'

It was, after all, still early. The household
had retired late to bed.

But the few intervening hours had yielded
little sleep. Sarah had not yet finished
dressing, and as she bent over the small chest
of drawers to peer into the mirror she was
dismayed at the haggard face that stared,
hollow-eyed, back at her.

'Have you done summat you oughtn't?'
Ellen was nothing, if not blunt.

Sarah's heart lurched with the fear that
had kept her awake half the night. He
couldn't have seen her with James, surely.
They were well hidden in the shrubbery.
Perhaps Mrs Hawthorne, or someone else,
had said something which reflected badly
upon her? She tried to bolster her courage at
the prospect that Mr Hawthorne might end
the interview championing her, rather than
chastising her.

Sounding as jaunty as she could, she replied, 'Mr Hawthorne received distressing news last night but he wants to talk to me about Caro.'

Ellen nodded, apparently satisfied. 'I'll send a message you'll be down directly,' she said, disappearing.

Sarah set to work, remedying the damage of a sleepless night and low spirits with all the artifice at her fingertips. Fear and trepidation soon turned to anticipation. Perhaps his disappointment at matters beyond his control would lead him to seek solace in the arms of a woman he desired.

No longer sallow and hollow-eyed, Sarah appeared before him, roses blooming in her cheeks.

'You wished to see me, sir.' She smiled as she bobbed a curtsy. She had exorcised her fear. She was filled with vigour and expectation.

He pushed back his chair and rose from his writing desk. There was no answering smile as he waved her to a chair. Yet his eyes appeared to drink in every detail, from the curls she'd arranged with such care to tumble from her Greek knot, before travelling the length of her best sprigged muslin.

Finally they returned to her face as she settled herself in a chair. Her heart beat wildly in confusion. He looked as if what he saw pleased him not at all.

'That is correct, Lady Sarah.' His tone was cold and formal.

She felt a moment's sense of disembodiment; as if she were looking at him through a waterfall. She blinked. He appeared to grow indistinct while the thundering torrent filled her head with noise.

She closed her eyes, gripped the sides of her chair and whispered through her dry throat, 'How did you find out?'

'From your own lips.'

When she opened her eyes it was to see his trained on her as if she were a spy who had infiltrated his household. 'I overheard you and your . . . lover . . . out on the terrace last night.' His disgust was evident.

'My lover?' She swallowed. 'James is my friend. My childhood friend. You misunderstood — '

'Have I misunderstood that you are here on false pretences, impersonating a dead woman? Have I misunderstood that you are not, in fact, the daughter of my late foster-brother but the daughter of the man against whom I have fought tirelessly in the parliament for so many years?'

Shame burned her cheeks. How underhand and wicked he made her actions seem.

'I did not set out, intentionally, to deceive anyone,' she murmured, plucking at her sleeve. 'I was misidentified after the ship went down. And . . . I had my reasons for not wishing to return to my father immediately.'

'Well, your father's on his way here to collect you, madam. So you had better prepare yourself.'

Sarah gasped. 'No! Please, Mr Hawthorne. You don't understand — '

'There is no deficiency in my cognitive powers.' His voice was chilling. He began to pace before the fireplace. 'I understand perfectly that you have been acting out a charade in my household, taking us all for fools. Having been deceived once before, Miss Morecroft — I beg your pardon, Lady Sarah — I am in no hurry to be taken advantage of again.'

'But . . . but I don't want to go. Please, Mr Hawthorne — '

'Having crossed swords with your father myself, so to speak, I am not surprised you don't want to go.' He finished on a snarl. 'But go you will.'

There was no hesitation or wavering that could give Sarah encouragement.

'His anger's not the reason — '

'I do not care for your reasons, Lady Sarah. Your deception is enough.' Already he was turning back to his desk, dismissing her. He waved his hand towards the door. 'Please, go.'

She rose. Clenching her hands into fists at her sides for strength, she made one more appeal.

'It was because of *you*, sir, I continued the charade. No other reason.' She took a step towards him, widening her eyes in entreaty, although his back remained towards her. 'Don't send me away, I beg of you. I cannot bear to leave you!'

Slowly he turned. Hope reignited in Sarah's breast. She had never spoken the truth more sincerely. If he would just forgive her and let her stay she would gladly spend the rest of her life doing penance.

'I have heard enough impassioned promises of reform to last me a lifetime, Lady Sarah.' His voice was impassive. 'Good day to you.'

Blindly, Sarah rushed towards her room. Someone addressed her in the corridor. She ignored them, hurrying on until she had gained the privacy of her tiny chamber where she threw herself face-down upon the bed.

Oh, dear Lord, she exhorted silently. Make Mr Hawthorne accept her charade for what it was. He was drawing parallels between her behaviour and Venetia's. As bad, he suspected she was a spy. Clearly, he'd not considered her real reasons to be the truth.

After some time Sarah became conscious of a tapping on her door. A small dark head appeared, followed by a taller, red-haired one. Two pairs of eyes regarded her anxiously.

'Are you all right, Miss Morecroft?' Harriet asked, pushing open the door and padding into the room.

'Of course,' said Sarah as brightly as she could. She sat up, forcing herself to smile, then caressed Augusta's dark curls as the little girl rested her head against her arm. Harriet snuggled up close on her other side.

Sarah's contrived cheerfulness seemed not to assuage their concerns. They continued to eye her fearfully.

'Why would you think I am not? Caro's ball was perfectly delightful,' she babbled. 'Your sister was a credit to you all; and I am as hale and hearty as I ever was. Perhaps you are here to pester me to give you more French verbs to conjugate?'

They ignored her attempt at levity. 'Ellen was being strange this morning,' said Augusta. 'And then she just left us in the nursery . . . alone.'

'She never does that,' said Harriet. Her dark eyes were luminous with worry. 'And she said you weren't coming to teach us this morning. That something had happened and that you weren't our governess any more.'

172

'But if you're not our governess any more,' said Augusta, her bottom lip quivering, 'I swear I'll not conjugate French verbs for any other governess, ever again.'

'Come now.' Sarah hugged the little girl, who had started to sniffle. 'Ellen has made all this seem like the end of the world. I'll never leave you completely. I'll always be there for you in spirit. And even if I have to go away for a little while, I . . . I'll do my best to come back.'

It was hard to keep her voice from breaking. The thought of leaving her young charges, she now realized, was almost as heartbreaking as being wrenched from Roland.

'I knew it!' cried Caro, bursting into the room and confronting Sarah, hands on hips. 'I knew you didn't *want* to leave. And we won't let you! Whatever Father says . . . well, I don't know what all this is about, but he's *wrong!*' With a hiccupping sob, she began to pace.

It was all too much for Sarah. Unable to check the tears that rolled down her cheeks, she tried to comfort the girls, who were all crying loudly.

The door opened once more. This time it was Ellen, standing stony-faced in the passage.

'Lady Sarah, Mrs Hawthorne says your new bedchamber is ready for you.'

'What?' Sarah frowned.

'Bein' a lady an' all, miss, you can't be expected to sleep rough like a servant,' said Ellen, bobbing a respectful curtsy, although her expression remained cold. 'Mrs Hawthorne has had one of the guest rooms prepared until such time as 'is Lordship arrives to take you 'ome.'

'So, it's true,' said Caro slowly, drying her tears with her cuff, and frowning at her when Ellen had gone. 'You really are the daughter of Lord Miles. Papa said . . . you had deceived us all.'

Sarah found it hard to meet her eye. Taking a deep breath for courage, she said quietly, 'If you would allow me to tell you the whole story, I would greatly appreciate it.'

She left nothing out. The spoilt, pleasure-loving society darling had learned some hard lessons, and she was prepared to put herself forward as an example of what not to do when faced with an obdurate papa. At the same time, she needed the girls to know her affection for them and her employer was deep and sincere.

At last she rose with a sigh. 'I'd better prepare myself for my father's arrival.'

'What will your father do?' whispered Harriet.

Sarah considered a moment. 'Well, he will probably be very courteous and correct and polite because he will be a guest in your house. But later he will shout and stamp around, and probably throw a good many things.'

'At you?' Caro asked, horrified.

'No, at the wall. And then he will hug me so hard I'll hardly be able to breathe, and then he'll cry a great deal.'

The girls blinked in surprise. 'Men don't cry,' said Augusta. 'At least, Uncle Roland doesn't.'

'He does,' said Caro. Colouring, she mumbled, 'At least, he did.'

'When Aunt Venetia died, I suppose,' said Augusta. 'Well, that's allowed. Even men can cry when people die.'

'Oh, Papa never cried *after* mama died,' said Caro. She glared at Sarah before her face crumpled. 'But I'd wager he will now,' she said on a sob.

The door opened and Ellen reappeared.

'I shall take the girls now, m'lady,' she said briskly.

Sarah stared with longing at the young charges she might never see again, and the funny little nursery maid whose trust and dignity she'd so injured. 'Please Ellen, I —'

Ellen cut her off. 'Lizzie will be here shortly to pack for you.' The girl refused to look Sarah in the eye. 'Mrs Hawthorne says tea is in the drawing room whenever you wish to present yourself.'

★ ★ ★

Roland's hand trembled as he replaced the decanter, the sharp brandy fumes burning before he had taken the first sip. He hadn't felt like this since Venetia had left him the first time.

Or had the familiar loneliness that now consumed him been more a feature of his life *with* Venetia, while her departure had occasioned relief?

Roland was not given to detailed analyses on the state of his heart. He had lost it when he was twenty, and the mauling it had received over the next ten years of marriage had convinced him that hearts were best left to the domain of women.

To banish the thought of Miss Morecroft — Lady Sarah — he thought of his election campaign just around the corner. He was for the abolition of rotten boroughs.

He smiled grimly. Not an idea Lord Miles favoured. And why would he when he could exploit his position and be re-elected time after time with little inducement — just the threat of increased rents for his tenants.

Taking another sip, he stared down the gravel drive that wound through the gardens, disappearing into the darkness of the park beyond.

Soon Lord Miles's carriage would lumber up that driveway. He wondered at the nature of the inevitable exchange between them before it lumbered back down the drive again, Lord Miles's daughter ensconced inside in padded comfort.

It would be the last he would see of Lady Sarah.

As it should be.

He sighed deeply, wishing the exhalation and the refilling of his lungs occasioned some relief. But there was pain in every breath.

He was replenishing his tumbler when there came a knock upon his door.

Caro? He hoped not. He hadn't the stomach for more of her tears and passionate entreaties. She'd left him half an hour before, weeping and vengeful. He was still shaken by the encounter.

'Your harsh judgment of me is ill deserved, Mr Hawthorne, for all I admit I am guilty of deceit,' came a cool, formal voice.

Unannounced and uninvited, she entered the room, moving with her peculiar grace until she stood squarely before him.

Lord, she was beautiful. The light seemed

to have laid a rosy cast upon her perfect skin, set off by her gleaming hair which seemed tinged more with russet in this light. She had always been confident but standing here before him, as Lady Sarah, she seemed like an unobtainable goddess.

Unobtainable, like Venetia had once seemed. And little joy he had got from attaining what he had once believed was his heart's desire.

Silently, he digested the young woman's impertinence while he drank in the perfection of her form: full-breasted and wasp-waisted with the most kissable lips he'd ever encountered.

He glanced away, pretending to note the hands of the clock, so as to hide his aching desire. Longing tore at him, devastatingly familiar. He clenched his fists at his sides. Succumbing to his heart would be his undoing.

'I believe Mrs Hawthorne is expecting you in the drawing room.' He ignored her words, his expression impassive as he turned back to face her.

'Why are you doing this?' She took a quick step forward, her voice barely above a whisper.

He noted the effort it took her to keep it under control. Well, it was hardly surprising she was upset. She had been unmasked; her whole story was a fabrication. She had taken them all for fools, to suit her own ends — whether it was for a lark, or because she was acting the spoiled child who wanted to teach her father a lesson, or even if she was a spy, which he naturally no longer believed. Of course she would feel the need to justify herself. Her pride required that he forgive her and farewell her as his friend when she left on the arm of her father, rather than eject her in ignominy.

'I'm sorry?' He raised an eyebrow, his tone as disparaging as he could manage when sorrow and disappointment were equally in the ascendant. 'Why do I do what, Lady Sarah?'

He could see her barely contained anger in the rise and fall of her bosom as she stared at him through those exquisite, heavily lashed hazel eyes.

He answered his own question. 'Why do I expel an imposter from my household? A woman whose motives can only be under suspicion for failing to reveal herself?' He had not meant to insult her so directly. But his instincts for self-preservation were honed to the highest degree.

'I have explained that my reasons were entirely prompted by a spontaneous act of . . . desperation,' she said tightly.

He turned his head away from the sight of

her eyes bright with unshed tears. Silently he willed her to give up the fight and just leave. He did not have the fortitude to cope with another emotional female right now. Hadn't he spent the last few years ensuring that emotion — certainly that of a romantic nature — did not become the architect of his destruction? Ten years of Venetia was more than a lifetime of tears and tantrums. And one glance at Lady Sarah's damp, glistening lashes was a frightening prospect. What if she should cry . . . throw herself at him?

Good God! He would be undone. Under such heavy fire he didn't trust himself not to reveal what was in his heart and do something unutterably stupid. Like tell her he loved her. Then she'd never give up her fight.

She took a steadying breath. 'If you choose to put a more sinister slant upon it . . . ' Her voice was controlled, cold, even.

He didn't like to admit he was disappointed that she refrained from continuing in a more emotional vein. The heat had gone from the exchange. Reason had returned.

'Clearly, Lady Sarah, you cannot remain as governess to my girls,' he said. He tilted his head, awaiting her corroboration.

She bowed her own, her rich reddish-gold locks gleaming in the slanting sunlight. It took the greatest self-control not to brush his hand over her silken tresses and tangle his fingers in the soft curls that fell from her top knot. A tantalizing expanse of white, flawless skin extended from the nape of her neck to the back of her gown where a row of tiny pearl buttons began and ended somewhere — he swallowed — below her waist.

Roland closed his eyes as he fought to retain his distance. When she raised her head to fix him with her hurt, angry eyes, he had put the sofa between them.

She whispered, 'I shall miss them.'

Was the regret just part of the act? he wondered. They did seem fond of her, but an accomplished imposter surely did not form dangerous personal attachments?

'Then I'm sorry you set yourself up for such disappointment.' Though his tone was dismissive, he longed to continue the exchange. He realized with a wave of overpowering disappointment it may well be their last. 'Please don't paint me the villain for acting differently from any other responsible employer, or gentleman.'

At her look of entreaty, he added, 'What else would you have me do? Keep you on indefinitely as a most attractive houseguest?'

He wished he had not said that, just as he would have regretted anything else said to cause the rise and fall and the delectable swell of lily-white flesh above the low, lace-lined cut of her bodice. It was a direct assault upon his senses, upon his ability to utter words of reason. For indeed, his words were reasonable. What else could he do but send for her father to fetch her?

'Is that all?' She swallowed and bit her lip. There was a dangerous gleam in her eye. 'Do you mean to tell me that . . . before . . . you were simply taking advantage of an attractive . . . governess? If there was nothing else . . . ?'

She could not finish and he immediately felt put in the wrong. 'I am not that kind of man,' he muttered. 'I told you before.'

'Then if there were some . . . feeling behind your past words and actions, how can you dismiss me so coldly? Why are you unable to acknowledge — '

No, this was too dangerous. He cut her off, running the back of his hand across his eyes to ease the pressure pounding in his head. 'We are getting nowhere, madam.' He took several decisive steps to his desk. Pulling out his chair, he turned with a look of cool enquiry, as if daring her to detain him further. 'Thank you for your services. If you have any further requests, I suggest you direct them to Mrs Hawthorne. Good day.'

★　★　★

From the casement Sarah watched the crested carriage roll up the driveway and halt before the front steps. She felt a surge of guilt, fear and, yes, above all, joy at seeing her father's mane of grizzled white hair as he removed his top hat for a moment to give his scalp a good scratch, frowning up at the house as he did so.

Then she saw the hunted look in his tawny eyes replaced by echoing joy as he recognized her through the glass window.

Within moments he was indoors, thrusting his outerwear at Lavery, while Sarah was running down the curved staircase, throwing herself into his arms at the bottom.

Unashamedly, they both wept. Then Lord Miles raised his head and caught sight of Roland over Sarah's shoulder.

For an instant he froze. Sarah, still gripped in a fierce bear hug, felt the strange cocktail of emotions replaced by one dominant feeling: fear. What would her father do now?

He appeared to falter. For one ghastly moment she thought he was about to break down and would have to be led to a chair and revived.

That, she decided a moment later, would have been preferable to his finding solace in anger, his habitual refuge. It would be over in an instant, but she cringed as he directed his obviously confused emotions upon Roland.

'How dare you contain my daughter, a vulnerable unmarried female, under your roof for nearly two months while I am left with the unspeakable devastation of believing her dead?' he thundered.

Shaking his fist, Lord Miles took a threatening step towards Roland. Sarah wondered if Roland, too, would defend himself using his most comfortable defence: irony. She was surprised when he advanced towards Lord Miles, hand outstretched, a tight half-smile upon his face; surprised, and touched, that when her father refused to grasp it, Roland placed it instead in a most conciliatory manner upon the old man's shoulder.

'Lord Miles, may I offer you some refreshment — brandy perhaps, after your tiring journey?' he suggested. Already he was motioning to Lavery to expedite this request.

'Do you think I would accept refreshment from my enemy?' thundered Lord Miles.

Sarah held her breath and watched as Roland gently propelled Lord Miles through the hallway. Her father moved slowly, like an old man. Remorse cut through her like a knife.

'Our opposing political views and previous history,' said Roland carefully, 'do not necessarily make us enemies.'

'An enemy milks his advantage. For the past two months you have detained the one treasure I hold dearer to my heart than any other.'

He stumbled as he turned to look at Sarah, who was bringing up the rear. How feeble he appeared, she thought with horror. Surely he had not lost his mind? Dear Lord, she prayed, do not let her be the cause of that.

'My lord,' said Roland, taking a seat opposite Lord Miles once they'd gained the library, 'make what charges you will once you have spoken to your daughter. She's been recovering after a terrible ordeal at sea and, I fear, has not known, herself, who she really is. Had the truth been apparent, your Lordship would have been informed upon the instant.'

Sarah wished Roland had given *her* the benefit of such a plausible pretext.

The brandy revived Lord Miles. He sat up straighter and fixed a pair of small but intense eyes on Sarah. How well she remembered that look, terrifying beneath his beetling white brows. He'd often used it to great effect, quelling her when her opinion ran counter to his.

But now there was no firm conviction to defend; only his grief and pain to assuage.

Seated opposite her father, Sarah clasped

her hands in her lap and hung her head. 'Forgive me, Father,' she murmured. 'I accept all blame. I've taken advantage of Mr Hawthorne and his family who have looked after me so kindly, ignorant of the truth. And I have given you more pain than any father ought to bear.'

'Why, Sarah?' Lord Miles's confusion was pitiful.

Mr Hawthorne rose. 'I shall leave you for a few minutes.'

Sarah nearly wept at the regret on his face as he looked at her en route to the door. She wanted to leap up and throw her arms around his neck, delivering a different and far more passionate apology for her behaviour than the one she was making to her father.

So this was it. She would not be granted a reprieve.

He was nearly at the door when Mrs Hawthorne's raised voice issued from down the corridor.

'Roland!' she cried, sweeping into the room and wringing her hands. Without acknowledging her guest, she added breathlessly, 'Caro's gone! It's true; I found this upon your bed!' She waved a piece of parchment, its seal broken.

He took it, scanning it quickly. 'This letter is for me.'

'The door to your chamber was open, Roland, and when I saw it I thought . . . ' Her voice trailed off as she looked with unmistakable loathing at Sarah.

So, thought Sarah, she would have had no compunction in intercepting and keeping secret from Roland any communication Sarah might have attempted.

'You must act quickly, Roland! Oh, my dear Lord, what will we do?' Crumpling onto the nearest chair in a heap of lavender stripes, she began to wail.

Dry-throated, Sarah asked, 'Does she say where?'

Not looking at her, Mr Hawthorne carefully refolded the paper. 'She has gone to London,' he said in clipped tones, 'with Mr Hollingsworth.'

Sarah gasped. 'Does she say why?'

Mr Hawthorne ran a hand across his brow, while Mrs Hawthorne shrieked as she rose to her feet, 'She has learnt the truth, Roland. I don't know how she could have discovered — '

'There is no proof to be discovered!' snapped Roland. 'There has always been servants' gossip. It's not a plausible reason.'

Sarah caught her breath and wondered why it hadn't occurred to her before that Caro's parentage would inevitably be called into

187

question, given Venetia's faithlessness.

'Caro is highly emotional, particularly now.' He directed a pointed look at Sarah. 'If she has overheard something which threatens her sense of security in this household, I've no doubt her vulnerability has been compounded by feeling deceived by those she once trusted.'

Anger replaced Sarah's lovelorn passion of earlier and she trembled with it as she rose. 'I cannot leave unchallenged the insinuation that I bear some guilt for Caro's desertion.'

'There's nothing you can do,' he said roughly. Addressing Lord Miles in more civil tones, he said, 'Forgive my rudeness, sir, but I must leave urgently. Please consider yourself a welcome guest in my home for as long as you choose. Arrangements have been made for you to stay the night rather than oblige you to repeat your long and tedious journey in the darkness. Cecily — ' He turned to his trembling sister-in-law. ' — If you need me I shall be at my club.'

'You cannot stay there if you find Caro,' Sarah pointed out. Clubs did not admit women.

'At the Crown and Anchor, then,' he said tersely, his hand upon the doorknob.

'Please, Mr Hawthorne,' Sarah begged, 'let me come with you. Caro trusts me . . . '

Her voice trailed off at his withering look. She saw him close his eyes briefly, as if in pain, and run his hand over his face. 'Caro,' he said, 'trusts no one anymore, it would appear.'

12

They broke their journey at the White Swan after four hours of bad roads and inclement weather.

Lord Miles had managed to doze over the deepest of ruts and fords. Now that he had been reunited with his beloved daughter, Sarah supposed he probably had a few sleepless nights to catch up on.

As they waited in the parlour for the sumptuous feast Lord Miles had considered necessary, Sarah felt at a distinct disadvantage. Fatigue sapped her, as if she had not slept a wink in two days.

'A bottle of claret, a saddle of beef and a blazing fire will make words between us easier,' said her father.

Sarah nodded as she thought of Roland, galloping towards London to try and find his daughter, yet having no clue as to where she might be, and her heart convulsed. Vulnerable, overwrought Caro could not be in her right mind to have accepted an invitation to run away with Mr Hollingsworth. It was not even as if they were eloping. If they'd been heading north towards the border there was at least the consolation of assuming a hasty marriage was their intention. But London? Alone with Mr Hollingsworth? Surely she must know she could only be ruined by such folly?

Having polished off a bottle of claret, her father's mood was much more sanguine.

'So you were punishing me for meddling in the affairs of your heart, my girl,' he remarked, chewing on his beef and looking at her over the rim of his glass. 'Well, you couldn't have devised a better way.' Recrimination had been replaced by a soldier's acceptance of being bested in battle. 'I'll not interfere in your matrimonial affairs again. James is courting a young lass, I hear. Well, perhaps that's premature, but it was only this last week that he has resumed pleasure-seeking. Nevertheless, he'll be overjoyed to hear you're safe and well. But if he comes courting — '

'He won't, Father,' Sarah told him with conviction. 'We were never more than friends. Too much like brother and sister.'

'I've been blind to a good many things, Sarah. With you gone I realized how much I relied on your cool judgment to temper my occasional outbursts.'

'When have you ever lost your temper, Papa?' Sarah's mouth quirked before they both laughed. Lord Miles reached across the table and placed his hand on Sarah's. 'Never leave me again, Sarah . . . unless it's to be worthily wed. I've always wanted that but it appears you truly are determined to remain unfettered by the bonds of matrimony.'

'No, Papa,' Sarah said steadily. 'I have no aversion to becoming a wife . . . to a man worthy of me. Until that time I am quite content to pander to your vagaries of mood. I shall *try* and keep sufficient staff for our needs with the usual reassurances that the silver salver was aimed at the wall and not at their heads. It is a great relief,' she added pointedly, 'that you are prepared to sanction my ultimate choice of husband.'

'Looked to me like that young pup Hawthorne had a gleam in his eye when he turned it on you,' Lord Miles said reflectively, taking another sip of claret, apparently oblivious to the sudden flaming in his daughter's cheek. 'Not but that he didn't try to hide it behind his stern words. Had he gone on trying to point the blame at you I'd have called him out!'

'I believe you called him out once before, Papa.'

'Lily-livered girl didn't want to fight me. Had to, though, else it'd have been the end of that precious parliamentary career of his. Not but that we'd all be better off without his ilk — dangerous radical!' Lord Miles snarled. 'It's the quiet ones with their bottled-up passion you'd best be wary of, Sarah.'

'Your passionate outbursts can be spectacularly frightening on occasion, Papa.'

'Look at me and what you see is what you get. You'll have a much easier life with someone in my mould than a buttoned-up Puritan simmering with passion.'

By dinner's end Sarah had managed to keep exhaustion at bay by sheer effort.

Theirs was a discussion long overdue. She needed to explain the desperation and helplessness that had driven her to flight. She needed, also, to reassure him of her love and remorse. She did not lie by citing amnesia as a reason for her deception, however she was guilty of omission as to why she had maintained her charade. She could not reveal her feelings for Mr Hawthorne. Instead she told Lord Miles it was her sense of responsibility towards the girls, Caro in particular, which had decided her to stay.

Finally she crawled into bed and slept, her reconciliation with her father at least some consolation. Lord Miles had been more angry that Sarah believed he'd force an unpalatable marriage upon her, than he was at her deception.

Sleep claimed her the moment she put her head on the pillow after their early dinner. Less than an hour later, she was wide awake. But of course, how could she sleep when Caro was still missing and she and Mr Hawthorne remained estranged?

Wrapping herself in the counterpane to keep out the biting cold, she took herself off to the window seat.

The moonlight was blinding. Sarah dug the palms of her hands into her eye sockets, shivering. Her sleep-fogged brain whirled over the same points, without solution. If Caro's reputation were destroyed, she would never forgive herself. Was Mr Hollingsworth no more than a fortune-hunter? Had he deceived them all? Or did he have a parson with a special marriage license waiting in London?

Her frozen feet throbbed from the cold. Stiffly, she padded over to the old trunk at the foot of her bed to look for something in which to wrap them. No longer did it contain the shabby garments belonging to the poor late Sarah Morecroft. Through industry, energy and cunning Sarah had managed in a short time to invent a wardrobe worthy of the lady she was — Minus, of course, those little extras, like a rainbow-hued selection of dancing slippers and a fur wrap or ermine-lined mantle or pelisse, which would have been so useful at a time like this.

Her seeking fingers found the coarse woollen shawl Mrs Hawthorne had given her. In it, Sarah had wrapped Miss Morecroft's diary, but it held little interest. Poor Sarah Morecroft's life, despite her glamorous, dissolute father and exotic background, had been rather dull. Only her reverence for the rakish Godby had infused it with life.

Guiltily, Sarah fingered the soft, tooled leather cover as she resumed her seat. How amazing that it should have survived what its mistress could not. Only a few pages were rendered unintelligible by water damage, due to its thorough wrapping in oilskin.

She thought of the young woman whose life she had effectively commandeered for the past six weeks. They'd been friends during the few days Sarah had been aboard the ship which had carried Miss Morecroft from India.

Perhaps Mr Hawthorne's anger at her was born of his disappointment that Sarah was not the last link with his foster brother, after all. Perhaps he had believed a sense of kinship existed between them. Instead, he had decided she was nothing more than a pleasure-seeking society miss, out for a lark at his expense.

She flicked through the thick parchment

pages until she was close to the end. The diary had been started long before the young woman had known her family would soon be dead and that she would be setting sail for England to work for her father's foster brother.

Five pages from the end the ink had run and the smudged handwriting became difficult to read. Nevertheless, Sarah was soon absorbed by the young governess's thoughts regarding her impending journey.

She smiled wryly. So her namesake hadn't had a high opinion of the dreary gowns her mother had mended and stitched for her, either. Pity Miss Morecroft hadn't been blessed with Sarah's imagination and skill with a needle.

It was almost impossible to make out the final page. Sarah was on the point of giving up when three syllables in careful looped writing caught her eye: Hollingsworth.

Her smile faded. With growing foreboding she bent her head, straining to read the context. It took several minutes to make sense of it and by then her heart was hammering. She no longer felt the cold as she cast off the counterpane — only dread as she threw down the book and looked desperately for the clothes she'd worn last night. There was no time to lose.

Although the last sentence remained unfinished, its ramifications were clear enough. Miss Morecroft's final diary entry had been a girlish eulogy of the handsome and charming Mr Hollingsworth.

*　*　*

'Oi! Watch it!'

Roland sidestepped, just avoiding the wheels of the heavily laden cart rounding the corner. Heart pounding, he leant back against the wall and closed his eyes.

Time was running out. For hours he'd called on friends and acquaintances, and scanned crowds in his attempts to find his daughter.

His initial inquiries around Larchfield had turned up nothing. Clearly, Mr Hollingsworth had invented himself; had arrived in the local area with no intention of ever being traced.

The noise of shouting and rumbling traffic echoed painfully in his ears. He knew he should keep moving but had not the energy. Eyes still closed, he surrendered to the dreamlike state that had begun closing in on him since he'd arrived in the capital. He thought of lovely Miss Morecroft — Lady Sarah — and conceded for the first time since banishing her that her motives may not have been all bad.

It was too late, of course. The damage had been done. He'd refused to give her a hearing. Whether she was now a prisoner of her tyrannical father or just her own guilt, he'd not see her again. She'd made clear her affection for him was deep and sincere but he wondered how long under her own roof, feted by admirers, it would be before she forgot him.

Despair and self-recrimination curdled in his belly. How nearly he had become a fool in love, yet again. Lady Sarah wielded the same power over him Venetia had once had. If he gave her another chance, wasn't it likely she'd use it, like Venetia, to test his affections? Venetia had regarded the suffering her every betrayal caused as confirmation of her supremacy over him. He did not think his masculinity could withstand it happening again.

A tremor ran through him. He was not thinking clearly if he allowed his loss of Lady Sarah to override his concern for Caro.

Pushing himself away from the wall, he followed the pavement with unsteady foot-steps. Dusk blanketed his long-distance vision with a grey haze. Or was it weariness? His mind was not as sharp as he needed it to be. The hand he raised to his brow seemed made of lead. It was time to return to the inn and sleep. Sleep would be the restorative he needed so he could look at the problem with fresh eyes.

* * *

Roland awoke with a start. All was black. He had no idea what time it was, or what had wakened him. He thought he heard a tapping. Had he asked for a light supper to be sent to his room? He closed his eyes. Perhaps he'd imagined it. Sleep beckoned once more. The comfort of its soothing embrace competed with the insistent tapping.

With a growl of irritation he hauled himself off his bed. He noticed he was still dressed, even had his boots on. Rubbing his eyes, he stumbled to the door and opened it a crack.

'I do not wish to be disturbed — '

Quick as lightning a small hand darted through the crack and gripped his arm. 'Mr Hawthorne, it's me!'

'Caro!' Surprise and delight jolted him out of his foggy state, but before he could respond in a more adequate fashion he was subjected to a fresh assault of shock waves.

'No, it's . . . it's your wife.'

His wife? What dream was this?

Blinking as the thickly veiled figure tried to push open the door, his brain ached with the effort of seeking reality.

The woman was unrecognizable beneath the black hat; the sweet, husky voice, however, clearly belonged to that of his nemesis.

Lady Sarah Miles.

'Sorry to disturb you at this late hour, darling.' Her musical tone sounded over-loud. 'I was delayed but certainly hadn't expected you to have retired so early. Mr Hawthorne, I need to talk to you!' Dropping her voice to an urgent hiss, she made another attempt to force an entrance.

He stared at her, his boot firmly wedging the door against opening further. What was she playing at? She couldn't possibly come into his chamber.

He saw the publican in the crack of light taking the corridor to the west, and called to him. 'My wife has arrived unexpectedly and requires her own bedchamber.'

There were none to be had, the publican told him, pausing briefly. There was one room of ladies but the bed was already sleeping three. He could organize a truckle bed if m'lady desired that.

'No, no, I'll suffer my husband's snoring for just this one night,' Sarah said with a sigh, elbowing herself finally into Roland's room, and closing the door behind her.

'What the devil are you doing here?' Roland hissed. Of course she could not stay. And he could show no weakness. For both their sakes. Her actions were tantamount to social ruin. Her father would put a bullet through his head.

'I have news.' When she lit a candle he saw her eyes were wide with urgency rather than shining with the seductive gleam he had been expecting. She cast her hat upon the bed and said, as she raked her fingers through her hair, 'I think I know where to find Caro — '

'Why did you not tell me before?' he exploded, gripping her shoulders. He was aware his overwrought nerves sought refuge in a suspicion that was unjustified. But suspicion was so much easier at this moment than trying to make sense of the other confusing emotions besetting him in equal measure.

She looked at him, hurt. 'Do you think I, who care as much for Caro as you, would have kept from you *anything* that may have assisted in finding her? Listen — '

She stopped. Frowning, she tilted her head. 'Roland?' It was the first time she'd used his Christian name. Music to his ears. Gently, she shrugged herself out of his grasp, then helped ease him down into the comforting depths of the cracked leather armchair by the bed.

He opened his eyes to see her holding out a tumbler full of brandy. 'I don't know if this will do you any good, or if it is the last thing you should be drinking in your exhausted, muddled, state,' she said with a small smile. 'Do you mind if I help myself?'

Without waiting for an answer, she poured another measure from the cut-glass decanter on the mantelpiece before settling herself on the edge of the bed opposite him.

'I believe Caro's disappearance is connected with Sarah Morecroft.'

Lord, but she was a sight to behold. Liquid fire burned his throat as desire pumped through his veins. Miss Morecroft was in the past. All that mattered was the young woman sitting before him. He could drink her in forever, watching her recount her fairytale, admiring her burnished hair while her melodic voice provided the pleasant background.

'Miss Morecroft's diary was in the trunk that was rescued.'

He smiled. He liked the way her eyes fixed him with such intensity.

'When we broke our journey I could not sleep, so I read the last few pages which I had not read before.'

She stopped. Roland blinked.

'Are you listening to me?' Her tone was suspicious.

He frowned. 'Of course.'

He was trying. But the sleep he had snatched had done him more harm than good. Jolted into wakefulness by the very woman who occupied so many of his daydreams and nightmares, he now existed in a pleasant state of unreality.

Struggling to regain the urgency he knew was required, he leant forward. 'Go on.' He rubbed his chin and was uncomfortably aware of his dishevelment. Glancing down at his muddied topboots and limp neck cloth, he couldn't even remember when he had last shaved. The hours he had spent thundering through the countryside must have exhausted him more than he realized.

'Sarah Morecroft helped Mr Hollingsworth with Caro's kidnapping!'

Roland smiled at her preposterous words. 'You're saying my foster brother's daughter plotted — ' He waved vaguely. ' — all this . . . several months after her death.'

'Sarah Morecroft intended revenge when she set out from India. When she met Mr Hollingsworth on board the *Mary Jane* they hatched a plan — '

Judging by her exasperation and sudden sharpness, she had taken exception to something. Yet Roland had said nothing beyond 'Oh really', and nodded his head.

Perhaps it was his tone — some people took exception to his tendency to sarcasm. Miss Morecroft certainly seemed to, for she slid from the bed. Appreciatively, he sniffed her scent of orange flower water, and opened his eyes to find her standing over him. Her little white fingers dug into his shoulders as she tried to haul him to his feet. She looked angry and when she opened her mouth he expected her words to convey this.

Instead she froze. Slowly, her right hand travelled up his arm and then down, across his chest. He held his breath, a strange sensation pooling in the pit of his stomach.

'Roland, you're soaked right through.' Her voice was low, almost accusing. The dainty white hand continued its exploration. It was a pleasant sensation. He made no rejoinder, simply closed his eyes and enjoyed her touch.

'No wonder you've taken in nothing!'

Oh, he was taking it all in. Revelling in it. He blinked at the insistent tugging at his waistcoat. She was undoing the buttons!

'Take it off,' she said through gritted teeth when she was finished.

Weakly, he gripped her wrist to stay her, his sense of honour finally roused.

'Madam, I don't think you — '

'And your shirt.'

Before he could object, she'd rested her cheek against his chest. 'Lord, but you're chilled to the bone!' she exclaimed. 'You'll catch your death unless I can get you warm.'

He had not the energy to help her as she stripped off his shirt and bundled the counterpane round his shoulders. It was an effort for her to remove his boots but she succeeded. He suspected Lady Sarah achieved most things she set out to do.

Standing back, she raked him with a critical eye. 'Now get into that bed and warm yourself.' Her voice was sharp. 'I think it's probably time for me to go. I'm not going to have you accuse me of taking advantage so I can demand satisfaction at the altar.' Her voice was sharp. 'I think it's probably time for me to go.' Her voice was low and grim as she resumed her task of trying to haul him out of the chair and transfer him to the bed. 'Despite the fact that staying would be eminently pleasing to me.'

No, she had not said that. He had imagined it to complete his beautiful dream. He must not let his mind and body betray him into believing what he only wanted to hear. She'd betrayed him once. She had not the purity of heart he'd attributed to her before she'd shattered his trust.

With a final effort she had him on the bed, rolling him onto his back so that he looked right up into her eyes. Her beautiful, clear hazel eyes. She didn't step back. He swallowed, overcome by sensation. Lord, she was inviting him to take her into his arms. He closed his eyes, his honour engaged in a bloody battle with the exquisite sensations engulfing him.

'Roland.'

'Darling Sarah,' he whispered, opening his eyes. Gently he traced a finger down the side of her cheek and tucked a tendril of gleaming hair behind her ear. If the parson now came knocking with a special licence, he'd be the happiest man alive. He was almost the happiest man alive for the fact that her desire for him overrode the terrible risks. But she was as impulsive as she was beautiful. It was up to him to persuade her to wait. It took all his willpower. 'Flattered though I am, my love — '

'You're lying on my arm . . . '

'Oh, Lord,' he muttered, shame and disappointment colliding as she tugged at her arm trapped beneath the weight of his body. He heard the urgency in her voice, but it was the fear in her eyes that went some way to clearing the mists swirling in his mind.

With an effort he rolled to one side and she

stepped back, rubbing at her wrist.

'Roland, I think I may know where we can find Caro.'

Caro. He groaned, covering his throbbing eyes with his hands. 'What must you think of me?'

Amidst the rustling, he heard a chink of glass. There was another waft of the heady scent of orange flower water and the heart-stopping words, 'That you are the most wonderful and honourable man I've met but that you are also very ill. Drink this.'

His prayers were answered as she supported him behind the shoulders, then held a tumbler of sweet water to his lips. He fell back when he'd finished, but not before he'd planted a kiss on the soft white skin below her collar bone.

'Sarah, you are a gift from the angels,' he murmured.

Her soft, ironic laugh as she gently sponged his forehead filled him with longing. 'Tell me that when you're in your right mind. I'm going now, Roland. I have to find Caro but I'll be back as soon as I can.'

He wished he could open his eyes, but they hurt too much. Vaguely he held out his hand in her direction and she gripped it.

'Must you go alone? Perhaps — '

'There's no time to waste and you've not

the strength to pick up a kitten.' He felt her lips upon his brow and heard her tremulous whisper. 'If anything happened to Caro, I'd never forgive myself. I need you to know that.'

13

'Writing implements and parchment in the private parlour,' she demanded of the publican, searching in her reticule for a coin. 'And a hackney.'

Fear churned in her breast, but excitement, too, as Sarah scratched her note to Roland a few minutes later. She would find Caro. She would save the girl's reputation and Roland would give her the reward she craved.

The rest of her life in his company!

Hearing voices in the passage outside the door, she put her hand to her bonnet to pull down her veil while she hastily sprinkled sand upon the parchment.

The veil was no longer there. As the voices stopped outside the door she heard the stentorian tones of a formidable matron apparently admonishing an errant daughter. She shrank into the shadows, clutching the folded parchment as a stout middle-aged woman wearing a green velvet round dress with matching turban entered the room.

'What were you thinking, Millicent? You danced three times with him. A young lady's reputation is her most precious commodity.'

Horrified, Sarah realised the formidable Lady Bassingthwaite stood not three metres from her in the private parlour she'd been on the verge of departing. A stickler for observing the rules, she had in tow her plain and clumsy daughter. Although Lady Bassingthwaite was always scrupulously polite, Sarah knew she disapproved of her. She guiltily wondered if that was because word had filtered through to her ears of Sarah's charade impersonating the venerable lady. She'd poked gentle fun at the lofty ideals of propriety for which Lady Bassingthwaite was known when she had pretended that accepting a handkerchief from a gentleman was tantamount to accepting his marriage proposal. Sarah winced. How foolish she had once been.

Fortunately Millicent's tears provided the diversion Sarah needed. As the two women made for the fireplace, she sidled towards the door.

'I beg your pardon, madam. I did not mean to intrude.' Lady Bassingthwaite cast a distracted glance in Sarah's direction, but Sarah was not about to respond.

With thundering heart she dashed into the passage and thrust the parchment at the publican with instructions that it find its way to Mr Hawthorne.

To her relief a hackney carriage was waiting

by the front entrance and she plunged inside. The excitement of her near discovery had sharpened the edge of tonight's whole drama, limned by the fact that Mr Hawthorne loved her. After tonight's dealings with him she needed no further proof.

Sinking back against the squabs as the carriage lurched forward, relief enveloped her.

Mr Hawthorne had called her his angel. He'd made it clear that despite banishing her, his feelings remained as strong as ever. How Sarah had struggled to beat her impulses into submission when the truth became clear in that close, dimly lit bed chamber, she'd never know.

Lady Bassingthwaite's stern reminder to her erring daughter was a timely reminder. A girl's reputation was her most precious commodity and to lose it was worse than death. Roland had admitted that he cared too much for Sarah to jeopardise hers. Now Sarah lay back against the squabs in the happy confidence that once she delivered Caro to Roland, she would have her 'happy ever after' ending.

Travelling through the Haymarket at this time of night was a new experience. With fascinated horror, she watched street urchins beg for pennies, and streetwalkers in tawdry, gaudy gowns accost gentleman passers-by. She'd been shielded from the seamier side of life on the occasions her father had escorted her back from the theatre.

Soon, though, her bravado fell away, eroded by the frightening unfamiliarity of the environment once they'd left the entertainment district. Shouts, hisses and catcalls punctuated the night. She snapped the curtain closed when a glimpse of her face attracted a half-admiring, half-jeering response from a young man with a dirty face and blackened teeth. And when the hackney turned down a narrow side street and slowed to a stop, her courage nearly failed her.

Sarah Morecroft's diary identified the street in Marylebone where the widow Hollingsworth kept a girls' school, but not its number. Rapping on the roof, she put her head out of the window to quiz the jarvey.

'School for young ladies?' The jarvey had smelled of beer when he'd handed her in, and now he gave a scornful laugh as he mimicked her refined accent. ''ere? Not 'less you mean Sally Hollingsworth's nunnery wot we're standing a'front of. Guess yer could call that a school of sorts.'

'Nunnery?' There was little to suggest the ecclesiastical.

'Bawdy 'ouse, ma'am.'

Terror ripped through her. But no, the man was leering at her, drunkenly. If Sarah believed him, she was lost. She was calling on a respectable widow — one who'd be as shocked and upset as Sarah to learn her son had enticed a gently reared young woman away from her loving home.

The house looked respectable enough, and no different from the other four square buildings with neat iron railings in front. Its blinds were drawn and lights burned in the upper rooms.

But as the jarvey set down the steps she was beset by indecision. If this were a house of ill repute, she'd be a fool to venture out of the carriage. She should contain her desperate impatience and return with Roland later.

'So wot yer plannin' on doin' then, miss?' asked the jarvey, holding open the door. 'If you've the blunt I can stay 'ere all night.'

She glanced the length of the dim street. Caro was inside, she was almost certain. What choice did she have? Roland was gripped by fever and quite beyond moving further than the posting inn.

'I'll pay you half a crown if you'll come with me now. Double that amount when you return me to the Crown and Anchor.'

He responded with alacrity, though Sarah's relief was tempered by his difficulty in keeping his balance. Still, his intimidating size kept her fear in check as she waited for an answer to her knock.

The door opened and a young woman of about twenty regarded her suspiciously.

'What yer after?' she asked.

She did not look like a servant girl. Instead of cotton print she wore a flashy gown of mauve and yellow satin. Nor did she look — much less talk — like Mr Hollingsworth's sister and, in fact, laughed uproariously at that suggestion.

'Me name's Kitty,' she told her. 'If you's come looking fer him yer outta luck. He ain't in.'

'What about Mrs Hollingsworth?'

'D'yer mean his wife or his muvver?'

Sarah gasped. His wife? Could that mean Caro? Or did he already have a wife?

Whatever this place was, Sarah had come too far to turn back now.

'Well, mightn't be no matter to you as to which one,' said her informant in answer to her question, 'fer old Mrs Hollingsworth is out, too, and the young one won't see no one. But if yer that anxious then you might as well come through and wait.'

Sarah turned to the jarvey. 'Stay with me,' she whispered and, though grumbling that he 'ought to see she had the blunt to pay 'im

214

first', he stumbled after her down a dimly lit corridor and through green velvet curtains into a well lit room beyond.

'More privacy here where you and your . . . gennelmun friend can wait. They shouldn't be too long. Just a-visiting, and things don't get busy for a little while yet.'

Sarah glanced around at her surroundings, her eyes dropping quickly from the Bacchanalian oil painting above the fireplace.

Trying to retain a dignified composure, she said, 'Please tell the young lady upstairs that her old governess is here. She'll see me, I know it.'

Kitty looked Sarah in the eye and sighed. 'Tain't worth it to me, miss. Girl's not allowed to leave the 'ouse.'

Her words occasioned both relief and alarm. At least she'd come to the right place.

Sarah fished in her reticule and brandished a half crown at her. For a second Kitty stared at it longingly, but at the sound of new arrivals she dashed Sarah's hand away.

'Hide it!' she hissed, nodding at the coin and looking furtively at the curtained doorway. 'And don't go offering 'ticements like that to the madam. It won't go down well.'

'Ah, Kitty. Visitors so early?' chirped a female voice. The curtain was drawn aside and an enormously fat woman entered. Although well past her prime, she wore her hair in girlish ringlets, their golden hue contrasting strangely with the grey pallor of her skin. Her dress of red silk, too, looked as if it had been designed for a sylph. Cut indecently low, it clung to her rolls of fat, leaving nothing to the imagination.

But it was the man next to her who chilled Sarah's blood.

Like the woman he appeared surprised, before his face split in a sly grin. Not this time the charming boyish smile for the ingenuous governess, as he regarded Sarah, speculatively.

'What a deliciously unexpected surprise,' he purred, brushing aside the lock of brown curling hair that flopped over his forehead. 'Alone? Or is this . . . er . . . gentleman your companion? An unlikely coupling, I must say.'

'My friend has agreed to bear me company while I make enquiries about Caro. I believe I have come to the right place.' Sarah's tone was far bolder than she felt, but she had to take the risk. Although the bull-like jarvey was the worse for drink, he looked as if he could fell Mr Hollingsworth with an idle flick of the wrist.

'Caro?' frowned the young man, pretending to search his memory while ushering Sarah to a chair with unctuous care. 'Refreshment, Lady Sarah? Kitty, if you please — ?

'Kitty, love,' his mother cut in, 'you do realize the time, and that you're not yet painted?' With a thoughtful frown followed by a saccharine smile, she added, '*I'll* fetch our esteemed guests some refreshment.'

'And please tell my dear wife she has a visitor,' added Mr Hollingsworth.

Settling himself in a delicate gilt chair opposite Sarah, Mr Hollingsworth regarded her quizzically. 'Lady Sarah, I confess to astonishment. Both to seeing you here, and at the very ungallant behaviour of Mr Hawthorne.' He shook his head. 'Leaving you with the responsibility of tracking down his errant daughter. I can't imagine how he knew where to send you since I had not yet made contact with him regarding . . . ah . . . terms.'

Mrs Hollingsworth soon returned, followed by a child carrying a tray. Sarah accepted the wine she was offered, which she had no intention of drinking, and watched with dismay as the jarvey downed his ale greedily.

Mrs Hollingsworth settled her formidable bulk upon a gilded Egyptian sofa. 'Now, dearie, what's this all about?' she asked. But despite her smile and the fact her tone was designed to put Sarah at ease, there was the glint of steel in her small, pig-like eyes.

'Mr Hawthorne will be here to fetch Caro shortly,' Sarah said bravely, hoping the threat of reinforcements would help her cause. Burying her clammy hands in the folds of her primrose skirts to hide their trembling, she went on, 'I came ahead to this address, believing that you, Mrs Hollingsworth, would be horrified to learn of Caro's disappearance in company with your son. However, as Mr Hollingsworth is already married, I see we misread the situation and should be grateful to you both for providing Caro with a refuge. If she was running away, please tell her she is forgiven. It would be best for everyone if we took her home now.'

Unfortunately, the Hollingsworths were not inclined to take the avenue with which Sarah had provided them.

'Best leave the negotiations to Mr Hawthorne, dear,' said Mrs Hollingsworth with exaggerated condescension. She was about to go on when soft-slippered footsteps sounded in the passage.

'I'm glad to see you in such good health, Lady Sarah.' The familiar brown-haired young woman framed in the doorway acknowledged Sarah with a thin smile. 'It has been a while.' The voice, soft and slightly breathless, was as Sarah remembered, but the lively Miss Morecroft she'd known on board ship was now a dispirited creature. Although she no longer wore homespun, the tawdry green satin gown looked out of place against her sallow complexion and plainly dressed hair.

Conscious that her own behaviour was not unblemished, Sarah nodded warily at the woman whose identity she had assumed these past six weeks. When Caro failed to appear in her wake, she took the offensive. Sarah might have acted the opportunist in upholding the assumption she was Miss Morecroft, but Miss Morecroft's actions had been far more calculated and wicked. She levelled an accusingly look at her. 'I believe I can thank you for leading Caro to this place.'

'You attribute too much to me,' the young woman protested softly, looking away.

But Mr Hollingsworth, who had risen at her entrance, took her elbow and drew her to the seat beside him, declaring, 'Such modesty, my angel, for I could have achieved nothing without you. Let us toast Divine Providence for joining our fates upon the slippery deck of that doomed ship.'

Sarah seized her opportunity while their attention was for the moment elsewhere. She was halfway to the door when Mrs Hollingsworth purred, 'You're surely not leaving us, my dear?'

Sarah swallowed. She had to get out of here. The cloying atmosphere of cheap perfume and the smoke from the coal fire was nauseating. 'If Caro is sleeping I would not have her disturbed. Mr Hawthorne will be here shortly.'

Mr Hollingsworth smiled. 'Where *could* Mr Hawthorne be?' Rising, he cast a quizzical look at Sarah. 'Somehow I fancied a lady of your determination preferred the more forceful type.'

Sarah glared, silently ordering the jarvey to his feet with an imperious look. Rubbing his drink-sodden eyes, he followed her to the door. With her hand finally on the knob, Sarah gave them her haughtiest look. 'Mr Hawthorne is the consummate gentleman — something you will never be!'

'Dearie me!' said Mrs Hollingsworth, her brassy ringlets bobbing as she leant forward. 'It seems you're uncommonly taken with our esteemed friend — ' A great crash drowned her words.

With dismay, Sarah watched the skittering shards of the porcelain urn which the jarvey's head had collected on his way to the ground roll across the floor.

'Can't hold his liquor, poor feller,' sighed Mrs Hollingsworth, looking sadly at the body slumped against the wall. 'Thank you,

Barnabus! Take the gentleman out. Lady Sarah, you mustn't worry about your friend. Barnabus'll take care of him. Now sit down and drink up. I'm enjoying our little chat.'

'No.' The walls were closing in on her. The Hollingsworths with their speculative smiles, and Miss Morecroft in her trance-like state, threatened all she held dear. They would keep her here against her will. They would take Mr Hawthorne, too, and then she had no idea what they planned. They were evil.

She tried to force her way past the door and into the passageway where she hoped for a clear run, but Mr Hollingsworth's hand was upon her elbow.

'Lady Sarah, you can't possibly rush into the darkness in a neighbourhood like this. Mr Hawthorne would never forgive us. Ah, good evening, Caro.' His smile was very different from the one he'd reserved for Caro's birthday, as he ushered the terrified girl into the room.

Caro's wan, pale face lit up when she saw Sarah. With a sob she threw herself into her arms.

'Very touching,' observed Mr Hollingsworth, closing the door firmly behind them and leading them to a green settee. 'Now, I must dispatch one more note. There is a gentleman who has, for the past six weeks, been all eagerness to meet the lovely Miss Caro. The fact that a lovely imposter' — He looked pointedly at Sarah. ' — has sweetened the dish is sure to garnish my reward. Now, let us have another drink while we wait for our happy little gathering to be complete.'

14

Roland woke with a raging thirst.

He needed water, or he would die. Swinging his legs over the side of the bed, he attempted to rise. But his legs buckled and he landed on his face upon the floor.

It took all his energy to struggle back onto the mattress where he sat a few minutes, his head reeling, as he tried to recollect what had brought him to this indifferent London posting inn. If he was in London, as he believed he was, he ought to be enjoying the rarefied atmosphere of his club. This place smelled of musty linen and cheap candles.

He noticed his boots were off and he was shirtless. But there was a basin of water and a sponge still damp on the washstand. His valet had not accompanied him on this apparently hasty, clandestine trip, and yet he had been attended to.

A vision of Lady Sarah swam before him, though he couldn't imagine why. While he searched in the gloom for the water jug, wisps of memory drifted through his muddled brain. The image of her was so very strong.

When he lit a candle and saw her veil upon

the bed, he put his hands to his head and groaned.

Dear Lord, if she'd been with him last night what atrocities might he have committed? If — as clearly had been the case — he was not in full charge of his mental faculties, the beast within would have taken over. He'd have given free reign to the lustful desires she inspired and which had consumed him during the past six weeks.

He groaned again. If she had been here last night, where was she now?

Caro!

Guilty fear galvanised him into action, but as he reached for his shirt, nausea gripped him and he fell to his knees on the wooden boards.

First Caro had disappeared. Now Sarah was gone. It was starting to come back to him — Sarah's tender ministrations; but there had been an urgency about her, too. Yes, something about Caro. What *was* it she had said? Something about knowing Caro's whereabouts? Surely he hadn't dreamed that?

If she really had been here at all? Surely Lord Miles would never have released her to travel, unescorted, to London? Surely Sarah would never have been so reckless as to have come, alone and unchaperoned, to his bed chamber?

Never! he reaffirmed, nodding decisively in part to shake his disappointment. The veil belonged to someone else and had inadvertently appeared on his bed. It was as simple as that.

He pulled his shirt over his head. He was feeling a little better, though he had no idea where he'd start his search. It was all so hopeless.

Then he saw the note pushed under the door with his name written clearly on the outside. Thank the Lord, he thought as he struggled to cross the room and pick it up. It must contain news regarding Caro's whereabouts. Perhaps, even that she'd been found safe.

But all it contained was a single address.

★ ★ ★

Twenty minutes later he stared with revulsion at the two-storied residence. No gentleman of fashion could be ignorant of the notorious Sally Hollingsworth's nunnery. That his daughter — and Sarah — might be inside was almost more than he could bear.

He shuddered, stepping up to grip the brass door knocker. What would he say? He'd never been in a bawdy house before. When he'd told Venetia something to this effect,

225

she'd laughed and said, well then, wasn't he the lucky one since out of the goodness of her heart she'd show him all the things girls in bawdy houses did. He didn't want to dwell, right now, on what she'd taught him.

He was still hesitating as to whether this direct approach was even advisable when a metal grille slid open.

'What's yer business, then?' asked the owner of a pair of eyes that regarded him with suspicion.

'That which brings most gentlemen to a house like this,' he said in bored, clipped tones.

The door opened a crack and stepping inside, Roland found himself in a dimly lit vestibule.

'Yer won't find better'n this, then. Come,' said an old man with lank, shoulder-length grey hair. Holding aloft a tallow candle, he led the way down a narrow passageway, dragging his club foot.

It was the early hours of the morning. A pretty girl in yellow and mauve was descending a flight of stairs, yawning. She caught herself up when she saw Roland, and smiled. She had nice teeth, he noticed. Like Sarah, he thought, and his heart contracted with fear and longing.

'Don't tell the missus,' she said in a

collaborative whisper as she lounged against the newel post and waited for Roland to draw level, 'but would the fine gennelmun like a glass of sommat?'

Roland did not answer — he guessed he looked as dazed as he felt.

'Now my 'andsome,' she said, taking his arm. 'You don't look at all the thing. Just come from a ruckus with the missus? Needin' someone to love yer? Well, Kitty's yer girl. A nice drink to start us orf? No? So it's right down to business, is it? Well, ain't so often I'm lucky enough to snag such an 'andsome fella, and I don't say that lightly. Come along a' me and Kitty'll look after yer.'

Roland's first instinct was to recoil, just as he did regularly from the lightskirts who plied their trade in the Haymarket and the streets near his club. But a combination of his reeling head and the sudden hazy thought that perhaps he could pry information more easily from this young woman than he could from the brothel madam — and that the truth was more likely to be reliable — made him surrender his arm and allow himself to be led up the stairs to her room.

'There now, if you'd like to make yerself comfortable and tell us yer fancy,' she said.

Dazedly, he watched her preen in front of a small tarnished-looking glass. The room was comfortably furnished, dominated by a large bed with a thick pink feather bolster.

He must have been frowning unconsciously and fingering the satin cover with unusual concentration, for she said in her pert, friendly voice, 'Like it, then? Stitched it meself. Makes things a bit more homely, like. Not that 'ome's a place I'm likely to visit ever agin.'

'Why?' he asked, distracted.

'Well, now . . . ' Kitty looked at him, startled. 'Daren't darken the doorstep now, do I? Not now I've taken to a life of . . . of bringing pleasure to gennelmun what can do with a mite cheering up.'

The next moment she was on his lap, coiling her arms around his neck and nuzzling his cheek, easing his coat from his shoulders and marvelling in a low, intimate murmur at his muscles, and his fine and handsome physique.

It was not until she took his hand and guided it under her chemise, that he jerked into awareness.

Rising abruptly, he was unable to prevent the girl from falling to the floor with a thud. She looked up from where she lay amid a tangle of skirts, her face full of fear.

'Now sir, playing rough ain't my game,' she said. 'I'm 'appy to pleasure you any way you want, sir, but I don't like playin' rough.'

'Forgive me,' he said, helping her up. 'I . . . I . . . you've got to help me.'

She must have seen the genuine anguish in his eyes, for her fear appeared to abate. Smoothing her dress and putting a hand to her hair, she curved her small body against his and nuzzled his neck. 'Course I'll 'elp yer, sir,' she purred, leading him to the bed and gently pushing him down.

'No, no, not like that,' protested Roland as she began undoing the buttons of his waistcoat.

'Oh, I'll give no cause for complaint, sir, if yer just bide yer time a wee bit,' she said.

Taking a steadying breath Roland gripped her wrists and pulled her away.

'Well, if yer want to do all the work, that's fine by me,' she said, lying back and starting to pull up her skirts.

Averting his eyes, Roland blurted out, 'I'm looking for my daughter. Please . . . I need to know if she's here. I'll pay you handsomely.'

He was conscious of her sudden stillness. When he turned, her eyes were black with terror. 'Lower yer voice, sir.' Her own was thick with fear as she sat up and smoothed her gown. 'You don't know what yer askin'.'

'I believe my daughter has been tricked by a scoundrel who gained her trust and — '

'You mean 'ticed?' Kitty asked, rising. 'But

a girl what's been 'ticed ain't got no respectability left and can't *possibly* go 'ome. 'oo'll 'ave a girl like that? I suggest you just leave 'er be. Might even take to the life . . . like me.' Regaining her composure, Kitty draped herself over his shoulders.

He shuddered as he felt her small tongue dart into his ear and was about to shake her off when he realized she was whispering. 'There's spies everywhere,' she hissed. 'Every word is listened to and there's eyeholes in the walls and door. I suggest you let me tend to you like you was any gennulman takin' yer pleasure and we'll 'ope your words of just now weren't overheard.'

'Please, I don't want — ' he started to protest as she pushed him back down.

'S'orright, sir,' she soothed, loud enough for any listeners to overhear. And then, lowering her head she again whispered, 'Pity, cos yer just the kind of genulman a girl like me could fancy.' Then more loudly, 'Oooh, yes, sir, very nice,' before adding in another undertone, 'Tell me her name. Madam's got all sorts of gals, and we're not all common like me.'

The situation was surreal. Good God, it had been so long since he had had a woman, and to have one so willing, squirming on top of him . . .

But she was not Sarah.

'Sure you don't want what yer paid for, since yer goin' to 'ave to pay for it anyway?' Her breath tickled his ear but it was not hard to decline. Only Sarah had the power to make him feel like a man.

'I'm looking for two women,' he whispered against her neck, pretending to embrace her. 'Caro, my daughter and her governess, Lady Sarah, or perhaps she might go by the name of Miss Morecroft. She came here about two hours ago.'

He felt the girl go rigid.

'*You're* the gennulman, then, they's bin waitin' fer,' she whispered. He had to pinion her with both arms to keep her on top of him, for if there should be spies to interpret her terror . . .

'I'll pay you well for your information,' he managed hoarsely. 'Obviously you know something — '

'Yeah? I know a lot, but I ain't spilling nothin', for it ain't worth me pretty neck. And money won't buy me, fer I get searched, and so does this room. Ain't *nuffink* I can keep from the missus.' She seemed more angry now, than frightened.

'Just ask what it is you want, then.'

'I want to get out of 'ere, but you certainly ain't goin' to be able to 'elp me do that!'

'Of course I could — '

'No, I signed a piece of paper wot gives Madam and Mr Hollingsworth 'normous power over me,' she whispered. 'And I'd rather be here than Newgate, for that's where I'll go if I don't do what I agrees to in that there piece of paper.'

Relief mingled with horror. 'So, Mr Hollingsworth is part of all this?'

'Mr Hollingsworth is Madam's son and they's downstairs waitin' fer ya. There'll be hell to pay when they realize you're up here with me an' all, 'stead of frontin' up to them direct.'

'Stop! Please don't go.' Roland struggled to hold her in his embrace. 'I *must* find Caro and Sarah. Tell me where they are and I'll do all within my power to help you.'

'I's well past savin', sir, and 'sides, 'tain't no good since your precious Caro and that other gal's wiv 'em as we speak. So you got no choice.' She paused as she buttoned her dress, then followed up a rather assessing look with a coy smile. 'Sure you don't want to get yer money's worth, now?' Frowning, she added in a more concerned tone, 'You orright, sir?'

Ignoring her, Roland tried to ignore the reeling of his brain as he steadied himself with his hand on the doorknob. 'I presume

I'll find the people I'm after if I continue down the passage and through to the back?'

''sright. And thank yer, sir,' she said, pocketing the money he placed on her dresser. 'You bin most generous.' Kitty's words filtered through the open doorway as he hastened towards the stairs.

15

Blinking at the sudden brightness of the gaudily decorated room, Roland found himself the focus of a small party seated around a cosy fire.

An enormously fat woman was seated on an Egyptian sofa decorated with gilt winged sphinxes. Her garb screamed her calling. Dear God, Caro didn't even know of such practices! Or, she hadn't two days before.

But it was the man next to her who caused the bile to rise up in his throat and his weakened frame to almost buckle. This time he was not taken in by the charm of his boyish smile as he had been when the personable Mr Hollingsworth had requested permission to lead his daughter in the next dance.

'Mr Hawthorne, so delighted you could join us. We are quite a crowd,' Mr Hollingsworth's caramel tones penetrated. 'Pray, allow me to introduce to you my wife, the fair Mrs Hollingsworth . . . '

Relief that the lady in question was not his daughter was short-lived. For when he opened his eyes again, there was Caro, in the gloom where the light cast by the oil lamp barely penetrated, huddled on a green velvet-upholstered settee.

She did not greet him but stared, unfocussed, like a frightened animal, her hand clasped in Sarah's. Beautiful Sarah, who regarded him calmly through liquid hazel eyes which clearly conveyed her relief.

Dear Lord, the two of them looked to him to save them from this hellish situation, yet he could barely keep them in focus. He found the back of a chair for support and his gaze returned to the young woman introduced as Mrs Hollingsworth.

'Good evening, Mr Hawthorne. It's been a long time,' she murmured.

At first he did not recognize her; he had not seen her since she was a child, after all. Then Sarah's words drifted into his consciousness: Miss Morecroft, Godby's daughter; for it could be none other. His heart turned to stone. She was behind all this. Back to haunt the next Hawthorne generation as her father had bedevilled his. He held her gaze before she looked away, her face an impassive mask.

She had her father's grey eyes fringed with jet-black lashes, and his mouth set in a pretty, round face framed by light brown hair. But she looked a pale, irresolute imitation of the Godby he remembered, and he felt a pang of disappointment. For her father? For what this had all come to?

Disappointment, however, was an insubstantial word for the way he felt as he returned his gaze to Caro and Sarah. Motivated by the determination to fight to the death to save them both, he was almost felled the next minute by another wave of dizziness.

Using the manner of one gentleman to another, the effete, self-assured Mr Hollingsworth introduced his mother — the fat, evil woman who regarded him speculatively, her eyes tiny pinpricks of steel in their folds of fat.

The sight of her made his skin crawl. She had grown fat on the profits of the flesh trade; on human misery. How many fallen women like Kitty upstairs would willingly have embraced lives of bondage, slaves to the lusts of men and the greed of people like the Hollingsworths?

'How much do you want for the girls?' Roland did not trouble to hide his disgust.

Mrs Hollingsworth's hand fluttered to her throat. 'Why, the language of common bartering sits ill with the likes o' us,' she said. 'We was just protectin' your dear 'uns, now, weren't we, Mr Hollingsworth? Til you got 'ere, though I must say you've taken yer time about it.'

'I'm not in the mood for games. Name your sum,' muttered Roland. The relief in Sarah's eyes only made him more wretched.

'As pecuniary reimbursement for the care of your daughter? Or for the governess, also?' asked Mr Hollingsworth. 'Leaving Lady Sarah out of the transaction, I'm sure we'd soon come to some mutually agreeable negotiation. But you see, Lady Sarah's style of beauty is particularly sought after at the moment.' He smiled. 'She is beyond any price.'

'Don't insult Lady Sarah unless you wish to earn more than my anger.' Though he spoke through gritted teeth, Roland feared his anger was something that would be difficult to translate into overt action in his current state.

'Ah, now, isn't it wonderful when a real gentleman champions his lady-love in our establishment?' crowed the fat old crone. 'If I were ten years younger — '

Her son cut in. 'The problem, my dear fellow, is this — '

'I don't care how much,' Roland snarled, closing his eyes as he swayed.

'Well, money's one thing, but it ain't goin' to please our esteemed guest whose company we presently await,' purred Mrs Hollingsworth. 'Ah, Sir Richard!' She simpered up at a new arrival whom the clubfoot ushered into the room with a great deal of supercilious care. 'Mr Hawthorne has been ever so impatient to get down to business. We thought you'd never get here.'

'A street urchin delivered your message when I was up to my wrists in gold coin at The Hellraker.' The newcomer rose from kissing the back of Mrs Hollingsworth's hand, a sardonic smile curling his thin lips as he surveyed the company.

Roland blinked at the man who'd inhabited so many of his nightmares.

Sir Richard Byrd.

Trickie Dickie, as he was commonly known.

Back from exile.

About five years older than Roland, tall but powerfully built, he was still a handsome man, although dissolute living had made its inroads.

'Not even a run of good luck could have enticed me to stay, knowing what other . . . enticements . . . were on offer here.'

His gaze slid over Caro, his velvet tones at odds with the lack of empathy in his cold, hard eyes, though he smiled as he bit his lip in apparent contemplation. 'This frightened-looking damsel must be Miss Hawthorne. Venetia's child without the fire and ice.' His eyes travelled to Sarah. 'And this lush little morsel must be the governess, yes?'

'How dare you!'

With a laugh at Roland's ineffectual outburst, Sir Richard went on, 'Mrs Hollingsworth and her son have been maintaining these two young women at their own considerable expense. Knowing my interest in the welfare of any Hawthorne family member, they kindly requested my presence to help resolve an adequate means of recompense . . .'

Roland waited. A weary acceptance that matters were about to become very complicated settled upon him.

Sir Richard moved to the fire to warm his back. He looked at home, an image he upheld as he said, 'Being a regular patron of Mrs Hollingsworth's esteemed establishment — '

At Roland's look of derision, Sir Richard laughed. 'Do not make the mistake of calling me inconstant. Venetia did that. No, my dear Hawthorne, I have but one fair and faithful creature whom I visit here regularly: the magnificently endowed Queenie. So it was an unexpected and delightful surprise when Mrs Hollingsworth sent me the message this evening informing me that Lady Sarah's quest to find your daughter had led her here.'

'The last person we'd expected to see!' exclaimed Mrs Hollingsworth, clapping her hands and leaning forward.

'Certainly a lucky chance I'd never thought would fall into my lap,' murmured Sir Richard.

Moving stealthily around the back of the small sofa upon which Sarah and Caro were huddled, Sir Richard took up one of Caro's smoky ringlets between two fingers. Lowering his face, he brushed the curl across his face, breathing deeply before he released it with a kiss.

Roland's fury ignited at Caro's frightened intake of breath. He took a step forward but the menacing effect for which he was striving was marred by his unsteadiness.

Sir Richard gave a bark of laughter. 'So you intend defending the girl's honour as you never did her mother's?' He caressed Caro's neck and his lip curled. 'Though it would appear Venetia's daughter is not as willing with her favours as her mother. Darling Venetia was ... so very accommodating.' With an assessing look, he added, 'Nor does she have her mother's ripe sensuality, but she is very young and that may come.' Leaning further over the sofa, he reached towards Caro's bodice.

'How dare you?' Sarah hissed, batting away his hand. Sobbing, Caro sank against her shoulder.

'If you're after vengeance, not money, then pistols at dawn,' Roland managed hoarsely.

'You'll not find me hard to negotiate with when the safety of Caro and Lady Sarah hang in the balance.'

It was an exhausting speech. Dear Lord, just give him the strength to endure what he must in order to rescue the women.

'I don't think Sir Richard was entertaining thoughts of duelling, but rather had in mind some other kind of challenge.' A tremor of excitement rippled through Mrs Hollingworth, like a gentle blow to a blancmange. Widening her eyes and biting her lip like a child barely able to keep a secret, she turned to Sir Richard. 'Are we to play our favourite parlour game, Sir Richard? Do you wish all of our large, happy company to participate, or just you and Mr Hawthorne and the two young ladies?'

'No one will play any parlour games!' Roland was surprised at the energy he managed to inject into his voice. He slid his gaze across to Sarah and she smiled. To his amazement she raked her eyes upwards over the length of his body in that lazy, maddeningly sensual manner she had, and then pursed her lips slightly.

He could barely believe it. There they were, in the direst danger, and she was flirting with him.

Yet was that not her way of bolstering him? Her feelings were reflected clearly in her gaze.

Despite the depths to which Roland was now reduced, she was reaffirming her desire, sustaining him at this moment when his manhood had never been more vulnerable. He felt a surge of love and appreciation for the woman he had banished from his household so recently.

'I am taking my daughter and Lady Sarah home now,' he told Sir Richard quietly. 'If neither money nor satisfaction at the end of a sword are what you want — '

Sir Richard began to clap his hands in a desultory fashion. 'Heroic words! And yes, satisfaction is what I'm after, but not at the end of a sword. Rather, upon the roll of the dice.'

Roland closed his eyes.

'Yes! I've in mind a very diverting parlour game which I think we'll all enjoy. I can see you're not up to much, Hawthorne. I'm surprised and disappointed, I must say, to find you in your cups, but as it's not a game of skill it hardly signifies.'

Roland ran the back of his hand across his eyes. 'The young ladies are very tired,' he said wearily. 'It's time we took our leave.'

'Come! I can see Lady Sarah is eager to enjoy some sport with you, Hawthorne.' Sir Richard kissed the top of Sarah's head. 'Damned fine filly this one,' he murmured. 'I don't wonder you're on fire to bed her.'

Steeling himself against the unwise impulse to lunge at Sir Richard and thereby provide the man with the perfect excuse to fell him with an easy blow, Roland blinked at Sir Richard's yelp of pain.

'The bitch bit me!'

'I'll do more than bite you if you don't let us all leave,' hissed Sarah. Her beautiful eyes were blazing. 'If you were a man of any substance you'd realize your warped plans for revenge could hardly be satisfied by pitting yourself against a man who is so ill he can hardly stand up!'

Roland's fear intensified. 'Stop, Sarah!' he begged. If they could suffer in silence just a little longer; if he could only lose consciousness, even if it was at the cost of his dignity, perhaps they could walk out of here relatively unscathed.

Sir Richard crossed his arms and directed an admiring look at Sarah. 'The young lady has fair got my blood up, Hawthorne. However, to prove I am indeed a gentleman, first choice this evening is yours.' He smiled. 'Name the stakes. Shall it be the lovely, innocent and retiring Caro,' he asked, caressing her shoulder, 'or this little filly, the fair and fiery Lady Sarah?'

Roland did not think he had uttered his

horror but Sir Richard answered as if he had.

He chuckled. 'It's merely a popular party game, old chap, which I've no doubt Lady Sarah has played countless times. Let me explain. Upon the roll of the dice an item of clothing from the chosen damsel is either removed, or replaced.'

'The ladies do not wish to play,' muttered Roland. His eyes were hurting from the light. 'Gaming debts sent you into exile once before, sir; I assure you, your insistence on this route will send you to a place far worse.'

'I did what I had to do . . . for Venetia,' snarled Sir Richard. 'I sacrificed *everything* for Venetia.' Violence lit his eyes. 'And I paid the price, by God! These past seven years I have been paying the price as she haunts me from the grave. She was beyond pearls, that's what she told me. A string of pearls that cost a king's ransom is what she demanded. Yet when I risked everything to give her what she wanted, she prettily accepted the gift with the most half-hearted of favours — ' Sir Richard's face contorted grotesquely as he hissed. ' — and then left me!' His eyes were pinpricks of malice as he looked at Roland. 'Left me and returned to her husband.'

So that was it. Relief kept Roland upright. He might have known money would ultimately guarantee their freedom.

'I cannot give you Venetia,' he said, feeling the world closing in upon him, despite his sudden illumination as to what Sir Richard really wanted. 'She was never mine to give . . . but I can give you the pearls — '

'The pearls are mine by rights and I mean to claim them. This little entertainment is the interest upon what you already owe me.'

Mrs Hollingsworth clapped her hands. 'Oh, this *is* sport.' She quivered with excitement. 'Do let us begin. There's the table, gentlemen, and there are the dice.'

'I refuse to play.' Roland eyed the die suspiciously. 'Certainly, not with those.'

'Always happy to oblige, Hawthorne. If you have them, we'll play with yours instead.' Sir Richard pulled a delicate gilt chair into the centre of the room. 'Lady Sarah, if you please?' With courtly exaggeration he assisted Sarah towards it.

She shrugged off his grasp and faced him with loathing. 'Not only must Mr Hawthorne play with loaded dice, but you can see he is seriously ill. If you force any of us you must know that your title will not protect you from the law.'

'What a fearsome and tempestuous creature you must be between the sheets,' he sneered. 'Just like your gentleman friend's admirable predecessor.' He turned to Roland.

245

'I have to tell you, Hawthorne, I've bedded lusty wenches in my time but your Venetia put the most enthusiastic whores into the shade. Why do you look at me like that? Perhaps she did not provide the same excitement in the marital bed? Was she as great a disappointment to you . . . as you were to her?'

'Oh dear! The table!' clucked Mrs Hollingsworth as it toppled over in Roland's haste to get his hands around his tormentor's throat. 'Archie, won't you help poor Mr Hawthorne to his feet? Poor fellow's in his cups.'

Nauseated, Roland suffered the grip of the young man's hands beneath his armpits. He was in no position to struggle, he realized, as he was set back onto his feet, only to stumble backwards as the world tilted once more on its axis. His inadequacy was compounded as Sarah, refusing to sit, taunted, 'Perhaps, Sir Richard, you were a disappointment to *her*, since she so willingly returned to her husband once she'd tired of you.'

Sir Richard's eyes flared. 'Young Miss Hawthorne will suit my purposes just as well, though her retiring ways are not so pleasing to me.' Lamplight glinted on the shaft of steel he pressed to Caro's throat. Roland and Sarah froze.

'Ah, finally you understand I will not be

gainsaid.' A voice of velvet in keeping with the charade. 'Once more, Hawthorne, I ask you to make your choice. Remember, it's just a game. A game of chance, a roll of the dice, your luck against mine. Just tell me, who shall be the stakes? Your daughter?' He grinned. 'Or this luscious wench?'

He gripped Sarah's shoulder with his free hand.

'*Still* you refuse to choose?' Sir Richard glared at him. 'Perhaps I need to press a little harder.'

Caro gasped and Roland had to close his eyes to the entreaty in her look.

Think! he exhorted himself. One wrong move and three lives could be in ruins.

'Please, Father.'

'Mr Hawthorne has too much honour to put *either* of us in your hands!' With dignity, Sarah relaxed in an attitude of defeat, sinking in the gilt chair set out for her. 'If you must choose, choose me, though I warn you, you'll regret it!'

Roland gripped the back of the settee for support. 'No, Sarah,' he whispered. But what could he do? He was powerless. Emasculated. Defeated before the game had begun.

'That is against the rules of the game, my dear.' Still smiling, Sir Richard removed the knife from Caro's throat. 'Mr Hawthorne must make his choice.' He looked at Roland enquiringly. 'Or must I choose for him?'

Pressing the knife once more to Caro's throat, he drew her up from her seat. She made a strangled sound, like a trapped bird.

'There's something fitting to my breaking in Venetia's spawn, though it's to be expected you'd place a higher value upon the very delectable Lady Sarah, since your parentage of the sadly dispirited Miss Caro has always been in doubt.'

'No!' It was all he could do to utter the word. He felt sweat crawling over his body, like an army of ants on his chilled, trembling frame.

Sir Richard cocked an eyebrow and his lips curled in a rictus of a smile. 'No? Not Caro . . . ? Or no, you dispute my assertion?'

'I am her father,' Roland managed hoarsely, raising his head. 'I will kill anyone who suggests otherwise.' The entreaty he saw in Caro's eyes was agonising. He'd do anything to protect her. The doubts fed her regarding her parentage had led to this. Had led them all to this. He could not let her think he had forsaken her.

'The lovely Lady Sarah, then. Yes, an understandable choice. Knowing how you've lusted after her I can imagine what it will cost you to watch me arrive first at the finish line.

So you've made your choice then. Lady Sarah . . . ' He paused meaningfully. 'Come, Hawthorne, say it. You've chosen Lady Sarah as the spoils tonight. Is that right? Then say it!' Angrily, he jerked Caro's hair, the knife still at her neck. She began to cry.

'Yes . . . Lady Sarah,' gasped Roland, defeated, as he slumped over the back of the sofa, his head resting on his folded arms. *Stand up like a man,* he exhorted himself once more. But he could do no more than keep his flickering, light-sensitive eyes open for a few seconds at a time. The scene was reproach enough for his cowardice. Caro's whimpers contrasted with Sarah's admirable bravado were equally intolerable. Sir Richard was now fondling the dice as he stood beside the baize-topped card table set up near the fire.

'Garth!'

At a nod from Mr Hollingsworth, the bullet-headed thug left his post at the door and pushed Sarah roughly back into her chair. Roland caught the flash of bravely concealed fear before she bowed her head.

So, she could no longer look at him? He didn't blame her. With difficulty, he raised himself at the rattle of dice.

'First throw is yours, Hawthorne.' Sir Richard beckoned to him, then strode over to his side. 'Let me help you; you're done in, old fellow.' His voice was full of feigned concern. 'That's right, steady does it. Got a head like a sore bear, have you? A nice warm fire will make you feel better. Isn't the lovely Lady Sarah a sight to behold?'

Roland cast her an imploring look. She looked like a queen on her throne with her haughty eyes and lips curled with disdain. Longing and despair slashed his insides as he feasted his eyes on her for as long as he could keep them open.

'Lady Sarah will appreciate your cooperation. Ah, luck appears to be on your side, which refutes your offensive charge that I am not a man of honour. Yours is the higher number.'

'I forfeit,' said Roland, who was glad he could now see only throbbing pinpricks of light in front of his eyes. His overloaded senses were at breaking point. The best he could do was remain upright.

Dimly, he registered the heavy bulk of another of the brothel heavies just two feet from him.

'But not I,' crowed Sir Richard in the next round. He circled Sarah, savouring her obvious loathing, and the terror she could not entirely hide. 'Of course, I could simply request the young lady divests herself of her gown.' He trailed a bony forefinger over Sarah's exposed throat, caressing her collarbone and closing his eyes in ecstasy, as he murmured, 'Soft womanly flesh. But no — I am, and remain, a gentleman. If the lady would just point her toe I shall merely remove her dainty slipper.'

Dropping heavily to his knees, Sir Richard slipped off Sarah's shoe. Caressing her foot, he held it against his cheek, murmuring, 'The anticipation is nearly killing me.'

It did not surprise Roland to lose the next throw. He watched, his disgust and horror equal to his helplessness. As much as he struggled to remain clear-headed, he wondered if losing consciousness would put an end to the nightmare for them all. What pleasure would Sir Richard gain if Roland were unable to witness it? This whole spectacle was designed purely to humiliate him.

Sir Richard eyed Sarah lasciviously. 'And now for the lady's stocking.' He laughed as Roland was held back, this time by a chuckling Mr Hollingsworth.

On his knees again, Sir Richard held out Sarah's foot, as if parading it before them. Roland tried not to look but his gaze was drawn to the dainty white silk-clad leg before travelling to Sarah's face. Her brave attempt to mask her fear with contempt, and then the hope he saw when her glance locked briefly with his, was almost too much to bear.

He blinked open his eyes at the sound of Sarah's shocked whimper.

'The ribbons are a delight, don't you always think?' Sir Richard addressed Mr Hollingsworth in a matter-of-fact tone, as his arm disappeared up Sarah's skirts. 'That join between silk stocking and flesh, just above the knee. I cannot help myself, but I must explore a little further — '

With a roar Roland tore himself away from his captor and hurled himself upon Sir Richard. 'Blackguard!' he managed between gritted teeth.

Caught unawares, Sir Richard was thrown on his back. However, Garth and his compatriot exerted little effort to return both men to their feet.

Sir Richard quickly regained his composure. 'So glad you appear to enjoy this as much as I had hoped,' he said smoothly, dusting himself down. 'Hawthorne, you win the next toss. Congratulations! I await with anticipation your choice. What? You wish to have the lady's stocking *back*? I had thought to keep it as a souvenir, but — ' He shrugged ' — it is within the rules.'

With trembling fingers, Roland took the insubstantial garment Sir Richard withdrew from his pocket. He had never replaced a lady's stocking before. Of course he had undressed Venetia many times. She'd enjoyed all forms of bedroom sport. Dismayed, he reflected this may well have been one of the party games his late wife had enjoyed in company with Sir Richard and which her erstwhile lover was now enjoying at his expense.

No words were exchanged but Sarah pointed her foot obligingly so Roland could roll the stocking over it with clumsy, trembling fingers.

'You tie it,' he whispered, leaving the slip of silk to fall slackly over her ankle. Not only did he feel incapable physically, but honour dictated. The lady had suffered enough indignity. She'd not want to feel yet another man's hands climbing her leg. How she must despise him now. His manliness had been torn from him with as little effort as her stocking.

'I can't,' she responded unsteadily. 'Please . . .' And she held out her leg again. A spasm engulfed her and he realised her fear was far greater than she displayed.

Feeling the contours beneath the smooth silk he eased up and over her calf was little consolation. His fingers were clumsy and tying the bow almost beyond his capabilities. Pausing in his difficult task, he glanced up at her face. 'I'm so sorry,' he whispered. He felt the light pressure of her hand on his head as he finished his task. An exoneration? A farewell to what they might have shared? Unable to stand, he had to be helped to his feet.

'Douse him with cold water!' Mrs Hollingsworth's command echoed stridently through the room.

Blinking at the shock, Roland opened his eyes in response to Sarah's sudden cries. Until now she had been self-controlled in her bravery. But now she sobbed as Sir Richard removed the pins that secured her hair and which now fell in a mass of thick, chestnut curls over her shoulders. It was glorious: glossy, abundant, with a life of its own. Roland's heart rejoiced at the vision of splendour, then shrivelled. Memories of this corrupt toad would forever mar whatever might have been between them. Roland had been stripped of his honour, and without honour his life was meaningless.

With another cry of helpless rage, he lunged forward. A glint of silver caught his eye as his fists made contact with Sir Richard's skull.

And then the murky darkness that had punctuated the last hour or more enveloped him and he surrendered himself to the oblivion that so effectively extinguished his honour and dignity.

16

Sarah and Caro huddled together for warmth beneath the thin blanket. Neither spoke, although Sarah knew sleep eluded Caro, who so desperately needed it.

In the silence of the attic she soon became accustomed to the sounds of the house: the insistent scratching of mice, the muffled thumps and groans of its occupants plying their trade, and the muted sounds of the city.

After what seemed like hours she became aware of a new sound from behind the adjoining door — muffled groans, but not like those others.

Joy banished her fears. Surely it must be Roland.

Though it felt like days, it had probably been only two hours since they'd been dragged up the stairs by Garth and locked into this hole of a room.

There was no light. Sarah had no idea how long it was before dawn, if they would be released or what their captors' plans were. Her greatest fear was reserved for Roland. He had been unconscious, blood trickling from a wound to his temple throwing into relief the pallor of his parchment skin as he'd been carted out of the room while they had all looked on. The indignity of it. To be humiliated before his own daughter and the woman he loved would be a near-mortal wound to his pride.

The mood of the evening had quickly degenerated after Roland's departure. Mrs Hollingsworth clearly felt cheated of her sport and Sir Richard had become despondent. Slumping into a chair, apparently more in his cups than Sarah had suspected, he looked liverish as in answer to the brothel madam's question he'd muttered, 'No, I haven't the faintest idea what we should do with 'em. Lock 'em up and we'll worry about it in the morning.'

Sarah feared Sir Richard might consider the girls and Roland posed too much of a risk to be allowed their freedom.

Yet surely he would release them? Any petitions for Sir Richard to face justice would be dismissed as the manufactured grievances of a cuckolded husband towards his late wife's former lover.

Another, equally insidious thought intruded. If Sir Richard really were arrogant enough to believe he could get away with his crime, would he decide to prey upon the girls once more, now that Roland were out of the way?

Or was it really only entertainment if Roland bore witness?

Sarah's ears were so busy monitoring Roland's laboured breathing that it was Caro who jerked upright at the faint scrape of a key in the lock. She gripped Sarah tighter as the door eased open on rusty hinges.

Someone moved stealthily towards them.

'Quiet! I've come to help you escape,' came a breathless whisper. 'If you have money and take me with you I know how it can be done.'

'Miss Morecroft!' whispered Caro.

'Hush.' The young woman raised her candle. In its dim glow she looked frightened. Wearing only a thin nightgown, her feet bare, she shivered. 'There are ears everywhere.'

Sarah rose from the bed. 'Of course you want money.' The softness of her voice did not hide her anger. 'Isn't that behind this whole charade? You wanted revenge, Miss Morecroft — for your father's well-deserved banishment. I have read your diary.'

The candle flickered and Miss Morecroft's dull countenance flamed. 'Mr Hawthorne destroyed my father, but I wrote of my anger, not revenge. I'm as much a prisoner as you, thanks to the dreadful day I met Archie Hollingsworth. Do you want me to help you? I assure you, there's no one else here who will.'

'Yes, please,' whimpered Caro, shivering

beneath the blanket.

Shifting restlessly, apparently to get warm, Miss Morecroft continued in her frightened whisper. 'I want ten pounds upon your safe deliverance so that I may buy respectable clothes.' Her teeth chattered. 'I'll need a reference, too, to secure a position. Do I have your word?'

'Respectable?' Sarah went on. Doubt had formed as to Miss Morecroft's role. 'Surely you've been well-rewarded for orchestrating the whole plan?'

'Well-rewarded? I've been ruined by a sham marriage. Duped into believing Archie's questions about Mr Hawthorne and his family were husbandly interest. Now, come. Dawn is nearly here and with it our only chance.' Leaning across the bed, she drew back the curtains.

'First we have to find Mr Hawthorne,' Sarah said.

'There's no time.'

'If Mrs Hollingsworth finds us gone, she's more likely to dispose of him in the Thames than provide him with the proper nursing he needs,' argued Sarah. She glared at Miss Morecroft, ready to do battle. 'I think he's in the adjoining room, only the door's locked. At least just try the key you used for this chamber.'

'And if he's ill?' Miss Morecroft asked, looking in two minds as to whether to object as Sarah took the keys and candlestick from her. 'I'll not let *Mr Hawthorne* jeopardize our only chance.'

Striding towards the adjoining door, Sarah turned to whisper angrily, 'Do you know why your precious father was banished? Not because of his affair with Mr Hawthorne's wife, or that he gambled freely upon old Mr Hawthorne's generosity. No! It was because he put his men in the greatest danger on the battlefield through his ineptitude. It was only thanks to Mr Hawthorne that he wasn't court-martialled and shot!'

'Liar!' Miss Morecroft hissed. 'All right, I'll take my chances alone. Believe me, I'd not put it past madam to dispose of you with as much impunity as . . . as the chickens whose necks she breaks for Sunday dinner.'

Both froze at a new sound. Stealthy footfalls.

'We came as soon as we could,' came a breathless whisper.

In the gloom Sarah could just make out the tawdry gold and mauve gown of the young girl who'd let them into the house.

'With stockings,' came a deep, throaty voice which trembled on a chuckle. 'I saw Her Fat Ladyship strip the sheets from the bed, so if leaping from the window was your plan, Miss Morecroft, you'll need these.'

Raising her candle, Sarah stared with amazement at a tall, flame-haired woman with the most enormous pouter pigeon chest she'd ever seen. From her hands dangled a pile of variously coloured stockings.

'I can't countenance what Dicky's gone and done to you girls,' she said, drawing her painted brows together disapprovingly, 'so I'm donating the spoils he brings me.'

'This is Queenie,' whispered Kitty in hurried explanation, though her tone conveyed a certain reverence. Queenie was certainly impressive in her tight fitting-gown of gold topped off by a matching turban sporting half a dozen peacock feathers. 'She's Sir Richard's favourite — '

'His One and Only,' Queenie corrected with a haughty toss of her head. 'But Queenie's not one to abide an injustice, though there's also me job to consider, an all,' she said, crossing the room to deposit the stockings on the bed. 'They're all nicely knotted, too. Did it mesel' while I was passing the time waitin' fer Dicky to come to me. Serve him right for the humilatin' things he was doing downstairs.' In another few strides she was back at the door. 'Dicky was asleep last time I checked but I ain't taking any more risks. Wicked he might be, but he's me bread and butter. Come, Kitty. You gotta consider yer own skin, too.'

Sarah watched the door close behind them before turning to Miss Morecroft. 'Why don't you start tying them to the bed post? It crossed my mind to wonder if the hay carter could be relied upon.'

Miss Morecroft's scorn followed Sarah from the darkness as she struggled to locate the keyhole of the door to the adjoining room. 'Very clever, Lady Sarah. Yes, he parks his wagon in the same spot every morning at dawn. But hurry, for if the key doesn't fit — '

'It does!' Pure, sweet relief surged through Sarah as she pushed open the door and raised the candle, her eyes drawn by movement to a pile of sacks in the corner. There was Roland, sweat-soaked and shivering, lying beneath a thin coverlet. His sunken eyes flickered the faintest recognition as she cast herself at his side and held one of his limp hands to her lips. He managed hoarsely, 'Are you alright?'

'Better than you, I'd wager,' Sarah murmured, kissing his knuckles and stroking his lank hair back from his forehead. When she skimmed her hand over his sweat-soaked shirt, she shook her head. It was freezing outside and he had nothing warm or dry to wear. 'Put your arms around my neck so I can

261

help you up,' she whispered. 'Caro and Miss Morecroft are waiting in the adjoining room for us. We're going out through the window.'

He gave a weak laugh as he obeyed, and she managed to haul them both to their feet. 'I'll go — inasmuch as I'm able — on one condition.'

'There's no time for conditions,' she said, struggling under his weight as he managed a few unsteady steps. 'I will not leave you.'

He stopped, panting with the effort of their progress, and Sarah was dismayed by the heat from his burning forehead when she laid her hand upon it. 'I need to rest,' he rasped. 'Sarah, I'm too ill. I'll . . . just hinder you.'

She'd have stamped her foot at his stubbornness were there not the need for silence. 'I said I won't leave you,' she repeated. 'Freedom is just through that door.'

'Sarah!'

'Roland, please!' she burst out, stopping when she saw his pallid face limned with dawn light. Suddenly she was afraid. 'Roland, you'll be well soon,' she told him as he sagged against her. 'You will!'

'Perhaps.' With a ragged breath he drew himself upright again and managed to drag another footstep across the bare boards. His hand struggled to her cheek and touched it briefly, before falling away. 'But swear you'll not sacrifice your freedom on my account.'

'I'll promise, if only to urge you on. When this is over,' Sarah panted, 'you'll realize all that matters is that you love me.' With relief, she reached the doorway and they collapsed against the frame. 'And I love you.'

He did not reply. His head was upraised, his eyes closed. He looked as if he'd lost consciousness on his feet. Then, with lips barely moving he managed faintly, 'Love does not last.'

Anger gave her the energy to drag him the final steps to the bed by the window. 'Give me the chance to prove you wrong.'

'I'd not be so cruel,' he rasped as Caro rushed towards him.

'Papa!' she cried, joy turning to alarm as she helped him to the mattress where he crumpled.

The clank of harness and clopping of hooves entering the courtyard cut the morning air.

'Roland!' Sarah shook him. 'The cart's below. You must get yourself to the windowsill.'

Moaning, he struggled to follow her directions, his eyes vacant as he grasped the knotted rope of stockings Sarah thrust into his hands.

'Into the darkness,' he managed between cracked lips. Weakly, he gripped Sarah's wrist. His eyes flickered open. 'If I miss my mark, I hold you to your promise — ' His voice was now so hoarse she could barely hear him. '

263

— to ensure your safety before mine.'

'I promise.' Sarah knew it was the only way to secure his cooperation as she and the two girls helped him into position.

She looked down past his shoulder. It was as Miss Morecroft had predicted. The cart, laden high with hay, provided an ideal landing pad.

'I'm ready.' His eyes flickered open for the briefest moment as Sarah gave him a gentle push.

To her relief, he landed well before dragging himself to the side.

Caro quickly followed her father to the windowsill before easing her way down the length of makeshift rope.

Tensely, Sarah waited for her to drop.

Grimly, Caro clung on.

'Caro, let go!' Sarah whispered urgently. She could hear the early stirrings of the servants.

Frozen by fear, Caro stared up at her as purposeful footsteps sounded on the stairs at the end of the corridor.

'Caro!' urged Sarah, but still the girl did not release her grip.

The footsteps came closer. There was no choice. Leaning dangerously far out of the window, Sarah prized open Caro's fingers and with a scream, Caro dropped the distance, landing safely amidst the hay.

'Your turn, Miss Morecroft! Hurry!' cried Sarah, running back to the door, her trembling fingers battling to fit the key into the lock as Mrs Hollingsworth's strident tones came from the other side.

'What's going on?' demanded the brothel madam, beating upon the door before managing to force it open a fraction. 'Let me in!'

Sarah screamed when she realised she'd been too slow in turning the key, her weight insufficient against Mrs Hollingsworth's determined bulk. She swung round at the sound of more running footsteps, this time inside the room, gasping with relief as Miss Morecroft threw her own weight against the door and at last Sarah was able to grind the key, locking them in.

She'd earned them a reprieve but there'd be little time before Mrs Hollingsworth arrived with reinforcements in the stable yard.

'What the devil!' cried the carter, running towards his vehicle as the two girls hurled themselves into it from the window, Sarah scrambling from the box to take possession of the reins.

With an expert flick of the ribbons she coaxed the cart horse into movement, fending off the pursuing carter with a crack of the whip.

★　　★　　★

'She's gone.'

Roland was hardly surprised by this. What did surprise him, however, was that Miss Morecroft — the real Sarah Morecroft — was bending over him, her familiar features arranged in a look of concern.

'Her father fetched her yesterday.' Miss Morecroft set a tray before him, then lowered herself onto a chair by the side of the bed. 'Eat your soup, sir. It's been some days — '

'Did Lady Sarah say if she'd return?' His throat was dry and his head ached. But his thoughts, at least, were lucid.

'No, sir. At least not that I heard. She'd been here four days. She couldn't stay longer.'

Four days since they'd left the Hollingsworths? The sketchy details of their escape were not something he cared to dwell upon. Certainly not the indignity of being helped by two young women through an open window, although the image of Sarah driving a hay cart through the streets of London was one he would treasure. The carter had caught up with them soon enough and been easily bribed to take them to safety.

He stared at the steam rising from his dinner, unable to return his gaze to Miss Morecroft's face. She seemed content, however, to sit in

266

silence and to help him when he struggled with his mug of water.

Five days since he'd banished Sarah. Barely four since she'd shown him how ill he had served her.

'The Hollingsworths,' he murmured. 'Are you one of them?'

He couldn't make her out. She looked like Godby but there was none of the mobility of feature which, in Godby's case, had always provided strong hints as to what he was thinking. This young woman had regarded the entire proceedings at the Hollingsworths' with stony-faced detachment. And yet, she was here.

'I met Mr Hollingsworth aboard the *Mary Jane*. I did not know it at the time but he'd been soliciting girls from the Continent to work in his mother's establishment.' With an ironic pursing of her lips she added, 'Apparently there is a craze for French mademoiselles.' She sighed as she twisted the wedding band she had moved onto her right hand. 'When we were the only two washed ashore near a small Belgian village I thought Providence had entwined our fates. We were married by special license but soon I was living a nightmare. It was a sham marriage.'

Although she told her story calmly, her eyes revealed the extent of her trauma.

'Perhaps it was better that way.' He looked at her with sympathy before forcing down a spoonful of soup. Losing one's virtue to a Hollingsworth might be preferable to being legally bound to one.

'Yes,' she agreed mildly. 'While I was incarcerated with Mrs Hollingsworth in London I had no idea Archie was at Hawthornedene preparing to entice Caro away.'

Soup splashed onto the tray. He felt as weak as an infant; even eating was an effort. 'What splendid story did he weave to make her go with him?' he asked. If Miss Morecroft were going to reveal every sordid detail, he wanted to know if Caro's dubious parentage were in the public domain.

'She did not go willingly, sir.' Miss Morecroft looked at him, surprised, as she wiped up the spillage. 'Surely you must have known she'd never leave you like that?'

Roland cast aside his napkin. Exhausted, he lay back against the pillows, unable to meet Miss Morecroft's eye. 'I have not been a good father,' he murmured. When she didn't reply he swallowed. He hadn't even asked. 'Where *is* Caro?'

'Sleeping, sir. She's very fragile.'

That was hardly to be wondered at. Roland closed his eyes. They were all fragile. What his darling Sarah must have endured, he could barely imagine. But his darling Sarah was gone now, recovering from her ordeal in the bosom of her family.

It was best she stay there. She would find it difficult to look upon him without reliving the past. His own inadequacy. A spasm of pain tore through him. He couldn't bring himself to ask Miss Morecroft the extent of Sarah's humiliation.

'You may take away the soup, Miss Morecroft,' he said. He barely cared whether he ever ate again, but of course there was Caro. He needed to be strong for her.

'Sir?'

'Yes, Miss Morecroft.' Wearily he dragged his gaze to meet hers.

'I have a letter.'

From an oilskin pouch she withdrew several folded sheets.

'My father wrote it after four of the little ones had died. When he felt the beginnings of fever he bade me bring him pen and ink.' She handed him the brittle, sealed parchment. 'He said it was the most important letter he'd ever written and I must guard it with my life.'

Roland scanned the few lines. Tears burned his eyes.

Miss Morecroft twisted her hands in her lap. Turning in her chair, she fixed him with a wavering gaze. 'I've done you a terrible disservice, sir,' she began haltingly. 'Not only for my part in what happened to you, and to Caro and Lady Sarah.' She paused, struggling with the words. 'I never knew, until recently, why my father was sent to India. And — ' She swallowed. ' — I understand now he owed you his life.'

Roland drew in a ragged breath. At least this time he was not the villain. He felt as if a great load had been lifted from his shoulders. 'Your father was young and he lost his nerve under fire. I'd challenge any of his superiors who were so ready to make an example of him to prove they would not do as Godby under similar circumstances.'

'Yet he blamed you for banishing him?' Miss Morecroft's lip trembled.

'He thought I was doing it for other reasons,' said Roland, recalling that dreadful night he had discovered Venetia in bed with his foster brother. Roland and Venetia had been married only a month, and she was already pregnant with Caro. He'd not thought he could survive her betrayal.

'Are you able to . . . forgive him, as he asks?'

'I only wish he was here to hear it from my own lips,' muttered Roland. Taking refuge in brusqueness, he added, 'You'll stay here, of course. This is your home now, Sarah.'

To his amazement, Miss Morecroft kissed his hand and burst into tears.

*   *   *

Sunlight glanced off the snow-capped mountain. Roland sat back in his chair on the terrace of the chalet and savoured the now-familiar backdrop of the Swiss Alps that had helped calm his disordered spirits for nearly two months.

For the first few weeks he had missed his customary eggs, bacon and haddock. The strange foreign food would have been unappetizing, if he'd had much of an appetite. But then, it had been a long time since his appetites were of any consequence.

He'd taken Caro to this place on the advice of his physician, who believed Caro was at grave risk of succumbing to her mother's emotional excesses. Though Caro had exhibited no such propensities, Roland considered time away from Caro's critical, prying aunt as important as the need for a period of calm reflection for himself. Time, age and maturity had given him an understanding of what had angered and perplexed him before: Venetia's addiction to the poppy. To some extent, Lady Sarah's youthful and innocent desire for instant gratification had helped him put

271

Venetia's desperate pleasure-loving into perspective. But while Sarah's natural sensitivity and generosity towards others tempered her impulses, Venetia's wild, untutored spirit had been allowed to develop at will, becoming warped in the process. Her father, addicted to drink and gaming, had lost his wits and his fortune through both.

Was it any wonder that Venetia's appetites were what they were? Or that she'd traded on her beauty, becoming venal and selfish in consequence?

Was it any wonder that Roland had failed miserably as a husband when he, himself, was so green — a slave to his own youthful desires, as yet untempered by the wisdom that came through age and experience?

He felt the rough parchment of Godby's letter in his coat pocket and the words chased themselves around his head.

'I make no apologies for what happened between Venetia and myself; from the moment I saw her, reason was beyond my power. Now I am older, and wiser, my heart breaks at the knowledge that my passion for Venetia destroyed your love for me, which I have come to value so much higher. Forgive me.'

'Father, you'll catch your death!' Caro's admonition came upon a cloud of frosted air as she seated herself opposite him at the breakfast table.

Roland transferred his gaze from the magnificent, snow-covered Matterhorn, to his daughter's green eyes. It was nine o'clock in the morning. Caro rarely made her appearance before noon.

'Come,' he said, rising. 'Let's walk.'

She tucked her gloved hand into the crook of his arm and they left the terrace, taking the snow-covered path Roland was in the habit of taking, alone.

And as they talked, his soul, which had felt a dry and shrivelled thing only hours ago, began to grow and thrive. He felt hope for the future, both for them, and for the reforms he believed would one day improve the lives of all.

Lady Sarah . . .

Sarah was one topic on which he dared not dwell. He acknowledged the great good she had wrought in his daughter, but that was as far as he was prepared to let his thoughts wander in that direction.

The nightmares that resulted from that ghastly evening at the Hollingsworths' were too brutal, too vivid to revisit willingly. Whenever his thoughts turned unexpectedly to Sarah his breath caught and his body burned with desire, only to be extinguished by shame.

Caro smiled up at him. The crisp air had put roses in her cheeks and he no longer doubted his wisdom in removing her from Larchfield's cloistering atmosphere and the carping of her aunt.

'You look so much better, Caro.' He was uncertain if it was the right thing to say. He did not want to spoil her lightness of spirit by fostering unhealthy introspection.

'I am,' she said simply, adding after a silence, 'I've been talking to a doctor of the mind. I realize how much worse things could have been for me but for your care and concern.' Her eyes filled with tears. 'But now *you* appear to be the brooding invalid.'

He looked at her with amazement.

The gentlest of breezes loosened the snow from the branches of the fir trees. It fell like powder, and caught upon Caro's lashes so that he fancied she looked like a wood sprite when she turned her large eyes upon him once more. Her words cut him to the bone as she said wistfully, 'I wonder whatever happened to Lady Sarah.'

'Lady Sarah.' He could do no more than repeat her name with longing.

Caro glanced up at him quickly. 'You were fond of her, weren't you, Papa?'

Roland shot her a narrow look. What was this? For nearly two months Caro had shown

274

little interest in her surroundings; had not uttered a word about her ordeal. Now she was dredging up the past and it was intruding uncomfortably on Roland's own blurred understanding of events after he had lost consciousness.

It was bad enough to have to remember his lack of heroism while he could still stand; unbearable to consider what might have happened after he had passed out, despite Miss Morecroft's reassurances.

'She was a fine young woman,' he conceded, embarrassed.

'She saved our lives, Papa.'

At Caro's reproachful look he added hastily, 'I wrote acknowledging that. She is still with her father.' Then — for Caro continued to look accusing, 'A very long letter, thanking her for all she did for you, Caro.'

'And you, Papa!'

Roland looked away. 'I'm sure I thanked her very properly,' he muttered, wanting to turn the subject. 'Miss Morecroft tells me you were very brave.'

'Brave! Lady Sarah was the brave one, for leaving her father once she had learned my likely whereabouts, and venturing alone to the Hollingsworths'. Miss Morecroft — the real one — was only brave in taking a risk to escape. Her very life depended upon it. After Mr Hollingsworth grabbed me when he found me walking in the park, then pushed me into the coach and tied me up, I did nothing but quiver and cry.' She bit her lip. 'He made me write that letter, you know. You believed I went with him willingly, didn't you?'

'It would have been understandable if you had,' he said, squeezing her hand, 'considering the lies I thought he'd told you about me — ' He broke off, realizing he had said too much.

'What lies?'

'It doesn't matter. Let's turn back; it's freezing.'

But Caro wouldn't let him off so easily. After some moments in silence she said softly, 'You thought he'd told me you weren't my father.'

'I am your father.'

'I know.'

The silence wasn't broken after that. The path took a circuitous route and they returned to the hotel just as luncheon's enticing aromas wafted out to greet them.

17

Sarah sat stiffly in her crimson and gilt chair and stared at the guests enjoying this evening's charades. Once she, too, would have added her laughter to the peals which greeted Miss Emmeline Farquhar's racy charade, but now she felt wrapped in a cocoon of misery and loneliness, disembodied from her old friends. They'd welcomed her back with a rapture born of her novelty, but as she remained withdrawn, they too had ceased to make an effort. Sometimes she almost felt a growing hostility. Perhaps they saw that she despised their thoughtless frivolity. Knowing the depth of pain that came from loving, she certainly despised the use of charades to so publicly mock the pain of a fellow house-guest.

She slid her gaze across to Lady Stokes. On stage the attractive Lord Stokes, playing the Duke of Cumberland, was in an intimate clinch with Miss Emmeline Farquhar, who played his mistress. Lady Stokes's jaw clenched with the effort of appearing to find the charade as amusing as everyone else. Clearly, she did not.

Sarah turned away in disgust as the audience broke into rapturous applause.

'And now for True or False!' Lord Stokes, tearing himself from the arms of his lady-love on stage, addressed the audience. 'The charade will first identify the three people chosen to take part in tonight's quiz. They will then have to answer questions put to them upon the roll of the dice.'

'Lady Sarah? Are you alright?' Lord Giles, beside her, touched her arm. His frown was full of concern.

She smiled weakly. 'I'm just a little weary.' How could she admit that games involving the roll of the dice brought back terrible memories?

'Perhaps we could take a turn around the supper room?' he suggested, and although Sarah knew he had no ulterior motives, she shook her head. His admiration the past few days had been balm to her anguished soul after Roland's devastating letter, but she had no intentions of pushing the boundaries of propriety. Who knew where a turn around the supper table could lead?

Another spasm of anguish gripped her as she reflected upon Roland's words. Indirectly, they were the reason she was here. At her father's admonition. It was he who had almost physically ripped her from Roland's side all those weeks ago and bundled her into his coach to take her home. But watching his daughter pine over Roland Hawthorne's silence had driven Lord Miles to the extremes of his limited forbearance.

'Worthless puppy if he can't appreciate a prize jewel like you, my love!' he'd fumed, forgetting that he had been strenuously against a possible match from the moment Sarah had finally hinted at her feelings for Roland.

'A girl with your wit and beauty mustn't squander her chances mouldering in the country with her cantankerous old Papa. Lady Mettling has invited you to spend the week at Middlebrook with a group of friends. You will write this moment and accept her kind invitation.'

There had been a fierce battle between the strong-minded Lord Miles and his equally strong-minded daughter before Sarah had finally given in.

However, the past few days only proved that she would have been far happier mouldering in the country with her cantankerous old papa. The frenetic gaiety she'd once embraced seemed stupid and pointless. Though she tried to enter into the spirit, she knew old friends and acquaintances whispered to one another that Lady Sarah was greatly changed — and not nearly so much fun.

To her confusion she heard several members of the audience cry out her name.

Lord Giles tapped her arm. He was smiling. 'It's a shipwreck, can't you see?' he told her, indicating the badly painted backdrop meant to represent waves and Miss Hemmersly acting out a brave attempt at keeping her head above water. 'They want you to go on stage.'

Fear gripped her. Dear Lord, this couldn't be happening. 'I don't think I can,' she whispered honestly. Her legs felt weak and her head reeled.

'Mr Roger Burbank, you are also required,' Lord Stokes called amidst general clapping and excitement. 'Come, Lady Sarah, you're not known as a shrinking violet. It's all in the name of honest fun.' He extended his arm and before Sarah knew it Lord Giles had pushed her forward and she was being helped onto the stage.

It was not the hostile grilling her overwrought nerves had envisioned. People were naturally curious about her ordeal and after a while she found it cathartic to answer questions like how cold had the water been and about the Belgian fishermen who had bravely swum out to rescue her.

'Many thanks for your brave answers,' Lord Stokes told her at the end of her ten questions, indicating she could now rise from her chair on the centre of the stage.

Smiling, Sarah inclined her head as she prepared to return to the audience amidst more applause.

'I . . . have a question.'

She turned at the interruption.

'Miss Bassingthwaite, why did you not speak up before?' Lord Stokes, still in his role as Master of Ceremonies, stayed Sarah with a hand. 'Lady Sarah, will you permit our shyest houseguest one final question?'

Frozen, Sarah stared at the girl, unable to answer. Millicent looked as plain in her blue round dress as she had the night Sarah had seen her at the London inn before walking into the trap laid for her by Archie Hollingsworth. There was a greenish tinge to her normally sallow complexion and her terror was apparent at commanding the attention of so many people.

Almost wearily, Sarah accepted her fate. It was clear enough. Lady Bassingthwaite had bullied her daughter into asking the question and Millicent, too frightened to disobey, had only now got up the courage to lay the foundations of a damning exposé. Naturally Millicent's veiled accusation would be given credence because of the kind of girl she was.

'What would you like to ask, Miss Bassingthwaite?' Lord Stokes prompted. His manner was expansive and congenial, like a master coaxing a nervous schoolroom miss. Sarah drew herself up proudly, smoothing down her sequin-encrusted crimson net skirts — a colour and picture she was sure the audience would always remember as Millicent blurted out, 'It's my mother who wants to know, actually, and I am so sorry, Lady Sarah — ' She swallowed, then stammered. ' — but she asks why you — '

She faltered, apparently unable to continue until Lord Stokes chivvied her in a friendly, encouraging fashion, 'Lady Sarah is not an ogre, Miss Bassingthwaite. I'm sure she'd be delighted to answer your question.'

Millicent swallowed and cast her eyes downwards as she continued in a voice that could barely carry across the room, but which certainly managed to be heard judging by the tumultuous response when she finally asked, 'She wants to know why you were alone at the Crown and Anchor when you said you were being looked after at Larchfield and . . . and why you then went unchaperoned to Sally Hollingsworth's address in Marylebone?'

18

'Well, you might have sent word more than two days ahead, for there's been such a to-do getting the house prepared and matters just as you would like them, Roland . . . Not that, but inconvenience aside, it isn't wonderful to see you back again. And you, Caro, in *such* rude health. Really, I don't know what your father was thinking, assuming your heart was so tender it could not withstand a simple rejection. As if it isn't something most of us have to bear at least once in our lifetimes. My dear, there are far worthier gentlemen than Mr Hollingsworth and you'd do well to bear in mind what you have to offer a gentleman disposed to taking a wife. You may not be endowed with such a pretty face and figure as my Augusta and Harriet but, unlike my poor girls, you have a handsome dowry to entice the most discerning gentleman — '

'I hope we need not wait too long for refreshment, Cecily,' Roland interrupted, stilling her words with a cursory peck on the cheek as he pushed his daughter out of her path. 'It's been a long journey.'

'I was hardly craning my neck out of the

window for the first sign of your arrival, Roland,' said Cecily tartly, preceding him into the drawing room and pulling on the embroidered bell rope. 'Bessie knows to expect you. I'm sure if you can be patient a little longer we can all sit down and enjoy a pleasant chat while we wait for tea.'

'So, Cecily, more than two months have elapsed, and yet your countenance and good humour remain quite unchanged,' Roland marvelled with an irony completely undetected by his sister-in-law.

'I'm surprised, considering the trials I've had to endure since you left me so abruptly with the entire management of this house and estate upon my shoulders,' she sniffed. 'Thank goodness we found Miss Morecroft — and I mean poor Godby's daughter — lodging with Mr Hollingsworth's mother so she was able to take up her rightful post. I've a mind to call on the good widow when I'm in London and thank her for her care; though I think that son of hers needs talking to for allowing Caro's tears to overrule his judgment. I daresay he was flattered by Caro's attention.' She ran a careworn hand across her brow. 'That aside, Harriet and Augusta have been sorely trying. I've threatened to box their ears if they so much as mention Lady Sarah's name. You can't image the difficulty I've had explaining to them events in such a manner as will not damage their delicate sensibilities by putting ideas into their heads, or poisoning the high esteem in which they hold their cousin. Not that I intend ever referring to this again, Caro. What's done is done. You've learned your lesson and you've been lucky. You still have your reputation intact . . . unlike that insinuating little baggage Lady Sarah, or whatever name she currently chooses to go by. Well, she's had her public come-uppance. The scandal! Exposed at Lady Mettling's house party for consorting with persons of ill repute!' she hissed before adding complacently, 'I daresay a nunnery might accept her if her father has deep enough pockets. Though it'll sit ill with her pleasure-loving disposition.'

'Lady Sarah has been publicly shamed?'

'Oh, don't you start, Caro,' said Cecily, irritated. 'I've had enough to put up with without Harriet and Augusta snivelling at the news. I'd thought to instil in them a healthy dose of terror rather than touch their tender little hearts. It's exactly as I said. She was an insinuating little baggage, a trollop, and there's no kinder way to put it.'

'How . . . dare . . . you?'

Shocked into silence, Cecily gaped at her brother-in-law. Then the gloating expression returned as she said, 'You always fancied yourself in love with her, didn't you, Roland? Well, I hear she is no longer received in any respectable drawing room, and that only yesterday she'd been given the cut direct by Lady Jersey.'

Hope flickered like a flame suddenly come to life in the cold, cavernous regions of Roland's heart.

Lady Sarah needed rescuing.

He swallowed, his mouth suddenly dry as he recalled the dutiful formal letter he had written her from Switzerland. His thanks for her bravery and subsequent care of him had sounded so trite. The words that followed were worse; a pompous-sounding death knell to all his hopes of what might have been: *It is my wish not to be distracted by life's frivolities so that I may devote my energy and passion towards furthering those worthy causes which remain the chief object of my life.'*

What he meant was that Sarah deserved to be happy and the kindest service he could render was to relinquish her.

What greater betrayal was there than to be discarded upon the roll of the dice? In the midst of the drama she had argued otherwise, but Roland knew that when normality returned, Sarah would come to despise him and his lack of heroism.

He looked beyond Cecily's shoulder. 'Ah,

Miss Morecroft,' he greeted the serious, brown-haired young woman who entered the room flanked by her young charges, Augusta and Harriet. They were trying hard to contain their enthusiasm at seeing Caro.

'I trust you have not been overwhelmed by your duties.' To his surprise he felt a pang as the little girls rushed to embrace his daughter. He'd missed his nieces.

'Not in the slightest,' she said with her usual calm. 'Harriet and Augusta have proved apt and diligent pupils, while Mrs Hawthorne has been nothing but kindness itself.'

Roland glanced from the demure governess, in whose manner he could detect no irony, to Cecily, whose lips were pursed in a prim, complacent little smile.

Good; it appeared he would not be required to arbitrate in order to keep a tenuous peace.

'Roland, where are you going?'

Roland had barely drained his tea cup before he was rising, inclining his head towards the three women.

'To London,' he said equably. 'You've run the household so efficiently in my absence, Cecily, I've no doubt you'll not miss my company another three days or so.'

* * *

'M'lady?'

Sarah, reclining on the Gothic sofa in her friend's small drawing room, glanced up from her deep introspection of the dancing flames as her maid put her head around the door.

'A gentleman to see you.'

James. Shame and embarrassment curdled in her belly. He'd written the moment he'd heard news of the uproar at Middlebrook.

She sighed. 'Show him in.'

Dear Lord, she'd never forget standing on the top step that led to the stage while the audience buzzed with excitement and Millicent wept, 'I'm so sorry, Lady Sarah.' Though if she really had been, and not such a wet goose to boot, she'd hardly have continued in imploring tones, 'Mother thought she recognised you at the inn and though I tried to stop her she went after the publican with some excuse and read the note you'd given him.'

Drawing her green Pomona shawl more closely round her, Sarah dragged herself off the sofa, wishing she had the freedom to fly abroad and escape the nightmare her life had become.

After a cursory inspection of her appearance in the looking-glass above the chiffoniere, and a weary adjustment to a flattened curl, she was ready.

She'd thought nothing had the power to

rouse her from her lethargy, but the sound of James's boots in the corridor outside the door made her feel suddenly ill. Not at what she'd done but at what he must be thinking.

She tensed, preparing herself for the moment James would thrust open the door and gaze upon her with reproach and disappointment.

'Gad's teeth, Sarah! You look like you've been sleeping in a haystack.' Striding to the footstool she'd migrated to, he crouched down to grip her shoulder.

It was all she could do not to cry. Instead, she took refuge in brittle pride. 'I do not need a lecture from you, James,' she said, turning away from him. 'I hoped you would not come.'

'That I'd give up on you at last?' he asked, rising and striding to the fire to warm his hands. 'Don't think you can ruin yourself without more than a murmur from me.' He twisted his head to look at her, dominating the room with his massive shoulders and red hair. But it was his look of puzzlement she found so hard to bear. Did he really think she was guilty as charged?

'Say your piece and then leave me alone,' she muttered, drawing her shawl close.

'Do you know what the gossips are saying? Not to mention the wags — ? A house of ill repute in Marylebone, Sarah?' He shook his darling shaggy head. 'Obviously there is some rational explanation. I, for one, do not believe you were enticed into the flesh trade. I'm sure most others who know you don't, either. So what I can't for the life of me fathom is why you don't defend yourself with the simple truth.'

For a moment she considered confessing everything. But that would mean revealing too much: her rash stupidity in venturing forth alone, her subsequent humiliation and her undying loyalty to Roland. If James learned of Roland's role in all this and the passion he continued to inspire in her, he'd belittle it all with demands like why wasn't he here? He might even resort to anger and seek Roland out.

Well, Roland just needed time. His duty was to ensure Caro could survive without him before he came courting Sarah. And as Roland was doing all in his power to protect Caro, so must Sarah.

'I was looking for someone about whose safety I was concerned.' She sighed. 'I'm sorry, James, but I have vowed to say no more. The truth would only damage her reputation.'

James narrowed his eyes at her, his disgust plain as he said slowly, 'You believe it worthwhile to sacrifice your reputation for someone who remains silent in the face of your ruin?'

Sarah stared mutinously into the flames.

'It's that Hawthorne girl, isn't it?' he asked suddenly. 'She ran away, or slipped up, and you went after her. That's it, isn't it? Now you're facing the music and she says nothing.'

Sarah held herself rigid. She would remain silent.

'Good Lord, and her father, that damned Whig Hawthorne — the Devil rot him — is happy to let the wolves devour you with nary a murmur in case it hurts his darling daughter or reflects badly on him, more like it.'

'James, please!' Finally roused, Sarah jumped up and gripped the lapels of his coat as she looked into his eyes. 'Terrible things happened that night at this house in — ' She swallowed ' — in Marylebone. Mr Hawthorne took his daughter abroad to recover. You really must not judge what you can't understand — '

'I understand that knave Hawthorne is letting you suffer the consequences of his daughter's mistakes. What I'd like to know is, where is he when you really need him?'

Raw pain tore through her. She'd like to know, too. Wilting against James's chest, misery settled upon her shoulders like a mantle.

James put his forefinger beneath Sarah's

chin and raised her head to look at him. 'Can't you see what you're doing?' he asked, more gently now. 'To yourself? To those who love you? Your father was beyond comfort when he thought you dead. Now this! Sarah,' he pleaded, 'go back to Lord Miles, now. I'll escort you. We'll call the banns. Do what we'd all agreed was in everyone's best interests before your — ' He exhaled on a disapproving grunt. ' — escapade under Hawthorne's roof.' He gave her a bracing shake. 'You know you'll be much happier at home with people who care for you than here — ' He indicated the room with its common, ugly furniture. ' — accepting the charity of fawning little Mrs Hargreaves, hoping your dissolute friends will invite you back into the fold. They won't, you know.'

'You're asking me to marry you?' she asked slowly, pulling out of his embrace to stand close to the fire. So it had come to this, after all.

'Well, no one else has offered, have they?' he asked pointedly.

She didn't know whether to laugh or scream. Instead, she gave him a long, considering look. 'Do you love me, James? Do you adore me? Does your heart beat faster when I enter the same room?'

'What nonsense you talk sometimes,' he

said, smiling down at her with fond exasperation. 'You know it doesn't and nor would I want it to. It would be like — ' He struggled for an analogy.

Sarah returned to her footstool, where she waited with interest. James was not one to wax lyrical at the best of times and he did not disappoint her now.

'I suppose it would be like having to mince around in diamond-spangled high-heeled slippers which pinched like the Devil.' He patted the top of her head and Sarah was reminded of the fondness he had for his cocker spaniel, Bessie. 'Give me a pair of comfortable leather slippers any day. Though, Sarah, you should do something about your hair. It's not like you to look so untidy.'

She let out a hysteria-tinged laugh. 'Well, how can I possibly say no to what must be the most romantic marriage proposal I've ever received?'

'Glad you think it's a good idea. I'm warming to it by the minute.' Rubbing his hands vigorously before the fire, he fixed her with one of his bluff, pleased-with-himself grins she remembered from childhood days after he'd winged a goose or shot a bullseye. 'We'll deal well together, Sarah. No inconvenient passion and bruised hearts, eh?'

It was hard to hold back the tears. His

generosity was so undeserved. She rose and crossed the carpet. Taking his wrists, she gazed at him with affection. 'That wasn't an outright yes. There's a caveat, James.' She paused. 'I cannot, in good conscience, agree to marry you when my heart is engaged elsewhere.'

'Well, why didn't you say?' He sounded more put out than heartbroken.

Sarah hesitated. 'Because I didn't think you'd approve. Papa doesn't, that's certain.'

'Good God! Hawthorne?' he blustered. 'After all that's happened and all he's done? Or rather not done, since he's the one who should be fronting up with an offer, though Lord knows what your father would say!' He shook his head, scowling as he repeated Roland's name with derision. 'Hawthorne! First he says nothing to defend you when he knows the truth; now he won't marry you when you're far and away more than the ungrateful blackguard ever deserved.'

Sarah hedged. 'James, perhaps he's not even heard the news. He's in Switzerland still, I think.'

'Well, you must tell him. Write to him. He deserves to know.'

She hesitated, unsure whether to elaborate, then added reluctantly, 'Before any of this drama at the Mettlings happened he wrote, telling me he was disinclined ever to marry again as he wished to direct all his energies towards his political career.'

'I told you — Damned Whig!' spat James, staring over her shoulder at the window as he digested her words. 'Well, there's nothing more to be said, then. Regardless of your feelings for Hawthorne, the very man who should be rescuing you from this debacle — though I daresay your father would rather see a bullet through his heart than his ring on your finger — he's not here. And clearly someone's got to save you, for I'll not stand by and see you ruined.'

Another surge of affection for her friend enveloped Sarah, but it was not love and it was so different from what she felt for Roland. She gazed at James, torn by shame and confusion. If she accepted him she'd be using him ruthlessly and shamelessly to save herself from a public disgrace which barred her from society forever. Yet without a timely marriage to save her, she'd never see another familiar drawing room or sip tea with a respectable matron again. The friends she'd once gossiped with would cross the road to avoid speaking with her. But worse than all that would be her father's hurt and humiliation. She didn't think she could do it to him.

'For goodness sake, stop snivelling, Sarah.' There was little sympathy in James's tone. 'It's time to face the truth. Hawthorne doesn't look like he's about to play the gentleman, in which case you really don't have much choice; for I can tell you now, I'll not see my dearest friend pay for a crime for which she's blameless.' Picking an imaginary piece of lint from his coat sleeve, he added with a grin, 'You'll make an excellent housekeeper and hostess at any rate, and if you pay more attention to your hair than you obviously did today, you're a diamond of the first water.'

★ ★ ★

Half an hour after James's momentous visit, Sarah stood at the window of the shabby drawing room wracked with indecision as to whether she was doing the right thing.

Though she wasn't sure she endorsed James's declaration that love was nothing but a load of codswallop invented to sell books and tickets to the theatre, she had all but convinced herself that theirs would be a comfortable union. She'd had to remind herself it was she who had pursued Roland; so if he held to his original stance that marriage was not on his agenda, she had no one to blame but herself.

Swallowing past the great lump in her throat, she traced his name on the fogged-up window pane.

Her father would be happy, and James was pleased enough, so now there was only her inconvenient passion for Roland to overcome. Surely, after the dramas of the past few months, a comfortable arrangement such as marriage with James promised, was to be commended.

She wrinkled her nose at the faux Gothic furniture and tasteless artworks of Mrs Hargreaves's drawing room. Suddenly she longed for the tasteful interiors of her childhood home. With a determined effort she banished the reflection that Larchfield had been just as beautiful.

'Darling Roland,' she said to the stuffed hamster in its glass box upon a table near her, 'where are you?'

She had attempted something with her untidy hair after James's criticism, but it still looked like a bird's nest.

The overloud rap on the door startled her and Betty Hargreaves's useless parlour maid put her head round. 'Gentleman to see you, M'lady.'

Sarah looked enquiringly at her.

'Can't say as I remember his name, M'lady, but he didn't have red hair.'

Life surged back, filling the aching void,

sweeping away her lethargy and snapping Sarah's backbone and lazy posture to attention.

It had to be Roland. No one else would call on her.

'Keep him waiting,' she ordered, flying to the door. 'I'll be down in five minutes.'

Heart beating furiously, she doused herself with orange flower water, enlisted the maid's help to button her into her best gold flecked muslin, and swept her curls into the most stylish *à la Meduse* coiffure she could manage in the seconds available.

Surely this meant he had finally heard, or come to his senses, or whatever the reason was for his silence? He'd only have to reflect on the eternal alchemy between them to realise he had no alternative.

Nerves jangling, she ran to the parlour. Her mind whirled with possibilities, but at the root of all was the knowledge that the only man she would ever love had returned. At the door she stopped to bite her lips and pinch colour into her cheeks, gathering her courage before signalling to the parlour maid to announce her.

'My dear Mr Hawthorne.' She swept into the room with as much regal dignity as she could manage, extending her hand, smiling. 'Welcome back.'

He took her fingertips and bowed, but it

did not escape her that his lips kissed the air, and his expression as he straightened was one she remembered well: wary, reluctant admiration, a throwback to the early days of her tenure at Larchfield.

'Lady Sarah,' he had said, his smile strained, 'I came the moment I heard news of your predicament.'

Predicament? It sounded as if she'd contracted some nasty disease. Then it struck her that perhaps he truly believed her fall from grace was in more than name only. That it was something unconnected to the night at the Hollingsworths'.

She dismissed the thought as nonsense, saying earnestly as she ran her hands along the top of the Egyptian sofa, 'I don't know what you've heard, but I am guilty of nothing other than being a party to the crimes committed at the Hollingsworths'.'

When he didn't immediately answer, but merely stared at her with a look she was unable to fathom, she grew afraid. She studied him, listening to the wind rattling the windows and the clock ticking. He was turned out with his usual care and attention to detail. The cut of his russet-coloured coat emphasised his broad shoulders and he wore a new pair of hessians with brown leather tassels. Though he did not exude quite his usual air of studied calm — frowning instead at the amber knob of his cane which he twisted in his hands — he'd managed to coax his cravat into an Oriental tie of utter perfection. Cosmo would have been green with envy. Calling on such irrelevancies was the only way she could stop herself from weeping, or throwing herself into his arms and asking him why he'd not come back to her sooner.

He advanced several more steps and stopped, putting his head to one side as he gazed at her. There was such sadness and sympathy in his expression that she felt her lip tremble; but instead of a smile, the lines of his face remained grim. He cleared his voice. 'Sarah,' he said softly, 'you know I don't believe you guilty of impropriety. I'd only just returned home when I heard you'd fallen victim to the gossips.'

She waited for him to draw her into his arms. Her body ached for the closeness they'd once shared but she steeled herself against her old impulsiveness. She had to know he felt the same way she did.

He cleared his throat again. 'When Mrs Hawthorne told me I came immediately.' Sarah saw the derision in his eye as he glanced at their surroundings. 'I've come to make you an offer.'

She stared back at him. Shock and disappointment churned in her stomach. Where was the impassioned declaration of love, the hoarse avowals of his enduring passion, his confession of surrender to the feelings he realised he was unable to deny?

'An offer?' She cocked her head, devastation making her flippant. 'To return to Larchfield as your governess?'

'Good God, Sarah, are you mad?'

He sounded suddenly so much like the Roland she knew that she laughed, asking, 'No, but I think you must be if you imagine I could be tempted by such an appalling proposal. It's even worse than James's offer only half an hour ago.'

It had not been the right response. The clenching of his jaw and narrowing of his eyes told that. Realisation crashed through her brain. Lord, his pride was as damaged as hers. She said quickly to ameliorate the damage, 'Do you know how long I've waited for you, Roland?' How she wished she'd never spoken those flippant, thoughtless, *stupid* words. It was no time to indulge in wounded dignity. Roland had *almost* just asked her to marry him and she wanted Roland more than she'd wanted anything in her life.

But the damage had been done. Desperate, she tried another gambit, pretending she didn't notice his withdrawal, his clouded expression, the clenching of his jaw. 'You came back to me, Roland, as I longed that you would. I did so hope you didn't mean what you'd said in your letter.'

He managed a reluctant smile. 'Of course I didn't mean it, though you surely understood what prompted me.'

She looked enquiringly at him. Oh Lord, was his prickly pride really going to get in the way of all this? They'd come so far.

With a growl of exasperation he closed the distance between them, only inasmuch as he gripped her elbows before releasing them in order to pace. 'Good God, Sarah, of course you do. I lost any credible right to claim you as my wife the moment I opened my mouth and sacrificed you to Sir Richard.'

'Roland!' She followed him to where he had taken refuge with an Egyptian armchair between them. Desperate to bridge the final distance, she whispered unsteadily, 'If you believe that, you're only playing into Sir Richard's hands. Surely it's what *I* think that matters?' She reached out to touch him. Though he looked warily at her hand as she rested the flat of her palm against his chest, he did not move away.

She craned her neck up to meet his anguished gaze. 'Sir Richard set out to humiliate you. If that is how you feel, if it is humiliation that now prevents you from seeking what you want, then victory is his.'

With a soft groan, Roland crushed her hand within both of his and brought it to his lips. 'I've told myself the same thing, over and over,' he whispered, his hot breath sending shivers of longing through her. 'It's the knowledge of my weakness, my *undeservedness*, that's kept me from returning to you all those days and nights of wanting you so badly I thought I'd lose my mind.'

For a brief moment she had dared hope, but his tortured expression stripped all that away. Too much still stood between them. She could see it in the rawness of his continued humiliation, and his refusal to forgive himself. She had no words for the pain that sliced through her.

'Sarah, don't you see?' He clenched her hand so tightly it hurt. 'I uttered the words that surrendered you to him; I made the choice to deliver you to horrors undreamt of. I have to live with that every day of my life.'

'You were *forced*, Roland.' She spoke through gritted teeth. 'By knifepoint.' She took a deep breath for courage and tentatively rested her head against his chest, melding her body against his, hoping to coax the loving softness from him for which she longed.

He averted his head, but stopped short of pushing her away.

'Roland, you came here to make me an offer — ' She pressed herself closer, raising her head.

He looked down at her. There was longing in his expression but still he resisted the invitation implicit in her pleading eyes, her pouting mouth.

'Captain Fleming is a good man,' he said gruffly, setting her away from him. 'In ten years you're far more likely to still be happy in a steady, reliable alliance with a man you're fond of than you would with me.'

'Nonsense!' she cried, reaching up to clasp her hands behind his neck. 'You know I've loved you — wanted you since I first came to Larchfield.' She was not yet ready to give up. If he could just accept that she did not share his fears. 'You feel the same, I know you do.' She raised her head and offered him her lips, but these gestures seemed only to increase his anguish and harden his resolve.

'Sarah,' he ground out, 'I owe you my life. Do you know how worthless that makes me feel after what I've done to you? Fleming has come to your rescue. If you love me, you must not hold me to the hasty and inferior offer I made you when I entered this room.' A muscle worked at the corner of his mouth.

Sighing, he ran his hand across his eyes. 'If you marry Captain Fleming you'll please your father. It's a sensible match. He's open and honest and holds you in the greatest affection.' He dropped his eyes, adding in tortured tones as he turned away from her, 'I can only be a constant reminder of the horrors you do battle with every day.'

A heavy, stifling lethargy crept upon her. He was resolved. Nothing she could do or say would change his mind. Dully, she asked, 'Or is it that you cannot gaze at *me*, Roland, without being reminded of what I was in Sir Richard's hands? Perhaps it is not your humiliation that stands between us. Perhaps *I* am the constant reminder.'

Defeated, she stepped back. It was like stepping out of the life embodied by all her dreams and hopes, and into another. One she didn't want at all.

Silently, they stared at one another.

'I love you, Sarah.' His voice was clear and direct; only the whiteness of his knuckles clenching the top of his cane betrayed the depth of his emotion. 'But when a man more worthy than I is willing to offer you comfort, security and affection, I refuse to stake my claim.' Bowing, he turned.

Sarah watched him through a sheen of tears. 'I marry James in six weeks,' she said brokenly as his hand gripped the doorknob. 'If you change your mind before then — ' She exhaled on a shuddering breath. ' — I will be waiting.'

★   ★   ★

Roland stumbled into the street. Self-disgust clawed at him. How could he have imagined they had a future in view of all that had happened? Weaving his way through the traffic, he made blindly in the direction of St James. Passers-by jostled him, and a dirty-faced boy in a greasy cap and coat too big for him tried to beg a penny. He was oblivious to everything but the pain that sliced through that treacherous, fallible organ, his heart.

'Have I got summat to tickle yer fancy!'

Roland stepped around the lightskirt who sought to detain him with an insinuating pout and thrust of her skinny bosom. Head down, he continued towards Whites, his club, intent upon burying his sorrows in a news-sheet.

An insistent tug of the sleeve made him look up in irritation. An instant later recognition dawned.

'Kitty!'

Smiling, she took his arm. 'Right glad I am to see yer got yer colour back, sir. Thought you was bound for your eternity box, I did, and that's the truth!'

'It was a close thing.'

'Yer still look as if you could do with a mite cheering up.'

Garnering his wits and his manners, he smiled apologetically, in a strange way glad of the diversion. 'I'm afraid I'm not in the market, Kitty,' he said, adding quickly at her crestfallen look, 'although if I were, I'd definitely court your kind offices.' His gaze skimmed the length of her, from her glossy brown hair and bright eyes to the boots in need of mending which peeped from beneath her tawdry lilac gown. 'So you've gone out on your own, have you? Escaped that evil den of vice and bondage?'

She frowned as she digested this, her hand still on his sleeve. 'Didn't I tell you I signed a piece of paper wot gives Mrs Hollingsworth rights over me person 'til I've paid her back in full? That ain't fer another three years or more. After that she says she'll 'elp me set up on me own.'

'Then you're not unhappy with the Hollingsworths?'

'Lord, I'd leave tomorrow if I weren't obliged to 'em!'

'Why don't you just leave now?'

Kitty looked at Roland as if he were queer in the attic. 'And get sent to Newmarket for me pains? The law 'ud be onto me in no time. Weren't you listening?'

'I daresay they've come to rely upon your trusting nature,' Roland said ironically.

'Young Mr Hollingsworth gives me special leave, s'long as I give him 'arf wot I earns in the street. The rest I gets to keep meself. The missus don't know; it's just his and my little arrangement and it ain't arf bad. I'll be able to set myself up right and proper, just like me friend, Queenie Featherlove, once I's paid me debt.'

Kitty batted her eyelashes and squeezed his arm. 'Come along, sir. Just for old times' sakes, eh?'

'And have half your earnings line young Mr Hollingsworth's pockets? Thank you, Kitty, but no.'

'On the 'ouse, sir. It 'ud be a pleasure.' She cocked her head and looked at him coyly. 'Ain't every day I gets to pleasure a gennul-man o' me choice. Tells yer wot — there ain't many what are as 'andsome and obliging as yerself.'

Roland gave her a wry smile. Then thrusting his hands into his pockets he withdrew, to Kitty's wide-eyed amazement, a pound note. 'Why don't you give that to your friend Queenie Lovelyfeather or whatever her name is, for safe keeping on your behalf. If she's what you aspire to, she's obviously doing something right. If you don't trust her, then keep it in a safe place until you need it.'

Kitty took the note from him and rubbed it against her cheek, eyes closed in rapture. 'I ain't never had a pound note afore, sir,' she breathed before letting out a regretful sigh. 'Contrary to expectations, poor Queenie ain't in no position to 'elp me, sir, since you might be interested to know she's got fiddle-stick's end of the bargain with our old friend, Sir Richard. It might make yer feel better to know he ain't just into trickin' coves what's got money. Although 'es done plenty more of 'em than just you, sir, and that's the truth!'

Roland's first inclination was to wince at the name. His next was to ask carefully, 'Sir Richard did the dirty on a deal with your friend? How was that?'

'Oh, all sorts,' said Kitty, warming to her theme. 'Queenie's a perticular favorite with a lot of the fancy coves, but she's the only one Sir Richard'll see. They had some kind o' 'rangement, only he's gone an' diddled her . . . feathered 'is nest at 'er expense, so she ain't about to set 'erself up, after all.'

Sadly, Kitty handed back the pound note. 'So it'll just line young Mr Hollingsworth's pocket after all, sir, and I ain't got nowhere safe to keep it.'

Roland folded the note and put it back in his pocket, looking thoughtful. Then he took Kitty's arm and began leading her towards a dark, narrow laneway which led off the main thoroughfare.

'Perhaps poor Queenie can realize her ambitions after all, Kitty,' Roland said, smiling into her questioning brown eyes, 'with you well-rewarded in the process.'

19

'The white lutestring is more appropriate, Caro, dear.'

Mrs Hawthorne put down her needlework and leaned back in her armchair with a complacent little smile as she surveyed Caro's choice of gowns for her grand come-out ball in a few days' time.

'The ruby velvet is more becoming to my complexion,' Caro protested as she caressed the gown's lustrous folds. It was draped, together with the white lutestring, over the arm of a chair in the drawing room of their London townhouse.

Though she had no intention of wearing scarlet, she was going to have to use all her wiles to avoid being forced to wear the white, which made her look even more sallow.

'Imagine wearing ruby velvet for a come-out ball! That sounds like something your mother would have done!'

Caro gritted her teeth as she gazed longingly at the dress in question. She thought it made her look more striking than she had ever looked.

She turned to her aunt. '*And* she'd have

put everyone else in the shade! Insipid pastels make me look like I'm permanently suffering the ague,' she grumbled, adding under her breath, 'Sometimes I wonder if that's your intention.' With a sigh she began to pace between the deep bay window and the fireplace, then stopped to look out into the sunlit street. 'Lady Sarah,' she said defiantly, though with a wary look at her aunt, 'says I need vibrant colours to ensure I'm noticed and that, surely, is the purpose of a coming-out ball.'

Mrs Hawthorne dropped her cross-stitch and stared, open-mouthed. 'How dare you mention the name of that disgraceful . . . imposter?' she snapped. 'If it were not bad enough that she impersonated a dead woman — or, at least, someone she thought was dead — in order to draw you girls dangerously under her influence, her recent disgrace has rendered her unacceptable to polite society. I doubt you will be seeing her at any *respectable* event this season.'

Caro's eyes flashed. 'Lady Sarah is a victim of injustice and the gossips. Since it is my understanding that the purpose of my come-out is to secure a husband, something I may do within six months, I believe I'm adult enough to speak as I choose.'

This time Mrs Hawthorne's eyes flashed.

312

The flowers adorning her bonnet swayed menacingly as she leant forward. 'Don't answer back, young lady! You are not out, yet! Roland, what have you been teaching your child?' she asked as the master of the house entered the room, looking for some mislaid article. 'Once I pooh-poohed your fears she would turn out like Venetia. Now she is the spitting image!'

Roland sighed, pausing at the escritoire in which he had been rummaging. Cecily was clearly very angry and he had not the energy for tact.

'Caro is as far from being like Venetia as is possible — with regard to Venetia's venal points to which I presume you allude, my dear Cecily.' He looked at her, a warning in his voice. 'Nor have I ever feared she was in danger of inheriting her mother's less than commendable traits. The only difference between now and a year ago is that Caro understands her own mind.' He nodded. 'Please excuse me.'

Gaining the sanctuary of his study, he stood by the French doors that stood open to the gardens and remembered the times he'd gazed upon Sarah taking a walk with the children along the path that led to the woods.

He might not have been able to save her from her indignities at Sir Richard's hands, but at least he was no longer wallowing in the self-disgusted lethargy that had plagued him during the months he had been in Switzerland with Caro.

After a lifetime spent fighting for justice for the disenfranchised, he was now fighting for justice for Sarah.

Revenge is a dish best served cold. He smiled. He had done his homework and laid his trap carefully. Sir Richard had acted with impunity for long enough; but he had not chosen his victims wisely.

Roland just wished Sarah would be around to witness the villain's impending fall from grace.

★ ★ ★

Caro wore a cream dress with a red velvet sash and three rows of red roses around the hem. It was a small victory but a victory, nevertheless.

She stared at her reflection in amazement. Even Aunt Cecily had marvelled over her transformation. The old termagant didn't need to know that the brightness of her eyes and complexion had enjoyed a little help from Tincture of Roses and Olympian Dew.

Long-ago gifts from Sarah, and unappreciated at the time, they had come into their own now. Nearly a year older, and a century wiser, Caro was determined to shine. It wasn't that she yearned for romance. In fact, right now she was decidedly wary of it, although Mr Hollingsworth and Sir Richard were rooted firmly in her past. Having survived the ordeal, she had been made stronger. She would never be a victim again.

She also intended to have her independence and follow her intellectual leanings — interests which hadn't been dampened by recent experiences. She remembered Lady Sarah's words: 'Marriage gives a woman status and independence the unmarried woman might never attain. A girl must just choose the right husband'.

Covering her face with her hands, she reflected on the night at the Hollingsworths'. She had forced herself to do so only through long training, yet she knew she had come through virtually unscathed compared with Lady Sarah. As if it weren't enough that Lady Sarah had suffered the indignities forced upon her by Sir Richard, she'd been recognised when visiting Caro's father at the inn where he'd stayed. She'd tried to learn more, but gossipy matrons did not readily divulge such details to innocents like Caro. Whatever was being said, Caro knew facts were unimportant compared with appearances. To be tainted by scandal was a crime in itself.

Twisting her hands together as she sat at her dressing table, while Mavis, her dresser, arranged her hair, she reflected on her poor unhappy papa. He must have been distraught when Lady Sarah had accepted Captain Fleming.

'Do you approve, Miss Caro?' Mavis pushed in a final pin and Caro surveyed the elaborate but becoming hairstyle, smiling. Rose buds had been tucked throughout her shiny black curls. The effect was charming.

'It's lovely, thank you. That'll be all, Mavis. I need — ' She hesitated, feeling such mixed feelings of excitement, anticipation and sorrow. ' — I need a moment or two to gather myself and then I'll be down.'

It had been more than a month since her father's abortive trip to London to propose to Lady Sarah. His behaviour had been erratic in the interim. Sometimes he had seemed distant and morose. At others it was as if the old fires burned within and he spoke to her like an adult, almost a friend.

Now here he was smiling in the doorway, telling her she looked exquisite as he offered his arm to escort her to her coming-out ball.

'You do me credit,' he said, as his eye swept from the curls that cascaded from her high crown, to the pearl-encrusted cream silk slippers that peeped from beneath the flounce of her evening dress. 'Your mother would have been so proud of you.'

'And Lady Sarah?'

He flinched but made a quick recovery, saying smoothly, 'She was a good mentor. Come,' he added as if he didn't want to be drawn on the subject. 'The carriage is waiting.'

During a rare moment of quiet later that evening, Caro surveyed the well-dressed crowd. How wonderful it would have been for Caro and her father if Lady Sarah had accepted his marriage proposal. Her rejection had had far more significant consequences for her father's state of mind than mere disappointment. She bit her lip, pondering.

Only since she had recovered her old spirit following her ordeal had she understood the extent of her father's suffering.

Within the first hour her dance card was nearly full. None of her fears of six months ago had been founded. She had not been the ugly duckling, forced to sit out dance after dance. The sallow complexion, once marred by spots, had become white and translucent, her dark hair had not needed coaxing with sugar and tongs to achieve the fashionable look of the day. It had just the right amount of curl and bounce. And her gangly, awkward figure, once rail-thin, had blossomed into a woman's body.

So it was easy to smile, to feel confident and almost happy this evening. Her father had told her in as many words how proud of her he was.

Still, something was missing.

She closed her eyes a second as she fluttered her fan in the midst of a conversation with a group of young ladies discussing the merits of feathers over artificial fruit as headwear embellishments.

Justice.

Although she and Lady Sarah and her father had survived their ordeal relatively unscathed, natural justice had been denied.

For the first time, Caro glimpsed the impulses which had driven her father his entire life. He could not bear injustice.

Philly Miniver pressed against her to compare dance cards. It seemed she, too, could not get over Caro's transformation, yet she was not mean-spirited. 'What magic potion have you been taking, Caro? Or was it all those months in the Swiss Alps? Your dance card is almost full. Much fuller than mine. Perhaps Sir Richard will ask me to dance.'

She simpered at a figure across the room.

'Sir Richard?' Caro's throat went dry.

'He's Papa's friend and ever so obliging.

Mama simply dotes on him and he's always so attentive to me. I'll get his attention. Perhaps he'll ask us both to dance — *if* you have room! Caro, where are you going?'

'I've lost a pearl button. Excuse me!' Caro whipped around, just as Philly signalled across the room.

Escape! She had to get out of here before she fainted. Before she embarrassed them all. Her mind was racing. She had to think clearly; had to be calm.

There was a knot of people gathered in the doorway. It would be impossible to simply barge past them out of the room. She veered to the left, walking fast but as gracefully as she could before she sank against the wall near a luxuriant and partially concealing flower display. A green curtain served as a partition separating the saloon from a small alcove, affording her the opportunity to nestle partially into its velvet folds and gaze at the milling guests. Taking deep breaths, she fanned herself energetically, terrified she might succumb to that most feminine of maladies: the vapours. Never, however, had any female had more cause.

Sir Richard had moved gracefully over to speak to Philly. Her friend was looking coquettishly at him from over the top of her fan points.

Surely Philly couldn't find him attractive? Caro wondered as her stomach rose up in disgust.

He must be at least twenty years older than her. Tall and thin with an insinuating smile, he had confidence but the charm of a death adder. He was a slug — a leech sustaining himself on the spoils from the underbelly of society, sucking out goodness where he could while he paraded himself as a gentleman, ruining the lives of people like herself, like Lady Sarah, like her father. People who had no recourse.

Helpless . . .

She closed her eyes, her breathing rapid. Then with one final, sustaining breath, her backbone stiffened; slowly she straightened up against the wall.

Helpless?

She took another breath. This time she felt almost calm. She blinked a few times, slowly scanning the richly garbed guests until her gaze alighted once more upon Sir Richard.

He towered over Philly. His body was bent slightly over her in a stance which, to Caro in that moment, suggested an attitude of brutal vanquishment of the female sex as a whole. Anger and revulsion swept over her and, at the same time, an all-encompassing feeling of empowerment.

It was too easy to assume that because she was a young girl she was helpless.

No, there were ways, other ways than the law — or breaking the law — whereby justice could be served.

She sucked in a short, sharp breath and her heart gave a nervous flutter.

Helpless?

Only if she lacked courage. And if she hadn't learned courage from her father, she certainly had from Lady Sarah.

Justice for herself. Justice for Lady Sarah.

She closed her eyes and thought of her darling, devoted father.

Most importantly, she wanted justice for her father.

* * *

'Hawthorne!'

Roland, striding down the passageway in the direction of the music, stopped as the red-haired giant, James Fleming, advanced towards him across the crimson Aubusson carpet. A deep flush burned the captain's throat and cheeks which, had Roland not been such a keen observer, he might have assumed was embarrassment. However the hardening of Fleming's eyes and the clenching of his jaw quickly disabused him of that notion.

321

Whatever Fleming's reasons for speaking to him, Roland had not the slightest desire to pursue a conversation with Lady Sarah's intended, yet the fact that it suggested Sarah was here made his heart beat faster. He marshalled a smile. 'Congratulations on your forthcoming nuptials. Lady Sarah is a remarkable woman,' he managed with admirable fortitude.

'She is.'

There was an awkward silence.

'I formed the greatest admiration for her character when she was a member of my household.'

'An irony, then, that the stain upon her reputation was, indirectly, on your account.'

'What?' Shocked, Roland could think of nothing else to say. He'd heard Sarah had been seen unaccompanied at a late hour and that some interfering matron had embellished this by suggesting all manner of outlandish hypotheses. Each time he'd enquired as to the exact nature of Lady Sarah's sins he'd received a different account. Certainly, he'd heard nothing which connected his name with hers.

'So you did not know, Hawthorne. I am glad to hear it, for your sake.' Fleming's look was slightly less condemning. 'Don't like your politics but didn't want to think too badly of you, if you weren't in the know. Lady Sarah's a mighty proud woman.'

When he'd gathered his wits, Roland asked, 'Why did Lady Sarah not tell me if my name were connected with hers, in the public domain?'

James grunted. 'Seems she didn't want to exert undue pressure since you'd already sent her a letter outlining your thoughts on matrimony. And that's fair enough, Hawthorne. Only I wasn't going to see such a diamond of the first water end up an ape leader through no fault of her own.' He sent Roland a challenging look. 'Well, Hawthorne, I must return to Lady Sarah.' He bowed. 'I'm looking forward to rusticating in the country. London is a cruel place.'

Still reeling, Roland returned his bow. 'I wish you well, Captain,' he managed. 'You are a lucky man.'

Captain Fleming turned on his heel and shot him a look not without reproach. 'Always been fond of the gel, and it didn't look as if anyone else was coming to her rescue,' he said pointedly.

* * *

Another trembling peacock feather.

Sarah watched it atop the emerald-green

323

toque as the feather responded to the haughty toss of its wearer's head. Plucked eyebrows arched heavenward, Sarah's erstwhile acquaintance passed by without a greeting.

The cut direct. Stock-standard treatment for those who had fallen from grace.

Except that Sarah was not a fallen woman. She had been painted as one, but thanks to James's loyalty her disgrace would be relatively short-lived, although there were those who would never receive her.

Like the peacock feather a moment ago, Sarah could feel her mouth begin to tremble.

She must find James. This propensity to tears that plagued her lately was out of character and she despised herself for it.

She wished she had not begged James to escort her to tonight's ball. He'd been right when he told her she was positively courting such reactions as the trembling peacock feather, and that she ought to stay where she was, in the country, with her father. She wanted, though, so desperately to encounter Roland one last time before she married James next week. Even if she knew seeing Roland was courting even greater heartache.

The card room was to her left, the supper room at the far end. She hesitated, scanning the crowd. James had said he would procure her a glass of champagne.

Her heart gave a nervous flutter as she surveyed the crowd. In all her life she had never felt so alone.

With her head held high she began her regal progress down the length of the room. She could just spy James, semi-obscured by a knot of gentleman.

She craned her head over a tiny voluble woman offering advice to a couple of gawkish girls, her staccato words like a volley of gunfire. Sarah almost smiled to hear her . . . until amidst a group near James she saw him.

The bourgeoning smile vanished and her heart rate sped into dangerous territory.

'I beg your pardon.' She vaguely registered spilling champagne upon a gentleman's sleeve but paid him no further heed as she negotiated the knots of chattering guests, all the while holding Roland in her sights.

He was not quite as tall as James, nor as broad-shouldered. But where James was large and forceful and brash of manner, Roland was well-proportioned, careful and reflective.

Advancing, she was conscious of the furtive glances in her direction and appreciated how Caro must feel as a fragile, vulnerable debutante. If possible her heart contracted even more. She wondered how Caro was faring.

And then she was able to see with her very own eyes, though what it was that distracted her gaze from Roland to the quivering girl in the far corner of the room she could not say.

Caro was alone, against the wall, one hand pressed against her chest, the other covering her mouth. She looked as if she were about to faint or, worse, be sick. Certainly, Sarah could see the waxy pallor of her skin from here.

Instinctively, Sarah glanced from Caro to the object upon whom Caro's gaze was fixed.

As she feared.

Sir Richard was engaged in intimate conversation with Philly Miniver in the far corner. His hooded eyes roved over her in a transparently speculative manner while Philly blushed and giggled, using her fan just as Sarah had taught her. Clearly, the young innocent was flattered. Sarah felt simply nauseated.

Caro clearly was.

Quickly, Sarah turned her footsteps in Caro's direction. She would be by her side within a couple of seconds. She would usher Caro into another room, soothe her, bolster her confidence. It was what Caro needed, but it was what Sarah needed also.

To be needed.

Her progress was interrupted by a couple of leisurely promenading dowagers, and when Sarah glanced again at the curtained alcove Caro was gone.

She frowned. Then she saw her.

Caro was advancing upon Sir Richard, looking like an avenging Valkyrie. Three more footsteps and she'd be upon him, with consequences Sarah dared not think of just now.

Altering her trajectory, Sarah hurried past a footman bearing a tray of drinks, jostled a scowling scion of the aristocracy and nearly floored a club-footed colonel.

Her hand shot out and she grasped a scrap of lace.

'Caro!'

She pulled the girl from her studied path, her own grasp stronger, and her subject more pliant than she had expected.

Caro had been wearing that mulish look of old. The consequences did not usually augur well. She extracted her from the crowd, orchestrating the potentially risky manoeuvre with all the skill of a consummate society hostess. Caro rewarded her with a scowl. But at least they were now partly obscured by the curtained alcove.

'I didn't like the look in your eye as you were advancing upon Sir Richard.' Sarah had not the time to formulate a more considered approach. Her words were blunt, her look direct. 'It will do your reputation and our cause no good if you make a scene.'

'Look at him!' hissed Caro. 'Talking to Philly like he's the most eligible man in the room, and unless one of us shows him up for what he is, he will continue to ruin lives.'

'But publicly condemning him is not the answer — '

'Credit me with some subtlety.' Caro's tone was injured. 'I was hardly about to rail at him like a Billingsgate fishwife.'

'What, then, were you about to do?'

'Entice him.'

'Entice him?'

'That's right.' Caro's eyes narrowed. Her breathing came fast and shallow. 'Entice him onto the balcony, alone. Then I was going to scream and succumb to the vapours, and when a large enough crowd was gathered I was going to accuse him of trying to . . . to kiss me.' She looked once more as if she were about to be sick before her expression became defiant.

'Caro . . . ' Sarah was lost for words. Her young, awkward charge had altered a great deal since Sarah had arrived at Larchfield. The coal-dark eyes shone with the fervour of old, but were set in a face that had matured and blossomed. Sarah had feared Caro's spirit had been extinguished by her experiences at the Hollingsworths'. She needn't have worried.

She reached out and touched Caro's cheek. 'You are an innocent. You do not know how dangerous this would be,' she said softly. 'Your reputation is your most valuable commodity. Nothing is worth endangering it.'

'Justice?'

Sarah winced, feeling the familiar ache in the region of her heart. 'Justice is never guaranteed,' she said softly.

'Clearly not, Lady Sarah, else Sir Richard would be in Newgate, not featuring on Philly's dance card.' She made a noise of disgust before adding quietly, 'And you'd be marrying Papa.' She sighed. 'But you're not, and I am more than prepared to take a risk to avenge ourselves against Sir Richard.'

Sarah frowned. 'Caro, what happened that night at the Hollingsworths' was something we are powerless to avenge. The risks we run in trying to prove the blackguardly behaviour of both Mr Hollingsworth and Sir Richard are too great to our own positions. And to your father's.'

'But if I were to claim Sir Richard guilty of enticing me onto the balcony and trying to kiss me, Papa would have no choice but to challenge him to a duel.'

So that was it. Sarah watched with dawning understanding as Caro warmed to her theme.

'Inaction is absolute anathema to Papa.

329

He'll just wither away if he's denied recourse to justice.' She hesitated, adding pointedly, 'Papa will sacrifice his own happiness if he feels he doesn't deserve it.'

Sarah knew this, but Caro's boldness had opened up new avenues of hope. It fizzed in her veins. Then she realised the futility of Caro's plan and the sudden excitement drained from her.

'Caro, do you know what lunacy your father considers duelling? Oh yes.' She interrupted the anticipated response. 'He duelled my very own Papa in his hot-headed youth, but he is wiser now.'

Caro opened her fan with an expert flick of the wrist and drew herself up tall. 'I'm very sorry we are at odds, Lady Sarah, but I love my father and would do anything to give him back his sense of honour.'

'You think I would not?' Sarah grasped her shoulder. 'Your intentions are good, but you are too vulnerable — '

Caro swung away from her. '*Someone* has to take risks,' she flared, marching into the centre of the room.

Sarah pulled her back. Caro was young with too much to lose; but Sarah had lost everything she held dear.

'It is a reckless, even stupid plan,' she countered, her voice low as she tried to conceal themselves from general observation. Caro could only be hurt if seen associating with Sarah. 'But if you promise me not to undertake it yourself, would you be satisfied if I did so?'

Turning with a slow smile, Caro touched Sarah's cheek with the tip of her fan. 'I believe that would be as effective.' There was a glint in her eye. 'Perhaps Papa would win, as a result, even more than simply justice.'

20

'You are not dancing this evening, Lady Sarah?'

Sarah ceased her regal progress across the salon and turned at the familiar voice, heart hammering, her breath catching.

Caro, declaring herself proud to be seen with her old governess, had insisted Sarah deliver her to Philly and Mrs Hawthorne, who were seated amongst a group of matrons and dowagers. Poor Philly. She'd blushed and stammered, terrified of acknowledging Sarah in front of Mrs Hawthorne, who had clearly delighted in giving Sarah the cut direct.

Torn between humiliation and amusement, Sarah had left them and was by a large potted plant several feet away from joining James when Roland stepped into her path.

His eyes raked her with appreciation, and his smile was confident. He seemed different, as if a great weight had fallen from his shoulders, and her heart soared with hope.

Bowing, he asked, 'Might I persuade you to make an exception and stand up with me for the next waltz?'

She felt the blush creep from her bosom

upwards. Unready to yield to her hopes, she inclined her head warily.

How dashing he looked in evening clothes. His hair, thick and dark, swept back from his high forehead, but she thought she saw a touch of silver at the temples that hadn't been there before. It only distinguished him more.

'Your magnanimous gesture might promote the rights of fallen women,' she said lightly, to hide her nervousness, 'though you court society's displeasure.'

'I take little account of the gossip mill, Lady Sarah.' Offering her his arm as the orchestra struck up a Viennese waltz, he led her onto the floor. 'Mrs Hawthorne is watching and I am sure you'd relish the chance to demonstrate the grace with which this fine art form can be executed.'

'I shall try to give satisfaction.'

That his smile was colluding offered another beacon of hope. When his arm encircled her waist, Sarah wilted against him. 'Embraced by society at last,' she murmured as he raised her up and they began circling.

How commandingly he held her. She could indulge in all the adolescent daydreaming she chose and he'd navigate her surely to her destination. It seemed an eternity since she'd last danced in his arms. And under such different circumstances. She closed her eyes, surrendering to the rapture of the music and the familiar warmth and strength of Roland's body inches from hers. Dare she hope this was the precursor to an even closer union?

'Why did you not tell me the whole truth, Sarah?'

The intensity of his softly spoken words jolted her back to the present. Before she could answer he went on, 'I knew you'd been seen alone and unchaperoned en route to a supposed assignation.' His look was heart-breakingly tender. 'But tonight is the first I'd heard my name mentioned.'

She clung to him as they navigated a tight turn, not trusting herself to speak. Out of the corner of her eye she caught James's disapproving look and saw Mrs Hawthorne fanning herself with a vigour unwarranted by the temperature. Beside her, Caro beamed.

Perhaps Roland saw James also, for he went on, 'I can only imagine you did not press me to do as honour dictated because you preferred Captain Fleming, after all. If that is so, I am glad you are marrying the right man. You deserve only the best, Sarah, for I've not met a braver, more admirable woman.'

'You know I don't prefer Captain Fleming,' she whispered, stumbling as her vision blurred. Roland whisked her skilfully a few inches from the ground, averting disaster as he negotiated his own footwork, then set her down again and resumed the dance with all the finesse of a gifted athlete.

Sarah's heart lurched at the quizzical, wondering look in his eye. He loved her. Minutes ago she'd not dared hope. Now hope had taken root and was flourishing in the warmth of his gaze. So how could he continue to deny her? To deny himself? Was his honour really more important than his happiness? She recalled Caro's plan in a new light. Perhaps it was not so foolish.

He squeezed her hand and murmured with feeling, 'How I long to repay you for all you have done for Caro and me.'

She closed her eyes, tensing as she strove for courage. He declared his love and his admiration, yet the caveat was always the same. His honour prevented him. 'Do you remember the last words I said before you left, Roland?' She heard the breathlessness in her voice.

He gazed down at her, silent a long moment. Then he said softly, 'They gave me hope when all hope was lost.'

The waltz was nearing the end. Desperation clawed at her. She couldn't let him walk away from her yet again. She opened her mouth to speak but he shook his head, his eyes yearning, but — it broke her heart to acknowledge it, regretful — as he murmured, 'Do you remember the last words *I* spoke to you?'

How could she forget? He'd sworn he'd not seek her out until he considered himself worthy of her. Well, time was running out.

Exhaling on a sob of frustration, she allowed him to navigate her towards the edge of the dance floor. Soon the waltz would be at an end.

Then what?

★ ★ ★

Roland studied her through narrowed eyes as she clung to him, the music thrilling to an end. He tried to make sense of it. She should hate him. Loathe and despise him. The sight of him ought to excite disgust. He'd failed her. Time and again. Instead, she gazed up at him with such transparent yearning it was enough to make him weep with frustrated longing.

He must dampen this ridiculous feeling of elation that was sweeping good sense before it. Regardless of the outcome of this evening, marriage to Fleming ensured Sarah's happiness. James Fleming was a good man: loyal and worthy of her. Roland's past matrimonial credentials hardly bolstered his cause. That aside, the bluff, good natured James would be a far better anchor for his free-spirited and headstrong beloved Sarah.

The knowledge that contact must soon be broken was almost more than he could bear. He thought of the entertainment to follow, the groundwork so carefully laid out. Later this evening would be a different matter, though the outcome was by no means assured. It would be foolish to get either of their hopes up.

But there she was, doing all in her power to convince him of her sincerity. Hadn't she already proved it? So much more than he deserved?

No. He must not weaken and take her somewhere secluded. It would be his undoing. He was entirely resolved to act only in Sarah's best interests. To take advantage of her misguided and incomprehensible tenderness would be an act of the greatest cruelty.

'What are you doing?' Sarah gasped the question as she was whisked off the dance floor and her arm was nearly dislodged from its socket as he dragged her across the room.

'Taking you somewhere secluded.' He heard the urgency in his own voice, and didn't care. Dear Lord, he had no idea what he was doing, much less what he intended doing. All he knew was that this conversation could not start and end on a dance floor in the public domain.

'I know a private alcove, a balcony,' she said, unresisting as he drew her along with him, delighting — it would appear — in the shocked expressions of those scions of respectability they passed. Certainly, the wicked gleam he saw in her eye when he glanced back, and the way the corners of her voluptuous mouth turned up, indicated she was delighting in something.

That was right, Roland remembered. Sarah knew the house better than he. Had attended balls here before.

The French doors clicked shut behind them, and they were greeted by a blast of cold air. And she without a shawl.

In his arms she would feel no cold. He would make sure of that.

He wasted no time. Without roughness — but without undue gentleness, either, for the clock was racing — he had her against the wall. One hand steadied himself against the cold stone, beside her lovely face, while the other gripped her shoulder, imprisoning her, before trailing down to encircle her waist. Her rapid breathing matched his, fuelled by the same energy. He was confident of that, now: desire.

Still he felt unable to act upon instinct: to thrust his body against hers and demand with a kiss, that she match him at all levels. Restraint was an integral part of his make-up and right now, restraint was all-important. Any future they might have together depended on what happened in the next half an hour. Succumbing to his passion now was premature.

And yet, wasn't hope the wellspring of Sarah's charm and vibrancy? It had sustained her through so much. Despite all she'd endured she'd never lost hope. The way she was looking at him now proved that.

With just a trace of tentativeness, Roland moved his face closer to hers.

'Sarah — ' he began. It was just above a whisper. He could hardly trust himself to speak steadily. The look in those limpid hazel eyes nearly undid him. All that he could have hoped for was reflected in their fathomless depths. She smiled tentatively but the invitation in the way she melded into him was implicit.

'Why do you not despise me?' he whispered, his lips a hair's breadth from hers. Her warmth and the hammering of her heart against his chest nearly drove him crazy.

'Despise you?' She cupped his chin with her hand, her look impossibly tender. 'When will you understand that you were as much a victim that night as I was? Stop blaming yourself. *I* don't.'

He hesitated, loosening his grip around her

waist, still unsure of the wisdom of this impulsive tryst.

'My darling Sarah, I want you more than I've ever wanted anything,' he ground out, restraining himself from plundering her mouth as he would have Venetia's, 'but I *must* give you this final chance to walk away.'

Sarah stamped her foot. 'For God's sake, Roland, was Venetia this patient? I've heard the gossip. The two of you couldn't keep your hands off one another. Is your reluctance towards me now a measure of your true feelings?'

Blood pounded in his ears. 'I was twenty-one, an innocent boy enslaved by love, but I *never* loved Venetia as I love you!'

'I'll say it again,' she whispered, nuzzling him, brushing her lips across his, 'If you want me, I'm yours.'

The featherlight touch was more than he could bear. Groaning, he crushed her against him, bringing his mouth down hard upon hers, extinguishing her gasp of surprise as he plundered the velvet cavern with his tongue, seeking, exploring, tasting and wanting more. And still more.

The rapid beating of her heart through the silk of his striped waistcoat drove him mad with wanting. The softness of her chestnut curls, the contours of her delectable body were like fire to a power keg. But it was the enthusiasm of her unleashed passions that most fuelled the urgency within him; the base animal instincts he'd spent years beating into submission threatened to vanquish him.

Yet the beast could not be unleashed, for he had not yet won her honourably.

With a final groan he set her from him. For several seconds they simply gazed at one another, breathless and shaking.

'Sarah!'

Guiltily, they jerked around to face James upon the threshold.

Only the faintest uprising of his eyebrows indicated he suspected anything untoward.

'I've been looking everywhere for you,' he said smoothly. 'I believe you promised me this dance.'

'I'm sorry, James.' She glanced towards Roland.

He saw the brightness of her eyes and the flush on her cheeks, noticed the faint breathlessness, and hoped Captain Fleming did not.

'Mr Hawthorne and I were just — '

'Discussing Lady Sarah's future,' Roland supplied smoothly. 'Perhaps we can continue our conversation during the next dance?' With a smile, he bowed himself out.

James turned to Sarah with a frown. 'You'll catch your death out here,' he said, taking her shoulder and propelling her indoors. 'Gad, but I'm glad it was me who stumbled upon the two of you, which is not to say I condone your behaviour, Sarah. Reckless, as always!'

Sarah bit her lip.

Out in the passage, James turned, softening at her expression. 'You bring your troubles upon your own shoulders, my dear girl.' He sighed, draping an arm about her shoulders and giving her a bracing squeeze before setting her in the direction of the ballroom. 'And I should remind you that you've already given Mr Hawthorne his chance. You are betrothed to me now, which gives me the right, I believe, to say I don't like to see you cosying up to him alone. In fact, I won't have it.'

'That's wounded male vanity, James, when you've made it clear you don't love me.'

'Yes, but you're about to become my wife. The contract has been drawn up, the matter is settled and the kind of behaviour I was witness to just now is simply unacceptable. Hawthorne is merely taking advantage.'

'I . . . I just wish I were marrying a man who loves me,' she said bleakly, ignoring the interested looks of a couple of society matrons.

James continued to propel her towards the ballroom. 'I hold you in the greatest affection. Isn't that enough?'

Sarah took a deep breath and turned, blocking his path. 'James,' she asked gently, 'would you be very disappointed if you *didn't* marry me?'

'Good God! Is that what all that was about on the balcony? Hawthorne's proposed at last? And you've accepted him?'

'No, he hasn't. James, please — ' Sarah tugged at his sleeve to bring him back to her. His wounded pride was hard to bear.

'He's toying with you, Sarah. He's made it clear he has no intention of being leg-shackled. Your admiration feeds his vanity. And he . . . ' Flushing, James looked away.

Sarah waited.

'Truth is, Sarah,' he said in a rush, his expression suddenly sympathetic as he looked into her eyes and patted her shoulder, 'the fellow has a *chère amie.*'

Sarah blinked. 'That's ridiculous,' she said scornfully.

'Oh Sarah,' he muttered, 'I knew you'd take it like that. You might think it's a bag of moonshine and I'm trying to bamboozle you because I don't care for the fellow. Only I know this to be the truth.' He hesitated, adding, 'Though you're not to think *I'm* in the habit of frequenting bawdy houses — '

Relief made her gasp, 'So that is where he was seen?'

The Hollingsworths'! Someone must have observed him enter the brothel.

'No . . . ' James appeared to be weighing up his words. 'Fact is, Lady Condon made it known. She was scandalized Hawthorne would carry his politics over the boundaries of what most people consider acceptable.'

Sarah waited, still sceptical.

'Lady Condon visited her seamstress and was forced to pass the time of day with a . . . female, clearly from the Cyprian corps, who was being fitted for a modish ensemble.' He sighed. 'Hawthorne was with her, offering his considered opinion. He . . . was financing her.'

'She must have been a friend.'

'She was no one Lady Condon had ever set eyes upon.'

'A visitor from abroad?'

James looked at her with even greater sympathy. 'I believe the violent orange hue of her glorious ringlets is not a colour favoured by the respectable. Besides,' he added, 'I saw Hawthorne with my own eyes lead a bit o' muslin into a dark alley off the Haymarket not three weeks ago.'

Sarah shook her head as if to clear of it of doubt. James did not lie, yet there had to be some explanation. With dignity, she took the arm he offered as they continued their

344

progress towards the ballroom.

'He's a dark horse,' James persisted, oblivious to her feelings. 'His wife was infamous. The betting book at White's is offering ten to one the daughter is going the way of her mother — '

Sarah swung round furiously, nearly knocking into a couple who had to sidestep past them. 'How dare you slander Caro!' she flared. 'Nor have you the right to cast slurs upon Mr Hawthorne's reputation on account of hearsay. If you want my opinion, the bit o' muslin he supposedly led away was a lass in distress whom he was offering assistance.'

'Sarah, that's doing it too brown,' said James, exasperated. 'All right, I'm sorry I slandered Miss Hawthorne. I'd forgotten she was your charge for three months. But really, Hawthorne doesn't deserve your slavish defence. Now where are you going?'

She had to find Caro. She'd been away too long and Caro was inclined to rashness.

'To mend a tear in my skirt, James,' she bit out.

Surely James's allegations couldn't be true, she told herself. Though what did a man plagued by loneliness do to ease his frustration? She didn't really know much about these things.

A cotillion was in progress as she entered

through the double doors, but it felt claustrophobic in the crowded ballroom. James had not gone after her. She knew he thought she was being ridiculous; that he didn't believe she'd end their betrothal so she could wed Mr Hawthorne. Well, he didn't believe Mr Hawthorne harboured those kinds of feelings. But he did. She knew he did.

She squared her shoulders. Marrying Roland Hawthorne was exactly what she intended doing. With a sigh she sagged against the wall near the supper room. That was if Roland could sink his pride or put a bullet through Sir Richard's head.

A footman bearing aloft a silver tray offered her a glass of champagne. She drank it too quickly, trying to find a reason for Roland's earlier behaviour. He'd surely not have kissed her like that if he was going to allow her to marry James? In which case, she thought, sudden excitement flaring within her, he must have come up with some plan to avenge himself against Sir Richard? That would account for the confidence she'd noted earlier.

Pushing herself back from the wall, she remembered the urgency of finding Caro. If Roland was forced into action against his better judgment he'd not thank his daughter for it.

Caro was no longer with Philly. When a

thorough search of the card room, ballroom and ladies' dressing room did not yield the girl, she became anxious.

Interrupting James discussing his latest horseflesh with Colonel Marshall, Sarah asked if they'd seen her.

'Heading for the balcony not long ago,' replied the colonel. 'Couldn't believe me eyes when she was pointed out as Lady Venetia's gel. Already rivalling her mother in the looks department, and it'd appear Sir Richard's as taken with her as he was with the mother.' He cleared his throat. 'Beg pardon, Lady Sarah. Forgot you'd spent time under their roof.'

Sarah hadn't waited for his apology. Almost running, she jostled her way through the crowd in the direction of the balcony.

Why had Caro not listened to her?

Because she thought Sarah had abandoned her with empty promises?

Perhaps an opportunity had afforded itself which, to the impulsive Caro, seemed too good to resist.

She heard voices on the other side of the door which led outside. With her hand on the doorknob, she glanced over her shoulder to ensure she was not being observed. She had almost pushed the door open by the time she registered the incredible sight in the ballroom behind her.

Roland was one of three gentlemen conversing in a knot in the middle of the room. Three gentlemen and one lady — if Kitty of the Hollingsworth nunnery could be called a lady.

Sarah froze.

Dressed in an elegant evening gown of lilac silk with roses upon the flounce, her dark hair curled at the front and drawn up in a modish topknot of ringlets, Kitty looked the epitome of the well-bred young lady she was obviously at pains to emulate. The three gentlemen were talking amongst themselves with the occasional nod of acknowledgement at Kitty, who smiled expansively.

Kitty and Roland?

Sarah's amazement turned to confusion tinged with anger. Not even Roland would be brazen enough in his pursuit of egalitarianism to bring Kitty to a society ball. Especially not when his daughter was making her come-out.

Jealousy vied with common sense.

What was he playing at? And who was the Cyprian with the violent orange ringlets James had mentioned?

At that moment Roland glanced up and caught her eye.

Then, he smiled.

It was such a candid, warm, transparent smile that Sarah was nearly undone. All her doubts and anxieties vanished upon the instant.

The gentle murmur of the room dulled to nothing, the moving throng of colour becoming a muted haze. Sarah was conscious only of the warmth reflected in his eyes, and the unbreakable bond between them. Seemingly physical, it spanned the distance from her heart as she stood upon the threshold of the balcony, to Roland, half a room away.

He raised his glass in a silent toast and his eyes crinkled in a smile. Slowly and clearly, he mouthed, 'I love you.'

Then Caro screamed.

21

There was little gratification in seeing Sir Richard pale and mute with shock as Sarah thrust open the double doors to the balcony.

Within seconds she became one of seemingly dozens of onlookers. Murmuring, they gaped at Caro, who stood with her back against the stone balustrade facing Sir Richard.

Caro was badly compromised. Sarah imagined Roland's devastation. His own daughter, compromised by Sir Richard? It would be more than he could bear. No man of honour or loving father could let this go unchallenged.

She watched Caro remove her hands from her tear-stained face and open her mouth.

To condemn Sir Richard?

So she had gone ahead with her foolhardly plan, giving her father no recourse but to defend her reputation through pistol or sword, thereby regaining his manhood in the process.

Except that Roland had no need to regain his manhood. He had matters well under control.

Sarah did not need this. Not when

happiness was so nearly within her grasp. Well, she was not prepared to stand by and watch Roland shot through the heart or forced into exile for taking honour to extremes.

'Caro,' she cried, sweeping forward to envelop the girl in her arms so as to stifle the anticipated diatribe. 'It was such a little spider.'

She raised her eyes to Roland, who'd just appeared, as she crushed Caro's face against her shoulder. Then, as if unaware of the crowd of goggling onlookers that flanked him, explained, 'Caro and I were taking the air when Sir Richard stepped onto the balcony . . . just as a great, big, ugly spider suspended itself from the lintel. You *know* Caro's feelings about spiders. I went to find something with which to kill it.'

Caro struggled within her grasp but Sarah was not about to release her. Not until Sir Richard was gone.

With a look of studied exasperation, she smiled at the man who had humiliated and ruined her, forcing down her nausea at the sight of his hooded eyes, wary and cold. How well she remembered them glinting with lascivious speculation, before he'd coldly condemned her to social isolation. 'My apologies, Sir Richard.' She stroked Caro's hair. 'You must have imagined you were walking in upon a couple of wild women.' With a shaky laugh, she turned back to Caro.

How empowered she felt at the sight of his confused silence. By taking the offensive, Sarah had put him on the back foot.

Responding to Sarah's silent signal, Roland bowed him out, together with the remaining guests, then came to stand at her side. 'What is the meaning of all this?' He sounded angry, but uncertain also.

Caro wrenched herself free of Sarah's embrace and faced her old governess with blazing eyes.

'You ruined everything!' she hissed. 'I thought you loved my father!'

'I love him too much for you to risk his life with your hare-brained scheme,' Sarah said, her expression softening as she turned it upon Roland. Caro, fiery and impetuous as ever, would thank her for it later. 'Now come, it's freezing out here.'

'Gratified though I am by all this talk of love,' said Roland as they stepped into the warmth, 'I would appreciate an explanation.' He tilted Caro's head up with a finger beneath her chin, adding, 'Though I shudder to think what your 'plan' involved.'

He shepherded them into a deserted passage just off the ballroom. Old masters stared down at them. Sarah moved to Roland's side, standing so close their bodies touched. A frisson of electricity charged through her, reinforced by a surge of exultation as she felt Roland stiffen with similar awareness.

'Caro was concerned you were in the grip of a crisis of masculinity — ' She was unable to resist stroking his sleeve. ' — resulting from your inability to defend us at the Hollingsworths'.'

Roland glanced between the two women. 'Caro is very perceptive,' he said, 'but it is not for her — or you, Sarah — to manufacture a situation whereby I can demonstrate my — er — manhood.'

He sighed, the noise of muted gaiety just beyond the double doors. 'I want justice as badly as you, but a public justice, more meaningful than that wrought at the end of a sword.' He turned to his daughter. 'Caro, if I were to demand satisfaction, what do you suppose might happen to me — and to the rest of you? Do you know what a crack shot Sir Richard is reckoned to be?'

'Such modesty,' Sarah murmured. She was well aware of Roland's skill with a pistol.

Roland pulled out a snowy handkerchief and offered it to his snivelling daughter. 'Now dry your tears,' he said gently, 'and look at me. I have a request, but if you feel you're not strong enough to oblige me, I'll ask Lady Sarah.'

They looked at him enquiringly.

'I have brought a companion with me tonight who will entertain the audience with a piece that has been — ' He slanted a smile in Sarah's direction. ' — carefully prepared. I had hoped, Caro, you might accompany her on the pianoforte.'

Caro didn't immediately pick up the nuance. Her recent humiliation was too fresh.

But Sarah clapped her hands and exclaimed, 'Why, Caro, you can play almost anything by sight and you've gained such confidence since that evening I instructed you in deportment.' Gripping Roland's arm, she went on, 'You may recall it. I had borrowed one of your late wife's gowns for the occasion.'

To her surprise he seemed reluctant to meet her look as he murmured with feeling, 'I remember it well.'

'Only I believe I did such a clever job at pretending to be your late wife, you actually believed I *was* your late wife, returned from the dead.'

Roland made a pretence of adjusting her hand upon his sleeve. 'That kiss was for *you*,' he said in a low voice, bending his head so his lips brushed her ear, 'though it took me a while to admit it to myself.'

She shivered at his touch, detaining him with a sly whisper. 'Are you sure you didn't wish it *was* Venetia? It cannot have escaped you that my response was not exactly lacklustre.'

He drew himself up and regarded her in silence. Then with quiet deliberation, he told her, 'I've *never* wished you were Venetia. That was the evening — ' He had difficulty uttering the words. ' — you broke through my defences and it was all over for me.' He glanced at his daughter. 'I was ashamed at how I scandalized and upset you, Caro,' he said. 'But that was the evening I realized I was unable to live without your governess.'

Caro blushed. 'I know.'

Sarah's heart swelled and she nestled closer to Roland. They were only a few feet from the double doors that opened into the ballroom. Anyone might appear but she didn't care.

Roland leant down to cup her face in both his hands. His voice was soft but urgent as he said, 'If this evening does not go as planned, Sarah, you are still betrothed to James.'

'No, Roland — '

He stayed her protest with a finger to her lips.

'This song,' Caro interrupted, frowning, oblivious now to her elders. 'Papa, if you don't think it too difficult I'm prepared to court the embarrassment of a poor rendering.'

He gave a short laugh. 'Let me reassure

you, Caro, your skill will not be under scrutiny.' Then, as he pushed the doors open and they stepped across the threshold, he added, 'I have worked very hard these last weeks to ensure the audience's attention will be focused elsewhere.'

★   ★   ★

Anticipation thrummed through Sarah's veins. What on earth could have inspired Roland with such expectation and fear of failure, in equal measure?

Since none of the guests this evening was inclined to engage her in conversation she sought out Kitty, who remained quietly within the ranks of the three gentlemen with whom Roland had been conversing earlier.

'Kitty?'

Kitty's eyes widened. 'Ssh, M'lady. I ain't s'posed to speak English.'

Sarah took her arm and drew her aside.

'I'm s'posed to be a Polish princess,' she said in response to Sarah's look of enquiry. ''twere Mr Hawthorne wot said I could come.' She gave a beatific smile as she clasped her hands to her scrawny chest. 'Said was there anything I wanted above all else in the world and I told him, 'to go to a grand ball like a princess and see real diamonds, only I know the likes o' me wouldn't never see summat like that.' '

'You wanted to go to a ball more than be free of the Hollingsworths?' Sarah asked in amazement.

'That's what Mr Hawthorne asked, too. I told him, 'course I wanted that, only that weren't never going to happen while that piece of paper gave them such a hold on me.'

Sarah smiled. 'What did he say to that?'

'Said he reckoned he could find a man o' law who'd be able to look into that piece of paper and do a deal with the Hollingsworths what would release me shortly.' Her eyes shone with excitement. 'Fact is, he reckons his lawyer chap'll have it all organized within the next few days. Then he said he *wanted* me to come to this 'ere ball tonight *and* paid for me dress.' Reverently, she touched the folds of her lilac skirts. As she returned her attention to Sarah, she added hastily, 'Weren't in the way of payment, like, M'lady, as in I weren't required to do nuffink in return.' Frowning, she added, '*My* fine gown weren't, leastaways.'

'And your friend's finery was?' Despite James's allegations Sarah was not perturbed.

'Well, a bit of bartering went on, I guess — ' Kitty shot Sarah a puzzled stare. 'Mr Hawthorne told you already? He said it were to be a grand surprise. Me lips were buttoned 'pon pain 'o death.'

'I was only guessing, Kitty. Just like my guess is that your friend is a striking redhead.'

'That's right. I'd forgot you'd met Queenie, then, M'lady. Didn't think you'd 'ad the pleasure.' Kitty smiled ingenuously. 'She's the star attraction this evening and weren't to show herself 'til she steps out and — ' She took a deep breath and frowned, memorizing the words. ' — 'strikes awe and admiration into the 'earts of all who behold 'er.' ' She gave a decisive nod. 'Oh, yes, and the fear o' God, too. That's quotin' Mr Hawthorne.'

'Sarah — ' It was James at her elbow. He bowed to Kitty.

'James, this is Princess — '

'Anna Pawlak,' Kitty supplied quickly.

Sarah explained, 'I've been naming various personages to her this evening, though she speaks no English.'

Before James could respond, Roland joined them. 'I believe the entertainment is about to begin.' He sounded calm, almost bored, and Sarah struggled to stifle all signs of her almost unbearable excitement. What could he have up his sleeve?

James gave a long-suffering sigh. 'Lord, I wonder what Lady Ponsonby has on the bill this evening: Miss Lavinia Longbotton swooning over her *Childe Harold* recitation?'

Roland gave Sarah a colluding look. 'I think the evening promises something a little less insipid.'

James's eyes narrowed. 'Hawthorne, might I remind you that Lady Sarah and I are to be married within the sennight. I trust you weren't offended at not receiving an invitation — '

'Not at all,' Roland reassured him. 'I'd rather stoke the fires of Hell.'

'Good Lord — '

Bowing, Roland turned to leave, then checked himself. 'My apologies, Fleming. That was discourteous. Nevertheless, I would ask to resume the subject of Lady Sarah's nuptials when tonight's entertainment has finished. Excuse me, but Lady Ponsonby is signalling, for I've the duty of introducing tonight's guest of honour.' His gaze caught and held Sarah's. Impulsively, he clasped her hand.

'Lady Sarah, my protégé, Miss Queenie Featherlove, is performing a work composed by me, in your honour.' He hesitated and there was urgency in his tone as he added, 'Listen closely, for it is my sincerest desire that her words find their way to your heart.'

Before James could respond with justified outrage, he put out a hand to his worthy competitor.

'Captain Fleming,' he said, 'though I deplore

your politics as you do mine, we do share a common interest: Lady Sarah's happiness. As one man of honour to another, may I be allowed a final opportunity to determine the lady's feelings with regard to myself?' He sent Sarah a heartfelt look. 'At the conclusion of tonight's entertainment that will no longer seem so outrageous a request.'

James responded with brittle pride. 'I assure you, Lady Sarah's happiness is paramount. I doubt you can convince me you are the better man, Hawthorne. But if you can convince Lady Sarah — '

A hush fell upon the audience as Roland strode onto the dais. Then a surprised murmur rippled through the crowd.

'Good Lord!' breathed James.

'Heavens! I don't believe — ' gasped a woman near Sarah.

Sarah couldn't help but silently agree. Queenie Featherlove was eye-catching, there was no doubt about that. Despite the costly accoutrements, including a spectacular string of pearls Sarah reckoned cost more than the diamonds worn by the duchess to her right, she made no secret of her trade. The way she thrust her bosom forward as she adjusted her plunging neckline, the turquoise feathers of her headdress swaying wildly, made no secret of her pride in it.

'Ladies and gentlemen,' Miss Featherlove crooned in a throaty but carrying tone, her arms sweeping wide to embrace the audience, 'It is my pleasure tonight to sing for you a song composed especially to honour a dear friend of mine — ' She twisted her head as if searching for someone. When her gaze alighted upon Sir Richard she gave a dazzling smile.

'Sir Richard, you were not leaving, I trust? My song is for *you*.'

Caught like a rabbit in a shaft of light, Sir Richard appeared to deliberate. His route to the open double doors was cut off as the interested crowd closed in.

A prostitute performing publicly in honour of a baronet? It was unprecedented. Not the least cause for curiosity verging on scandal was the fact that Roland Hawthorne, an MP known for his radical egalitarianism, was promoting the woman and the entertainment.

Caro made her way to the piano, Sarah joining her to turn the pages. Like the rest of the crowd that evening, they gasped as Miss Featherlove named the personage she honoured. Then they smiled at one another.

'Better than swords?' whispered Sarah.

Caro nodded as she sank onto the stool and struck the first chord. 'Better than swords,' she concurred softly.

Miss Featherlove inclined her head in response

to the musical introduction before launching into her song in a fine, strong contralto, her peacock feathers trembling with emotion.

Dickie Byrd sat in an old fir tree,
Gloating over his spoils, he rubbed his hands with glee.
Laugh, Dickie Byrd, laugh, there's plenty more money.

There was appreciable movement in the audience as people strained their necks to search out the hapless Sir Richard. From her elevated position to one side of the dais, Sarah could just see him, a lone figure scrutinized by the crowd. His hooded eyes roamed over Miss Featherlove before apparently seeking Roland, and his thin lips curled in a snarl as he ran a finger around his neck to loosen his cravat.

Dickie Byrd promised an equal half to me,
'To feather your nest,' he said tenderly.
Laugh, Queenie, love, laugh,
Together we'll have so much money.

Sarah turned the pages, giving Caro's shoulder a reassuring squeeze as she glanced around the room. Some people appeared mesmerized, others distinctly uncomfortable. She guessed there were more than a few gentlemen who had sampled the charms of the inimitable Miss Featherlove.

The meaning of the song was quite clear and Sir Richard, publicly unmasked for his duplicity, was powerless to refute her musical allegations.

Miss Featherlove's massive bulk swayed in time to the tune, her loving glance never once leaving Sir Richard's pallid countenance.

Dickie Byrd said: 'Use your charm, Queenie,
Ferret out those secrets, enticingly,
Then we can laugh, yes we can laugh, over
*   all that money.'*

He was powerless, thought Sarah with a thrill. Just as she had been powerless as his captive. Roland had engineered this situation to liberate her and to grant herself and Caro the satisfaction of seeing their tormentor publicly humiliated. Her heart swelled with pride.

The Duke of Lomar snuggled up to me,
Lord Basil Swain and Harry Stokes said: 'My
*   dear Queenie,*
How you'd laugh, love,
How you'd laugh,
If you knew how we made our money.'

The murmurs grew and the three men named in Queenie's song, young blades well known for winning and losing fortunes upon the turn of a card, wiped their sweating brows and fingered their collective stocks as if they needed more air.

No one, however, looked as uncomfortable as Sir Richard, whose compressed lips and narrowed eyes, as he fixed them upon Roland, made no secret of his loathing.

Sarah was glad of the protection her position on the dais afforded her.

Across the crowd her eyes locked with Roland's. Her heart turned a clumsy, lurching somersault before nestling cosily into position. A look of understanding passed between them. Though she was enjoying every minute of this, anticipation clawed at her. Soon Roland could declare himself publicly.

Miss Featherlove raised her voice to be heard above the din, snatches of song plunging others into the mire of scandal.

No matter how much more of Sir Richard's villainy was revealed in this little ditty, Miss Featherlove's performance promised a scandal of such proportions that he would never be received in respectable society again.

Roland's focus shifted and Sarah's gaze darted back to Sir Richard. She half expected to see him bolt through the French doors which opened onto the terrace.

He was halfway there already.

Then he hesitated. She saw him square his shoulders before he turned towards Miss Featherlove. In half a dozen strides he was up the stairs and onto the dais.

The songstress faltered only briefly as he approached her with angry deliberation. Sarah turned another page of music while Caro continued playing without a false note.

Only when Sir Richard put his hands to Miss Featherlove's throat did she falter. Caro stopped playing. The dowager to Sarah's right gasped.

'Release Miss Featherlove.' Roland spoke quietly, but his voice reverberated in the sudden silence.

'I'd rather handle a snake,' Sir Richard ground out, 'but perhaps you forget, Hawthorne, that the necklace belongs to me.'

With a cry, Queenie gripped the pearls as Sir Richard fumbled with the clasp.

A low, excited hum rippled through the crowd.

'Legally, my late wife's property is my property,' observed Roland, as he crossed the dais towards them. 'You should have thought of that before you bestowed such a handsome gift upon Venetia.'

Sir Richard's face contorted with rage. Roughly, he jerked Queenie within the circle of his arm. 'I was exiled because of debts incurred procuring Venetia that . . . tribute to my *enduring* admiration.'

'You did more than admire her,' said Roland calmly. 'You became her slave in the process. Do not blame me for that.' Glancing between the audience and his adversary, he indicated the door with a flourish. 'I think it's time to leave, Sir Richard.'

Sir Richard's hands dropped from Queenie's throat. She took an unsteady step backwards.

'Pistols or swords, Hawthorne.' Very deliberately the baronet flung down one black glove. It landed with a dull thud upon the stage at Roland's feet.

Sarah's heart lurched wildly and her knees went weak. No man of honour would refuse a challenge. Yet this was lunacy. And wasn't it what Roland had been striving to avoid?

To her surprise Roland smiled pityingly at Sir Richard.

'My point has already been proved. Why would I take up arms now that the whole world knows you for the villain you are?' Looking past Sir Richard, Roland found Sarah. In a moment he was at her side. She felt his comforting warmth through the thin fabric of her bead-encrusted muslin evening gown. Longing rippled through her but she fought the urge to sag against him. Let him deal with Sir Richard first.

'So you are a coward then, Hawthorne?' Sir Richard taunted. 'Venetia said as much. How many times were you cuckolded?'

Fighting her indignation, Sarah pushed Caro back down onto her seat.

'My late wife's memory is not under discussion.' Roland refused to be drawn.

It was clear Sir Richard's frustration was growing at the infertile ground upon which his taunts were falling. Yet Sarah was conscious of Roland's tenseness as he called on those reserves of restraint which had served him so well.

She was equally conscious of Caro's efforts to restrain herself and prayed the girl did not burst out with something inappropriate. Caro had grown in maturity but she was like a wound-up spring when her emotions were engaged.

Queenie, now standing halfway between Roland and Sir Richard, fingered the pearls nervously. Hardly surprising, observed Sarah, in view of the way Sir Richard was eyeing them balefully, as if he would pounce any moment and rip them from around her neck.

The baronet scratched the side of his large Roman nose. 'Here's the bargain, Hawthorne. Return my necklace and I'll not mention the . . . er . . . compromising situation in which I found myself with your *dear* friend, the most delectable Lady Sarah in a certain house of ill repute.'

Dear Lord, was she going to succumb to a fainting fit at the most inappropriate time of her life? Sarah closed her eyes as she swayed. She wondered how many in the audience would attribute the hot blush that crept up from her neckline as the stain of guilt. Not that it mattered; it would merely endorse what was already accepted as the truth.

Then she felt the wool of Roland's coat against her forearm and the surreptitious squeeze of her hand.

He was giving her strength and courage, just as she had given him the same that night at the Hollingsworths'. She stifled a sob as he left her to return to Queenie.

'Miss Featherlove, I hope you'll forgive such an ungentlemanly act,' he apologized, as his hands went to the nape of her neck to unclasp her necklace.

No. Sarah didn't quite say it. She was shocked; horrified. *It doesn't matter*, she wanted to say to him. He must not cave in, publicly, on her account.

She saw Sir Richard's triumphant sneer as Roland held the pearl necklace like a delicate, sparkling spider's web, suspended between his hands.

But the victorious scorn was replaced with confusion, then frustrated outrage as Roland resumed his place at Sarah's side. Only it was not Sarah he addressed, but a blushing Caro.

'This belonged to your mother and is, by rights, yours now. Its history is not a happy one, but its destiny is yours to decide.'

Caro rose slowly. Unable to speak, she stared first at her father, then at the assembled guests. A movement from Sir Richard made her turn her head.

Admiringly, Sarah watched as Caro stood her ground, for he looked in that moment as if he would wrest the necklace from her grasp if she dared take it.

Caro put out a tentative hand to touch the pearls, then recoiled as if stung. 'No, Papa! I don't want them!'

Roland nodded.

'Sir Richard.' He smiled as Sir Richard stepped forwards as if he expected Roland to relinquish them to him after all.

'Perhaps, Sir Richard, you wish Lady Sarah to have the pearls as a token of atonement. It was, after all, on your orders that she was detained at the address to which she was directed — ' He waited for the excited murmur this inevitably created before continuing. ' — used as a pawn for vengeance against myself.'

The low, excited murmur grew in volume. Above the din Roland continued, 'Lady Sarah should be honoured for her bravery that night.' He shook his head, his expression one of disgust. 'Instead, she has been pilloried, her reputation besmirched. She deserves far more than just those pearls, Sir Richard.'

Sarah clasped her hands to her breast as she gazed about the room. She could almost believe she saw the scales falling from people's eyes. Even the way Mrs Hawthorne regarded her thoughtfully through narrowed eyes suggested she was reconsidering her opinion of her. Nevertheless, Sarah knew there were many other crimes for which she'd not forgive the former governess.

James, as if sensing her focus, transferred his fulminating stare from Sir Richard to Sarah. The smile he sent her made her heart pound with joy and relief so that she nearly missed Roland's next words. James, like every other person in the room, now saw how things stood with her and Roland. And he condoned it.

'Lady Sarah, unless you object, I would like to give these pearls to Miss Featherlove. They will fund a charitable project patronised by a certain Polish Princess in our midst tonight.'

'Cor blimey, sir,' gasped Kitty, blushing

fiercely as all eyes turned on her, 'if that ain't arf rich!'

'No!'

Turning at Sir Richard's bellow of rage and gasps from the audience, Roland thrust the pearls at Queenie, sidestepping as Sir Richard barrelled towards him, manic desperation lighting his hooded eyes. Focusing on the pearls, Sir Richard altered his trajectory at the last moment.

There was barely enough time to act. Queenie screamed as her former lover, face contorted with malevolence, prepared to knock her off her feet and make off with the necklace. With a short, sharp upper thrust Roland sliced his fist into Sir Richard's jaw. Screaming with pain and rage, Sir Richard crashed to the ground.

'Can a member of the judiciary help our friend off the stage?' Roland asked.

A response came from several quarters accompanied by a smattering of applause as Sir Richard was picked up bodily and removed.

Roland inclined his head. 'I look forward to furnishing a statement of events involving our friend's villainy, however I still have unfinished business with Lady Sarah.'

He beckoned to her, his gaze full of love as she stepped towards him. Reaching out, he took both her hands and she caught her breath at the jolt of sensation which slammed through her at his touch.

Trembling, she smiled at him, her heart almost bursting with joy as they locked gazes and she witnessed the depth of his feeling for her.

'I denied you the pearls because of the evil with which they are associated,' he said clearly, for all to hear, 'but I want you to know you have *carte blanche* to choose whatever baubles take your fancy when we are wed.'

Sarah intended more than *carte blanche* with regard to baubles. Roland was hers now. Hers to love and cherish.

And to make her feel not only that she had met her match but that she was the luckiest woman on the planet.

'Caro, a final chord, if you will.'

As relief and love surged through Sarah, she returned the kindling look in Roland's eye, squeezing his hands and longing for the crowds to disperse so they could be alone.

He had staked a great deal on this, she knew. And her answer, though she could not utter a word, was for all to see.

Caro obliged with an elegant few bars and Roland, flanked by Miss Featherlove and Sarah, drew them towards the centre of the stage.

Sarah gazed out across the sea of rapt

faces, her heart near to bursting. She wished her father could have witnessed Roland's performance. It would make him revise his assessment of him as a buttoned-up Puritan, she thought. And he'd have appreciated his showmanship.

Like actors on a stage, Roland raised the two women's hands in the air and, to a final flourish of notes from Caro, they sank into a deep bow.

Rising, Roland brought Sarah's hand to his lips and kissed it extravagantly. 'Ladies and gentlemen, the show is over,' he said loudly. 'Thank you for coming here tonight.'

'And thank you, my love,' he murmured, his breath tickling Sarah's ear as she nestled against him, savouring his warmth as they watched the procession of carriages pass beneath their secluded balcony. 'You were most obliging.'

Sarah raised her hand to trace the watered silk of Roland's waistcoat. Wonderingly, she stroked his beloved forehead before cupping his strong jaw.

'Surely you knew, dearest Roland, I'd decided during my first days at Larchfield that you would be my husband?'

'I hadn't realized your feelings went to quite those extremes,' he said with a smile, 'though you hinted at a certain fondness for my company. But marriage? What would a beautiful, confident young woman want with a damaged, taciturn fellow like me?'

It seemed he couldn't keep his hands off her, stroking first her cheek, and now, tenderly, her throat and collarbone. Tremors of love and excitement rippled through her.

'I saw the potential, my darling.' Snuggling closer, she added, 'I knew I could mould that damaged, taciturn fellow into the hero of my dreams.' She gave a contented sigh. 'And what a hero you turned out to be.'

He looked down at her and the expression of bemusement on his lean, ascetic face, so much more handsome now that the lines of tension and worry had relaxed, amused her. She gave a short laugh. 'Surely you must have been entirely confident of my answer?'

He brushed a tendril back from her face, his smile heart-stoppingly tender. 'I certainly was not. Awaiting your response on stage was more terrifying than approaching your father.'

'What?' She gasped, twisting out of his grasp. 'My father has already given us his blessing?' Disbelief mingled with joy as she clasped her hands together. Her beloved, irascible father, whose determination to enforce upon her an unpalatable marriage had had such wide-sweeping repercussions. Yet he had already sanctioned her one true love? She could hardly believe it.

'What's this?' asked Roland, touching her cheek. 'You didn't cry just now when I told you I couldn't live without you.'

'You needn't sound so wounded.' Sarah laughed through her tears and hugged him tightly. 'Once I'd decided to marry you I knew the hardest thing to reconcile would be Papa's displeasure. Especially — ' She sent him a wry glance. ' — when I learned the two of you had been at each other like a couple of warring schoolboys.'

'I suspect your father would take as much exception to that undignified description as I do.' Roland drew himself up with exaggerated dignity. 'He certainly took exception, initially, to my presumption.'

Sarah shook her head wonderingly. 'I wish I could have been there. Did he throw anything?'

'I was a little concerned when he attacked the fire with such energy, then didn't set down the poker as he addressed me.' With a smile, Roland patted her hand which now rested against his lapel. 'But after a couple of brandies during which I explained the situation, rather as I did on stage, his mood became much more sanguine.'

'Oh, Roland,' Sarah burst out with feeling, 'I knew you'd win him over, just as you did me.'

'Well, there were differences, but as regards

timing, I hope you'll forgive my impatience.' He cleared his throat, suddenly awkward. 'I couldn't wait three weeks for the banns to be read, after all the time we've wasted.'

Sarah's eyes lit up with joy. Standing on her toes, she twined her arms around his neck. 'You've arranged a special licence?'

Clasping her wrists so as to ease the stranglehold she had on him, he said, 'Your father, in fact, offered to relieve me of the task, since I had so much to organise this evening.' His sigh held relief as he added, 'I'm glad you feel as I do, my darling. I was afraid you'd be disappointed at not preparing the event to your satisfaction. In about three hours, we'll be man and wife.'

'Three hours!' Sarah cried, wrenching out of his arms, her hand fingering the simple gold cross at her throat.

'Sarah, what is it?' Drawing her back to him, Roland's look was a study in anguished confusion.

'Two things, Roland.' She could see his suspense was agony and knew it was wicked to take advantage of the power she had over him. With an extravagant sigh she asked, 'Don't you remember your promise?'

He seemed at a loss.

'On stage when you gave the pearls to Miss Featherlove you promised I could choose any jewels I liked.' Maintaining her stricken look she went on, 'Surely you don't imagine I can be married with just this simple gold cross?'

'Sarah, it's three o'clock in the morning.' His brow still creased with concern, he added, 'Which is not to say I don't fully intend — '

Sarah laughed, and with a growl Roland snatched her back within the circle of his arms once he understood she was amusing herself at his expense. Narrowing his eyes, he asked, 'And the second thing?'

Sarah met his gaze with studied earnestness. There was no levity in her tone this time.

'I want a proper proposal, Roland.' Only as she made the request did she realize how important it was to her. 'Many men I've not loved have asked me to marry them.' She swallowed. 'James asked me, but he might as well have been buying a cow at market, and then you, Roland — ' She reached up her hand to stroke his cheek, willing him to understand. ' — You began to propose when you came to see me that day, though it sounded as if you were being forced because duty required it of you.'

Slowly Roland nodded. He understood. With a wry smile he said, 'And on stage I skipped the proposal, assuming you'd make your feelings clear if you objected.'

Sarah nodded.

Straightening to his full height, he drew her into the moonlight and for a long moment gazed down at her, as if the sight were to sustain him through all life's battles.

'Lady Sarah,' he said, his voice soft and impassioned as he lowered himself on bended knee, 'if I could be everything you ever wanted, I'd have no hesitation in asking you to make me the happiest man by agreeing to be my wife.' Kissing her hand, his smile was wondering. 'But if I let the fear of my shortcomings stand in the way of my happiness, I'd forever wonder what might have been. Sarah, words cannot express my admiration of your strength and courage — ' There was a quaver in his voice. ' — and above all, your loyalty. Nor can you know the extent to which they've sustained me.'

Sarah felt the great lump in her throat swell. Shocked by the depth of love and sincerity she saw in his fevered eyes, she needed the catharsis of being in his arms once more, but he was not finished.

'You taught me never to give up hope and to you I credit my salvation. If you would do me the honour of being my wife, history would know no happier man.'

'Oh, Roland!' cried Sarah, hurling herself at him as he rose, covering his face with kisses and catching him off balance so that he stumbled against the wall. 'That was far and away the best proposal I've ever had. Yes! Of course I'll marry you!'

For an eternity they clung to one another, savouring the joy of deserving one another, equally and forever.

Finally, when they broke apart, Roland decided there was time enough to grant Sarah's first request after all. She deserved to be married in something finer than her simple gold cross, and the grumbles of the nearby jeweller at being woken from his sleep were soon silenced by Roland's generous patronage.

When Sarah's gratitude far outweighed his expenditure, Roland wondered how he ever could have compared her with Venetia.

And later, when he brought her back to Larchfield as his wife, he watched with loving pride as she greeted his two young nieces with kisses and hugs and cries of delight. Sarah even received Mrs Hawthorne with dignified kindness, though Roland suspected this had the opposite effect of soothing the delicate sensibilities of the former mistress of Larchfield. And he suspected Sarah knew very well it would, too.

As love for his new wife and hope for their future replaced the doubts and insecurities that had flourished in his once-barren heart, Roland no longer questioned his right to a second chance at happiness.

Sarah had made him see the world through her eyes. Happiness was the preserve of everyone, but only those who strove for it deserved it.

We do hope that you have enjoyed reading this large print book.

Did you know that all of our titles are available for purchase?

We publish a wide range of high quality large print books including:
Romances, Mysteries, Classics
General Fiction
Non Fiction and Westerns

Special interest titles available in large print are:
The Little Oxford Dictionary
Music Book
Song Book
Hymn Book
Service Book

Also available from us courtesy of Oxford University Press:
Young Readers' Dictionary
(large print edition)
Young Readers' Thesaurus
(large print edition)

For further information or a free brochure, please contact us at:
Ulverscroft Large Print Books Ltd.,
The Green, Bradgate Road, Anstey,
Leicester, LE7 7FU, England.
Tel: (00 44) 0116 236 4325
Fax: (00 44) 0116 234 0205

LADY FARQUHAR'S BUTTERFLY

Beverley Eikli

Falsely branded an adulteress and separated from her child by her vengeful late husband, Lady Olivia Farquhar unexpectedly discovers a deep and mutual love for her son's guardian, Max Atherton. But happiness with Max can never be possible when Olivia is blackmailed into a union with her late husband's religious confessor. Unaware of the sinister motives behind the reverend's desire to make her his wife, or of Max's efforts to clear her sullied name, Olivia is bereft of hope. Can Max turn things around in time?

THE FOREVER OF ELLA AND MICHA

Jessica Sorensen

Ella and Micha have been through tragedy, heartbreak, and love; now they are thousands of miles apart. Ella continues to go to school and tries to deal with her past, desperate for Micha to be by her side, but she refuses to let her problems get in the way of his dreams. Micha spends his days travelling the country with the band. He wants Ella closer to him — but he won't ask her to leave college. The few moments they do spend together are fleeting, intense, and filled with passion. They know they want to be together, but is wanting something enough to get them to their forever?

FRANCES AND BERNARD

Carlene Bauer

He is Bernard Eliot, a poet: passionate, gregarious, a force of nature. She is Frances Reardon, a novelist: wry, uncompromising and quick to skewer. In the summer of 1957, Frances and Bernard meet at a writers' colony. Afterwards, he sends her a letter, and with it begins an almost holy friendship. From their first, witty missives to dispatches from the long, dark night of the soul, Frances and Bernard tussle over faith and family, literature and creativity, madness and devotion — and before long, they are writing the account of their very own love story.